ALSO BY AYAH ABDUL-RAUF

Paint

Say You're Sorry

The Fox and The Stag

by Ayah Abdul-Rauf

The Fox and The Stag

{a novel}

by Ayah Abdul-Rauf

Making Metafiction

first published by Ayah Abdul-Rauf
Copyright © 2024
shethewriter.com

ISBN: 978-1-7327773-2-3 (ebook)—ISBN: 978-1-7327773-4-7 (paperback)—ISBN: 978-1-7327773-3-0 (hardcover)—

Library of Congress Control Number: 2024908869

Any references to historical events, real people, or real places are used fictitiously. Names, characters, and places are products of the author's imagination.

First Ebook Edition 2024.

*This one is for those who blame themselves for suffering
at the hands of another.*

Contents

The Fox and the Stag

Author's Note

This novel, an artifact of my childhood, is over seventeen years in the making. There is no combination of words that can adequately express what it means to me, so I will not try.

I am indebted to the librarians and baristas who maintained, inspired and supported the environments where a young person could safely do this work. The support of these people kept me safe while I was ensconced—totally—in the all-consuming task of making this thing.

Many people over the years witnessed my obsession with this text; I am also grateful to those who responded with compassion and patience rather than condemnation and judgement, though it was often a mixture of both.

There are many drafts of this book. The one in your hands is not the most recent, but it is the most primordial—the most closeted. I knew when I finished this draft that there wasn't much I could do that didn't change the fundamental nature of what I was doing, or the salient fact that it came from the heart and mind of a young, unworldly person. This is also the draft most closely aligned with Alan's wishes for it.

While my name is on the cover, I can not take sole credit for the text. The epilogue—not penned by me—was especially hard-won. Let us meet these mysterious co-authors; I start by leaving you in Alan's very competent hands:

Prologue
Water, Water Everywhere

"If I could put a silver siphon between your eyes and suck out those memories, I would do it.

Art is mysterious, yes—but the feelings it gives you, those should not be. I agree with that—but listen—there will never be time enough. Do you think the abuse of innocence isn't a commodity of your world? Real people ignore the stroke of their own veins. Fuck coherence.

You ask, "why is this language so strange?" This is my preference. If my words are on stilts, it's because I walk among eggshells. You say the text is confusing; this is my preference. Those with no patience should read the text and despair—okay, okay. I hear you. I'll do it. I'll write the opening."

Hi. I see you have overheard some of my chat with the Author—sorry about that. I am no deity, and my grip on metaphysics is loose at best. So I'll start by introducing myself: I am Alan Cope. I'm the "main character" of this book. It is about *me*. (There, I said it).

The Author and I delayed this publication until we could come to an agreement about how to achieve coherence in it. Her proposition: to rewrite the novel (for the billionth time) as a letter to my family, and with a conventional plot.

We managed a decent go of it. I found it laborious, and she delightful. It was coherent, sure, but it was bogged down in detail and stupid Realism. And frankly, it was dishonest. My boyhood never felt sentimental, so why should a book about it be? Basically, I didn't like it.

The other option for publication was simply to wait longer for the zeitgeist to move forward; until people take the abuse of men and boys as something other than a morbid joke. (Or worse, some of you think that these things live in the realm of fantasy, which is doubly ironic to me). That, we thought, could open people's hearts to my literary performance, and thus we could publish my preferred draft pretty much as it is. I think we are about as far as we might get with that collective failing. I would be very surprised if this draft is more accessible than it was when it was finished seven years ago, but then again I rarely go on the internet so you can take my opinion with a grain of salt.

Eventually, we settled on this: what you're reading now. She would publish the book as I like it, but only if I write this prologue to give you as much of that precious *context, justification* and *coherence* as I can bear.

Still, you'll find things to be confused about in this pages. You might find it obscure, dark, and hopefully a little sad; I'm nothing if I can't show people how to live with misery. The Author says reading this book is like reading shadows through chicken wire. To which I say: you wrote it. To which she says: yeah, but this is what you wanted.

I do want it this way: You shouldn't feel closer to my experience than I felt myself. I was disconnected, out of body and disassociated for most of the events in this book. I hardly had access to my emotions and I won't give them up to strangers. If waiting could make me ready, the Author would wait forever. But I cannot unpack all my terrors.

Maybe there are feelings that you, too, never want to encounter again. How much of your childhood can you actually remember?

This book is the story of my dark and confusing youth: I was kidnapped by a villain and survived. I was (am) the younger brother of a man suffering the ghosts of his past from being kidnapped himself. I was coerced into addiction and did not find much safety in my homecoming.

My memories are not chronological, and the book somewhat suffers for it. Trauma makes memory unreliable. For instance, I know a great deal of things could only have happened during my capital C *Captivity,* but I distinctly remember them happening long after I came home. We made the editorial decision to split those experiences (and the "metaphors" of them) between the 2nd, 4th and 5th parts of the book.

And the final question to bear: If this is a story about a boy suffering abuse, where is the abuse? Why the forests, the bears, the antlers and the floods? Which of my memories actually happened to me, and which were imagined?

Why did I give my author such clunky metaphors, instead of the more sordid—and therefore more *coherent*—details of what I survived as a trafficked-poor-kid-from-broken-American-home?

I don't know why you will ask this. I find the answer obvious, I find it goes something like this:

Can you tell, from the distanced nature of my language, the strength of my affection for you? The dams I must throw between us, that I might not drown in my own love?

—Alan J. Cope, 2024

"And because I am happy & dance & sing.
They think they have done me no injury..."
—*William Blake*

I

Alan's Brother

Alan Cope wore black shoes with white laces. He wore a real jacket and rode a clicking bicycle. His messenger bag was real. Alan Cope was a real boy.

Alan's body had thirteen years on it. He rode his bike with just as much experience and discomfort as his age demanded: he maintained balance and contact with the brakes, and he thought that this would make anyone's hands hurt, because it did for him. He did not ride in a straight line, but weaved with Baroque abandon as he pedaled away from the small, locked house where he lived with his older brother, Roger Cope. The wind toyed with his hair. It dried the blood around his left eye.

Fifteen minutes into this, a dog observed Alan through a window. The dog quietly watched him dismount the skeletal body and pull it over the grass. It watched Alan approach the window. The dog belonged to Jenna and Arden Cope. They were Alan's cousins, on the side of his late father.

Alan rang the doorbell to his cousins' house and waited for Jenna to open it.

"Roger hit you," she said.

The dog followed Alan's entrance into the house with a lowered head and gently wagging tail. "Can I keep my shoes on?"

"You always do." Jenna's gaze dropped to the bag at Alan's hip, then back to his bruised face. "How long are you staying?"

"Not long."

She blinked. "At least one night?"

"He was aiming for the wall."

"Terrible aim, I guess." Jenna shut the front door. Alan looked at the dog.

While waiting for Arden to return home from her law firm, Jenna and Alan did their school work in the living room. They had the same 8th grade worksheets, and they looked up often but rarely spoke. Alan didn't realize he was grinding his teeth. Understanding subjects and objects. The bear attacked the young hunter. Put a square around the subject. Put a circle around the object. The young hunter was attacked by the bear. Put a square around the subject. Put a circle around the object. Alan felt sick. He thought about going to the bathroom but didn't. Jenna dropped her pencil.

"How about some tea?"

Alan nodded. "Yeah, please." The dog whined. Jenna left the room and Alan, hoping for a distraction, rifled absently through the mail on the coffee table. One envelope had an address he recognized. Someone had already torn into it. Alan pulled the letter out and saw the name Diane Cope.

His vision blurred before he could read it a second time.

The dog barked and Alan slipped the letter into his messenger bag. Jenna returned carrying tea.

"The cups match," Alan said.

"Of course they match. Are you okay?"

Alan's yawn was enormous. His eyes watered more. "I'm okay. Homework is boring."

Jenna nodded and put the matching teacups on the coffee table. Alan wanted to go to the bathroom but he turned to the worksheet on his lap. He drew squares and circles. He occasionally swallowed. They heard the garage door lift. The dog stood and paced at Arden's arrival. Alan could not bring himself to look at his older cousin. She talked at her cellphone and collapsed into an armchair.

Alan heard her rifle through the mail on the coffee table. He counted his teeth by feel. Arden's cellphone snapped shut and the rifling stopped. "Jenna," she said, "have you fed Butter?"

"Yes, I fed Butter."

"Then why is he looking at me like that?"

Jenna dropped her pencil again. She went back into the kitchen. Arden stood in front of Alan and he put a hand on his messenger bag. "Dog's not hungry," he muttered.

"I know, Alan. Did you go through my mail?" She sighed. "You're just going to ignore me and do your homework?"

"It's really hard and I don't get it."

"You do get it and it's not hard."

Alan finally looked at her. "Why didn't you tell me about my mom?"

"I just got the letter."

"But the date was a week ago."

"Why hasn't Roger told you?" Arden said. Alan frowned. He wished he had an answer.

"I'm going to kill him..." Arden leaned her head against her hand.

"Do they know for sure she's dead?"

"No."

"Then why declare her dead legally?"

"Do you want a lecture on the law?"

Alan shrugged, keeping his face turned away. "I just don't want mom to sneak up on me."

"I already hired a detective, she's not going to sneak up on you. She's not allowed within a hundred feet of you. Legal death is good. This is good news for you." Arden is not known for tact.

Alan started to put his homework away. He chewed on his lip. "I'd feel better if someone was looking for her." They heard Jenna cooing to the dog in the kitchen.

"Does Roger wear a ring?" Arden said.

Alan realized she caught sight of his face. "He threw the toaster at the wall. The plug hit me."

"Well Alan, I'll buy you guys a new toaster. You need a better one."

Alan stared at her. "No thanks," he said, "I like the one with the slots just fine, I understand how to use it." Arden crossed one leg over the other.

"Have you changed your mind about moving?"

"No. I want to stay with Roger."

They looked away from each other as Jenna reentered the room. "I can't believe he didn't tell you," she announced. She looked no more surprised than she always did; her eyebrows were naturally arched. Alan watched the sisters swing into an argument about eavesdropping. He left his tea unfinished. Arden and Jenna acknowledged his departure with hasty nods. At the front door Alan heard a whine and turned around with his hand on the knob. "I'm sorry, dog," he said. "Don't get sore; I'll be back soon."

Chills took Alan's body once he left the house. His facial injury would incite a phase of apologetic compatibility with Roger; Alan wondered how long it would last before the tension in his brother would once again manifest in a violent outburst.

When Alan reached his front door he dropped his bike and knocked and waited. Then he knocked again. Alan wiped his forehead with his sleeve and took heavy steps around the house so he could enter through the back door.

The back door opened to the kitchen. Roger lay facedown in front of the fridge. Alan leaped over the toaster on the floor and knelt by the prone figure. He said his brother's name and shook him. Roger's hair was damp from sweat. He groaned and pulled out his hand mirror.

"Are you okay? Don't do that. You scared me bad," Alan said.

Roger opened the mirror and rubbed his eyes. "Candy was right." His voice had the self-denouncing quality of a smooth, dark stone falling in a chasm: "I have a pixie-face. It's a stupid face. No one can love this face."

"What's wrong?"

"Nothing, I'm fine, kiddo. My head hurts." Roger smoothed his eyebrows. "How long has it been?"

"When did you hit your head?" Alan voice returned to its accustomed tenor.

"I didn't hit my head." Roger rubbed his eyes for a moment. Then he rested his cheek on his arms. "My legs went out after you left. I was just thinking on the floor and…I actually fell asleep." He laughed. His legs "went out" because he has intermittent paralysis.

Alan was smiling. "I should have left you alone, then."

Roger's eyes flicked to Alan's messenger bag and back to his brother's face. "You went to Arden's house, didn't you? I thought you'd stay there until tomorrow."

"So did I." A pause happened.

"I didn't know you were behind me when I threw it, kid," Roger said.

"It's alright."

"Your face is swelling."

Alan shrugged. "It's no big deal."

"But I scared you. You grabbed that bag and ran out the door."

Another pause. Alan dropped the bag on Roger's legs. "Can you feel that?"

"You put it on my legs?"

"Yeah...How long is this gunna happen, Roger?"

"It won't take more than three hours. I'll know when my legs are coming back. It hurts a lot." Alan could not bring himself to point out that Roger had misunderstood the question. He brought pillows into the kitchen.

"Thanks, kid," Roger said as he slipped them under his head. "Don't linger. Go finish your homework. I want to see if I can sleep again..."

Alan picked up his bag and hesitated. He stared at his brother's long, dormant legs. "Can I ask you something?"

"Hmm?"

"Why didn't you tell me about Diane?"

"What about her, kid?"

"Have you checked the mail?"

Roger opened his eyes. "No. Are we orphans?"

"I don't know," Alan said, "she's legally dead. No one's looking for her."

The phone rang and Roger looked at him. "Arden will fix that, Alan. Don't panic."

"I'm not panicked. But what if—," The phone interrupted with a second ring. "What if Diane finds out no one's looking for her?"

"That's absurd, Alan. She won't." The phone rang again and Roger sighed through his nose. "Listen, you're safe because—"

"Because of you, you won't let anyone near me blah blah blah."

"Don't *blah blah blah* me. Will you please just get the phone?"

Leena Strang was on the phone. Alan could tell because Roger's voice got the timbre he reserved for women; and especially for Leena.

"Hey there, doctor-doctor. I'm grand. How are you?"

Alan left his brother's sight but lingered on the stairs to listen. It was no secret that Roger was smitten with his doctor. But Leena never seemed to condone or discourage his affection.

"I'd like to check, sweetheart. I'd like to check my schedule. But the calendar you gave me is in another room and I'm quite paralyzed."

And what a curious thing it was. No one had yet been able to explain Roger's paralysis. Leena's attempt to heal him had made her nearly as famous as the phenomenon itself, or so Roger seemed to think.

"Yes, I suppose I was under stress... It's not serious, I promise.... Saturday? Are your sure that's the only day we can reschedule? Oh no, Leena! No, I need to see you this week for sure. I've been having the most horrible nightmares."

A survivor of kidnapping was already anomalous. But a victim who insisted that he'd spent his captivity in another universe posed an even more unique challenge. Alan was certain that any doctor would leap at the chance to study the first person with Cope Syndrome, but Roger wouldn't accept critical examination from anyone but Leena.

"Don't worry, *Doctor* Strang, I haven't watched the news. But you know my birth... birthday. Coming up. It's freaking me out. But not Saturday. Alan won't be in school. He can't be alone for that long."

Alan shook his head and a small smile snuck onto his face. He knew Leena would not indulge Roger's protective little habits.

"Arden works on Saturdays. And Jenna's always out with her girlfriends, I can't make him join, he gets shy."

That part was true. Alan loved girls. He loved the way they smelled and when they said smart things in soft voices and the many shapes of their eyes and he loved how plant-like they were, breathing everything in all the time. He thought often of botanical varieties in stem and blossom and pollination. It made him like a mouse in a bush.

Roger, on the other hand, was taller and rabbit-like and miraculously unafraid of women, even though they always looked at him first.

"....Perhaps you could come over for an in-house appointment? I'm sorry, Dr. Strang, I can't leave Alan alone. Please, please, you're here all the time anyway. You know I just can't do that...well, well Leena, the world *is* full of questionable characters, they might try to take advantage—,"

Alan heard the combined sound of Roger yelping and the phone hitting the floor. He ran back into the kitchen. Roger was biting his knuckles. Alan snatched up the phone and spoke into it:

"Hi Leena, this is Alan. Roger dropped the phone. His legs are hurting him. Yes ma'am, he's fine. Don't worry about Saturday, he'll be there."

Roger tried to grab his brother's ankle and Alan stepped away from him.

"Yes, ma'am, Roger's nodding at me. I expect he doesn't want to talk now. He's been a bit sore about his birthday next week, but—, oh, me? I'm fine. Yes, ma'am. Good-bye." Alan hung up the phone. Roger glared at him.

"You eavesdropping punk." He croaked, "don't interfere with me and her!" He rolled over on the floor.

"Why can't I just go to Leena's office with you?"

"You'll be with Jenna and her friends." Roger said, "I have to call Leena back now. Give me the phone." He stood up slowly, using the fridge for support. Alan wanted to help but was wary of doing so.

"I don't want to follow the girls, it's a pain."

"Give me the phone, kid."

"Take me with you."

A muscle twitched in Roger's jaw. He seized his brother's arm and took the phone from him. Alan stepped back with a hand on his stomach. Roger stared at him.

"What is wrong with you?"

"Nothing." Alan walked backwards.

"Where do you think you're going?"

Alan didn't answer. His arm burned. He went upstairs and the messenger bag thumped his hip with every step. When Alan reached his bathroom he dropped to his knees in front of the toilet. He saw big dark eyes in the water and closed them. Alan touched his tongue and the blaze spread to his neck. He reached beyond his teeth and probed tender flesh. The burning sharpened. He vomited for the first time in two weeks, finally, and felt like a fever was drifting off of him in waves.

Alan stared at his hands as he washed them, straining to hear if Roger was outside the door. He curled up on his mattress and pulled his jacket tightly around him. Alan listened to calm breaths and sensed a dry, gasping quality to his skin. The house creaked as Roger paced the ground floor. His voice echoed up the stairs:

"...it's under control. I organized my doses. I have that box with the days of the week on it."

Alan sighed. Roger was clearly referring to his own remedy; throwing up was one of Alan's deepest secrets, yet somehow, like constant aching of his hands, he assumed it was normal. It was everyone's secret. Alan shut his eyes tight and wondered how much Leena knew. He had tried learning about the nightmares which made his brother shout every night. But Roger wouldn't or couldn't explain them. He trembled and shook his head whenever Alan asked.

Alan rolled onto his back. Two strings hung from his jacket hood. He picked one up and started twisting it around the base of his index finger. The tip swelled and felt sore. He unraveled the string. April 15th was only eight days away. Roger would turn twenty-two. On his 18th birthday, Arden had bought him a trench coat. The following year it was a cellphone. When Roger turned twenty, he received a laptop that he never opened.

Alan started rubbing his eyes. On the 21st birthday, Alan had made cupcakes. He had frosted them with his head down and when he turned around he saw Arden and Roger sitting in the backyard. He wondered how they'd gone out without him noticing and then he saw a wine bottle by Roger's ankle—the sliding glass door cracked when Alan opened it. He kicked the bottle and screamed things until he tasted the blood pouring from his nose. Roger pulled his sleeve over his hand and tried to wipe Alan's face clean and Alan bit him.

Alan stopped rubbing his eyes. Stars scattered across the ceiling and disappeared. He heard his brother approach the room and sat up. His back was rigid. The door cracked open.

"What are you doing?"

"Nothing."

"You're doing nothing?"

"That's right."

The door slowly opened. Roger leaned against its frame. "We're both going to Leena's office on Saturday. You'll have to wait in the lobby. I couldn't get her to come over this time."

Alan nodded. Roger twisted the doorknob. "Did you get sick?"

"Why would I get sick?"

"I dunno, I grabbed at you."

Alan watched his brother's hand on the doorknob. He rubbed his jaw. "I'm not sick."

"So you're fine, then?"

Alan shrugged.

They stared at each other. Roger frowned. "Don't worry about mom."

"I'm not."

"I told Leena what happened. She said you should write a letter to her. I mean to Diane. Not to send it, but to process your feelings."

Alan stared at his tattered pants. They exposed his knees; this had been a point of contention with Roger until Alan tore all his own pants to shut him up about it. "What made her say that?"

"I don't know, kid. She's a doctor. I'm making dinner this time."

"Don't burn yourself."

Roger's chuckle sounded loose and frayed.

Alan frowned. "I'm serious."

"Come down for dinner." Roger closed the door.

Alan ripped a sheet up from a notepad. He wrote "To Diane" at the top of it. He crossed out "Diane" and wrote "mom." He changed it back.

To Diane:

I wrote you this before but I'm writing it again. I killed someone when I was five, right after you left and they put me in a f-house. He was a teenager. He was on me and I bit him and he bled to death in the forests of Pennsylvania. As usual, don't tell anyone. Roger had paralysis again this morning. He doesn't miss you.

Alan Cope

Alan sifted through old letters:

Dear Diane:
I was only five years old. I couldn't breathe. He died in the
forests of Pennsylvania and no one ever found out. Keep it a
secret. Roger misses you and dad.
Alan Cope

To Mom:
Remember I told you I killed that boy in the forests of
Pennsylvania. He bled to death. It makes me feel sick. Don't
tell anyone. Roger's okay. You shouldn't have left, he came
back eventually. I know it would be better if I was gone
instead, I'm sorry. Roger says he is more wanted than me; I
know I'm very lucky.
Alan Cope

In truth, Alan wasn't entirely sure whether any of
these things had happened, especially the bit about the
forest. But it was nice to have an upsetting story for his
mom. He liked to imagine that she might pity him. Alan
folded the letters and pushed them under his mattress

among their predecessors. He went downstairs and edged past the couch. He entered the kitchen. Roger stared into a pot on the stove. He stirred its contents while steam rose into his face. Alan peered into the pot. Vapor moistened him and he shook his head.

"You've overdone it."

Roger kept stirring. A narrow gap lived between his lips.

"The noodles are too soft. Roger!"

Roger's shoulders contracted. He dropped the stirring spoon and looked at his brother. His hair was damp.

"Sorry," he said.

Alan turned off the stove. He carried the pot to the sink. "Get me a colander."

Clanging filled the kitchen. "What, like the strainer?"

"The thing with holes."

Roger brought the colander to the sink. Alan poured the pot over it. Roger picked up the front of his shirt and wiped his face.

Noodles sat hot and heavy under sauce. Alan started to take off his jacket but Roger hissed and said no, *don't take it off*. Alan slipped it back over his shoulders. He looked at his dinner. It smelled good. Alan twisted his fork in the noodles and pulled them to his lips. He chewed on them until his throat shifted and they were gone. He filled his mouth again. Roger ate without words. Alan heard him swallow.

"Sometimes I miss dad," he said. Roger nodded.

After eating, the brothers sat in front of the television. The lights were off. Alan looked right and saw a rare phenomenon. Roger's long limbs were folded and calm. His breathing looked soft. He had never been so visible as he was in that fluttering half light. His eyes were attentive. The pupils gleamed enormous. His nose was pinched and gently freckled. It made him look younger than his age, yet he exuded a quality which suggested the opposite. Alan blinked and turned back to the television.

Commercials flashed. Low-fat yogurt. Brand new episodes now streaming live. Beat your virus before it beats you.

"I forgot what we were watching," Alan said.

Roger chuckled. A carton of cigarettes sat on the coffee table. He leaned forward to pick one out and paused in the act of lifting it to his mouth.

"Alan."

Alan looked at him.

"We were watching something. What were we watching, kid?"

"I just said I don't know. Have you had medicine today?"

"Of course I have," Roger mumbled. He put the cigarette in his lips.

Upgrade your phone plan now. Never clean your gutters again. Say good-bye to tinny tap water.

"It's dreadful." Roger took the cigarette out of his mouth. "It's a bad stick."

"It's not lit."

Roger rubbed his hands over his pockets. He arched his back and fingered them.

"It's by the phone," Alan said, "the lighter is."

Roger stood out of the couch and left. When he came back he breathed smoke. His jaw trembled. The body at rest was gone.

"You forgot how to smoke," Alan said.

"I don't want Sunday to come."

"You're going to see Leena."

Roger shook his head. "She doesn't. She doesn't know."

Alan crossed his arms and swallowed. "What doesn't she know?"

Roger reached across the couch to pick up the drawstring for Alan's jacket hood.

"Stop," Alan said, "stop that."

Roger released the string. He sucked on his cigarette and left the couch. Alan rubbed his right cheek against his shoulder.

The top of the staircase opened to Roger's bedroom. Alan followed his brother into it. Roger crawled onto his brass bed and worked his way under its blanket. Alan looked left and right. He looked back at the staircase.

"Where's the cigarette?" He asked.

"I don't know, I dropped it." Roger stared at the ceiling.

"No, you didn't. It was in your hand and now it's gone."

"Please please please go to sleep, kid."

Alan examined the stairs with big eyes. He returned to the living room. He looked for smoke and found none. Alan grabbed the stair railing and ascended. When he stopped in his brother's bedroom doorway, Roger sat forward.

"Don't go away," he said.

"I'm going to sleep. You said to."

"I'm afraid."

Alan's brow furrowed. "Can't help if I don't know what's wrong, Roger."

Roger leaned against a brass bar. He shut his eyes and breathed like air was painful. Alan approached the bed and pushed his hands under the mattress. He found the edge of the blanket and pulled it. Roger seized his bedding.

"Now stop, kid, I need that tight. I can't sleep without any sensor—,"

"You mean pressure."

"Would you shut up and stop talking to me like I'm an idiot!" Roger launched into his list of things he did not like about Alan, things he thought Alan should change, things that were (for the most part) untrue. Alan just kept plunging his hands under the mattress.

"What are you, having an idea?"

"Yes, actually."

"Don't be such a smart ass." Roger had a fault line in his brow. He scrutinized Alan's movements. "Be careful. There's nothing between the coils and the bed."

This, just days after Roger had screamed at him for not getting a box spring to endear himself to a social worker who never showed up anyway. How was Alan to get a box spring for his mattress? He couldn't even drive. Alan grit his teeth and dragged the comforter off of the bed and into Roger's bathroom.

"What are you doing?" Roger asked. "What are you —,"

"I can make it heavy." Alan dumped the blanket into the bathtub. He turned on the faucet. The blanket darkened under water and Roger's shadow. "You brilliant child," he said.

Alan's mouth twitched. Roger stepped into the bathtub and crouched. He stared at his brother. "It's natural on you, it doesn't show." he said.

"What?"

Roger nestled under his wet blanket. "The bruise. This is great, it's like a weighted blanket."

Alan looked left at the mirror. "I don't know what you mean."

"I mean your eyes look kinda bruised anyway, so it's fine. You're alright."

Alan nodded. "I'm okay. Can you tell me...what Leena doesn't know?

"She doesn't know why I'm afraid...of...the fifth... you know."

"You're afraid of your birthday."

"Yeah."

Alan sat on the bathtub's edge. He watched his brother's knees tent the blanket. "Is it the taxes?"

"What?"

"Taxes are due in April."

Roger shivered a little. "No, no. Arden does the taxes."

Alan pressed his ear against his shoulder. "Are you calm now?"

"Yes."

Water dripped. A tiny part of Alan wanted to be alone, but the consequences of not hearing his brother out in a moment like this were, as yet, unknown to him. He took a deep breath. "Tell me why you're afraid."

"Did you *know*, that used to be my jacket you're wearing. Dad bought it for me the day I turned ten. The sleeves were too long…"

"Leena says you're obsessed with me wearing the jacket because you're anxious."

Roger opened his eyes. "I am not obsessed—, wait, when did you talk with Leena about it?"

"When she's visited Arden and I've been there."

"She talks to you."

"Sure. She asks how I'm doing."

"Does she ask about me?"

"I tell her you're functioning."

"Thanks, kid. You're a gem."

Alan shrugged. "She's your doctor."

"She's my soulmate." Water dripped. "Do you remember when back when she wanted to be a social worker?" Roger chuckled. "Leena's not treating me because she's a doctor, Alan. She's a doctor because she wants to treat me." Roger smiled.

"You love her."

"Yep."

"But you can't tell her what bothers you about your birthday?"

Roger's smile disappeared. "I pretended not to know. I hoped she could give me a better explanation than the truth, but she let me down."

Alan squinted. "What is the truth?"

"She knows I'm upset about losing my childhood. She says I'm afraid of aging. But the truth...well. Um." Roger huffed and shook his head.

"You don't have to tell me."

"No no no, I need to tell. On my...the day I got the jacket you're wearing. I was...that's when he came. Actually."

"Who?"

"I can't remember his name," Roger whispered.

"Wait, no." Alan shook his head. "You were reported missing on April 22nd, Roger, you're just remembering wrong."

"No I know that. I know it was in the *news* on the 22nd, I have a copy of the paper from Tioga under my bed."

"But you're saying...you're saying you were kidnapped on your birthday..."

"Yes that's why *I hate my birthday.*"
Alan saw his brother swallow. "Oh, man. You want a hug?"

Roger held out a hand. It looked like a cradle. Alan brushed it with his fingers. Water dripped.

When Alan returned to his bedroom he locked the door. He took off the jacket. He stretched his arms. The crooks of his elbows cooled. Alan brushed his teeth until he tasted blood. He touched the swelling around his eye. He slept on a freezing mattress.

In the morning, Roger stood in Alan's bedroom doorway. He closed his eyes to the sound of breathing and smiled. "Like clouds," he uttered. Then he said his brother's name. He stepped forward and nudged the mattress with his foot. "Wake up, kid. Your school day awaits." Alan breathed clouds. Roger knelt down next to his brother and blew gently on Alan's forehead. The hair fluttered. The eyes opened.

"Time to get up," Roger said.

Alan rolled onto his back. "Did you sleep last night?"

Roger laughed. He picked up Alan's jacket and threw it at him. "I forgot to sleep. Meet me downstairs."

In the kitchen, Roger used a dark marker to print "ALAN'S LUNCH" on a paper bag. He wrote it with the type of precision Alan saw Arden exhibit while applying eye makeup. Roger spread lettuce and mustard on bread. He sliced a tomato and shuddered when the seeds slipped out of it. He was rinsing the knife when he said, "They were a lot less ugly before."

Alan tied his shoes. "What?"

"Tomatoes. When I was in Luna…"

Alan squinted. "Is this about the lighting?"

"Forget it."

"But you remember it." Alan tensed. Roger's stories about Luna, the imagined island where he claimed to be while kidnapped, were few and far between in the years since Arden caught him giving Alan a whispered account of his captivity there and she threatened to separate them.

Whispered though the stories were, Alan could never forget them: he was so young and his eyes were even bigger back then, he hung on to Roger's experienced and romantic words: *Luna's nights are so bright, there have three moons in the sky, I am so famous there...*

Roger opened the fridge. "Do you want turkey or corned beef?"

"I don't care." Alan picked an apple off the table. "Tell me again."

Roger sighed. "The lighting is different. It was better in Luna. Like you could taste it. Shades within shades." He dropped a bag of sliced meat on the counter. "There was a visual quality that we don't have on Earth. Like more texture, but it wasn't texture." Roger pulled apart thin slices of meat and made irritated sounds when they tore. "I can't explain it right."

Alan stared at the apple. "Was there a name for it?"

Roger plucked the fruit from his brother's hand. He added it to ALAN'S LUNCH. "Just forget it, kid, we'll be late." Car keys jangled. Alan followed his brother to the garage.

"Can I ride my bike to school next year?"

"Put your seatbelt on."

"You said I could this year and you changed your mind."

"I thought you'd have a new bike by now."

"But why does that matter?"

Roger's fingers travelled through his hair. He put the car in reverse. "Must we discuss this every morning?"

"I have a great bike already."

"That thing is about to fall apart."

Alan frowned. "You're paranoid."

"If you ask Arden for a new bike, she'll get you one. I'll ask her for you."

"Stop trying to change the subject," Alan mumbled.

"What was that?"

"Why is it okay for Jenna to walk to school?"

Roger flicked the turn signal. The car ticked. He pulled the steering wheel left and flicked the signal again. "She's too stubborn to let me drive her."

"Let me ride my bike!"

Roger turned on the stereo. He twisted the volume knob to the right. Alan pushed it left. "You think it's dangerous."

They were at an intersection. The car slowed, then stopped. Roger said: "Alan I *like* driving with you, okay? Why do you have to make me feel awful about everything?"

Alan stroked the volume knob to the right. He rubbed his thumb over the pockmarked loudspeaker beside him. He felt a drum solo. When they arrived at the school, Alan grabbed ALAN'S LUNCH. He pulled backpack straps over his shoulders.

Roger unlocked the car. "If anyone asks about your face you just tell them—," Alan slammed the door. Roger watched him go.

The students moved in one direction. Alan entered a classroom and sat. Behind him, students filled the room. A bell shrieked. Alan took off his jacket. The teacher started to babble. Alan heard "Cope, Alan." He raised his hand and dropped it. The babble went on. The teacher stood up and wrote numbers on a chalkboard. Alan stared. Every time the teacher met the boy's dark gaze he cleared his throat and turned back to the board. Alan looked at his backpack, and the duct tape which held it together. He drew a picture of his bike. A bell shrieked.

Alan entered other classrooms. He left them. When moving through the hall, he twisted and weaved. Voices shouted obscenities at him. He did not brush other bodies. In the afternoon, Alan peered into ALAN'S LUNCH and somebody flicked the back of his head. They said the worst things about Roger. Jenna used to bite back, but she hadn't in awhile.

"Ignore them, Alan. They're lower than the floor."

They sat in anonymous noise. "They don't even know him." Alan said after a minute.

"I guess what they do is on them," Jenna said, tucking into her cheeseburger. "You gunna eat? We have to go early for the assembly."

"But I thought we already had one this semester."

"Yeah, they think we need another one. Probably because of the serial killer."

Alan squinted. "A serial killer? In Cortland?"

"What, you're listening now? There's videos online of all the kids he took. Where have you been?"

"I can't put on the news. It scares Roger incredible. If he knew about this, I'd be locked in a closet or something."

"He would bubble wrap you." Jenna laughed and chewed on the edge of her cup. Alan shuddered. When he bit into his sandwich, he found the cheese still wrapped in plastic and set the whole meal aside.

Alan joined the assembly with his cousin. They sidestepped into a row of bleachers. "Gymnauseum," Alan uttered. He sat and stared at the lofty ceiling. "Very spacious." Noise protected his voice. He pulled at his collar and tried to unzip the jacket. Alan touched his collarbone. He looked at his arms.

"Jenna. The jacket's missing."

"Jacket? Which jacket?"

"The jeans jacket with the hood—,"

"I'm kidding, Alan! I know what jacket."

"It's missing."

"It's probably in your locker."

"But it's not." Alan stood. A woman stopped his progress at the exit.

"Where do you think you're going?"

Alan looked at his shoes. "I...can I go to the bathroom?"

"Look at you. You want another suspension? Go sit down, for heaven's sake, why can't you boys just sit down?"

Alan sat at the foot of the bleachers. He shook his left leg. Someone spoke about kidnapping. "It's my fault," Alan muttered. "It's my fault, Roger's going to kill me, he will kill me, it's all my fault..."

The next time Alan saw his jacket, it was under the hands of his math teacher.

"You left it in here this morning. I kept it in my desk so it wouldn't be stolen."

"So it wouldn't be stolen?"

"You left it."

"Yes, sir, yes, I left it. Thank you for keeping it safe. It is my only jacket." Alan took a deep breath for the first time in hours.

"I thought so. Please call me Mr. Boding, 'sir' makes me feel old."

"Yes, sir." Alan reached for the jacket.

The teacher pulled it back. "You haven't been squinting since I moved you to the front of the room, I notice. I hope your other teachers are as accommodating as I am. Have you seen a doctor about your vision?"

They stared at each other. The teacher opened his mouth, then closed it. Alan lowered his head. "I'm sorry, I shouldn't stare. Roger says it startles people because my eyes look fucked up. But I can see just fine."

"How is your brother?"

"Roger is doing well and he is an inspiration to us all. I have to—,"

"Is he still working on that memoir?"

"What memoir?"

"Please, Alan, use my name. Your brother mentioned a memoir in one of his interviews."

"Oh...the book about his...life." Alan's voice took on a clipped quality. Roger's progress on this memoir hadn't yet extended beyond a mess of (now dusty) notecards in his room. "Misdiagnosis. It's called Misdiagnosis." The teacher started nodding. Alan cleared his throat. "Roger is probably waiting for me out front, so..." The teacher pushed the jacket forward. Alan thanked him and slipped his arms into it.

When Alan stepped outside he smiled at the breeze. A group of girls loitered next to a brick wall. They watched a young man pacing yards away from them. The man smoked and gave them a friendly wave. One of the girl's whistled. Alan approached him. "I'm sorry I took long. I was talking to my math teacher."

Roger released a stream of smoke. His trench coat was slipping off one shoulder. "What does he want from you?"

Alan adjusted the coat. The girls tittered; one let out a little shriek. "He asked about your memoir."

"Ugh, don't remind me." Roger put out his cigarette on the bottom of his shoe, then cocked his foot. "Shouldn't have done that, I like these shoes...."

"They look expensive. Where are they from?"

Roger grinned. "A nice lady in Ohio."

"Oh my God."

"Her husband is a total bore, Alan, she just needs someone to talk to. Anyway, what's your teacher got like a crush on me or something?"

"He still thinks there's something wrong with my eyesight."

"Damn it, kid." Roger stepped off a curb and Alan followed. "That's your fault, don't look at him. Your eyes are like an animal." He unlocked his car. "Don't make me wait again. They don't let me in the building anymore."

When they were home, Roger curled up on the couch. Alan sat at the kitchen table and opened his backpack. He drew squares and circles. After finishing his English homework he entered the living room.

"Is Candace coming here?"

"Who?"

"Candy, your friend."

"She changed her mind."

"Oh."

Roger's arms were around his stomach. "She wanted to come over and watch my documentary."

"Didn't she see it when it first aired?"

Roger paused. "Hey, you're right. We watched it together. We had popcorn and everything. She wants to see it again!" He smiled. "Aw, she's so creepy. She's so messed up."

"I can get you a book."

"There is nothing good to read."

Alan blinked. "You've got a library in your room."

"I have read all the romantics already. There is nothing good to read." Roger launched into a monologue about his hopelessly bad luck in finding a good novel to read. It made Alan rather uneasy.

The garage door strained open. Keys rattled. Arden approached the living room. She had a piece of paper which she shook in front of Roger's face. Roger pushed himself into a seated position. He took the paper. He unfolded it. "That's a big number."

"Yeah. Anything else you have to say?"

"I thought I spent more than that."

"You might have if you bothered to go shopping."

"Do you know what month it is?" Roger rocked back and forth. Arden snatched the paper from him.

"This is my work, Roger. My education is sitting in a vault, gathering dust because you won't spend money like a normal person. Use the internet! Call people! I can't believe I have to tell you to spend money, I just, I can't!"

"I—I want to, Arden, I told them, take the money."

"You have to *pay the bills*, Roger, they don't just take it from you."

"I said they could do it auto-pay!"

"Then why aren't the bills paid?"

Alan picked a battery up off the floor. He found the remote. He popped the back open.

"You're bitchy, Arden. You're here at least twice a week just to bitch at me for not spending enough of your money. That's a case of extreme bitchiness."

The battery slipped and kept slipping. Alan was grinding his teeth.

Arden's voice lowered. "Don't start pulling that independent crap on me, Roger Cope. Nothing is going to change my mind."

"If I had a real job—"

"You can not hold a real job."

Roger shook his head. "I won't listen to you!"

"You're being such a baby! Do you want Alan sleeping on concrete?"

The coffee table flipped onto its side. Baby indeed—Alan didn't see who did it. He dropped the remote and ran into the kitchen. He grabbed his backpack and slipped into the garage. "Let them argue," he said, feeling through cobwebs. Alan pushed a button and light happened. He sat next to his bike and turned on his calculator. His pencil ran blunt. He chewed on it.

Arden entered the garage and stopped when she saw her cousin. "What are you doing in here?"

"Homework."

"Come with me, Roger wants to be alone."

"Did he say it was allowed?"

Arden groaned. Alan went in the house to get his messenger bag. He put the remainder of his homework in with the spare clothes and toothbrush. He buckled the bag shut.

"You don't need to bring that," Arden said from her car while Alan descended the driveway. The bag thumped his hip with every step.

When Alan arrived at his cousin's house, Jenna lit a candle and he realized he smelled like a trashcan. He showered with hot water. He used generous amounts of soap. Shopping bags filled the closet of his second bedroom.

"Thank you for the new clothes." Alan leaned on the doorway to Arden's office. It smelled like wood.

Arden waved her hand. "You need them, Alan. Throw the old ones out."

"I put them in the wash. I like your office."

Arden bit her thumbnail. "I haven't finished unpacking. This is supposed to be Roger's bedroom."

"I'm sorry. I tried to make him move. He's attached to the old house. Really attached."

"Leena will make him come to his senses eventually," Arden said, smiling. "There's a woman who knows what she's doing."

Alan nodded. "Jenna said I could make the fish in the freezer. I'm going to make it."

Alan spoke while using the kitchen. "You're hungry too, dog. I'll get your dinner." He poured pellets into a bowl labeled BUTTER. He washed his hands. He chopped vegetables and poured vinegar. Alan spoke to the animal. When the smells of the kitchen became the smells of the house, his cousins joined him. Arden closed her eyes when she ate Alan's food. "Who taught you to cook fish?"

"Why wouldn't I?"

"Never mind." Arden swallowed forkfuls of soft flesh. "Can you make this again next week, Alan, if I buy more fish?"

"Yeeeeees, ma'am. But I should go home soon."

"No," Jenna said, "you should stay and make dessert with me. There's this thing called a dump cake…"

"I could stay but I want to make sure Roger takes his medicine."

After eating, Arden put her plate in the sink. "Wash these, Jenna. I'm taking him back."

Alan's seatbelt clicked. The messenger bag sat on his lap, still buckled. When they came to an intersection, Alan watched a pale van make a slow stop behind them.

"I wonder how many kids could fit in there," Alan said.

Arden looked at the rearview mirror. "What?"

"Kidnappers usually have pale vans like that."

"Alan Cope, I am turning this car around."

"Why?"

"I warned you before."

Alan pulled his seatbelt. "I want to go home!"

"Roger is so toxic."

"He's not! It's got nothing to do with him. I just happened to wonder. Take me home. I have to make sure Roger's had medicine."

"When is his next appointment?"

"This Saturday."

"I'm making it an in-house session. Leena can talk to you both."

Alan stepped into a dark house. He turned around to wave at Arden's car, then pushed a button. The garage creaked shut. Alan crossed the kitchen and opened the sliding glass door. He looked at his brother. "Why are you gardening so late?"

Roger pushed his fingers into soil. "Leena says I should garden when I'm frustrated."

"Planting flowers?"

"Evidently."

"Did you take medicine?"

"Yes, Alan. I was a dutiful brother and took all my drugs. I'm calmer than the sea, bish." Roger tore open a seed packet.

"Okay." Alan walked backwards. He slipped into the house and remembered to breathe.

Roger could not sleep through the night. Screams woke him. They issued from his own mouth. He stood out of bed and met Alan in the hallway. "I heard you scream," Alan said.

"You were in my nightmare," Roger rested his hand on the bannister.

"I'm okay."

Roger held out his hand. Alan brushed it with a finger. He went back to his room. Roger leaned against the banister until it creaked. He shut his eyes. He grabbed the rungs. "I dreamt of broken bones."

When Saturday arrived, Roger paced. "In-house appointment? My Leena, in this house? Look at the state of it! Why didn't you tell me earlier, kid?"

"Roger, I did tell you. Many times. And you were happy, remember?" Alan craned his neck to watch his brother pace into the kitchen. "This means you don't have to leave me in a waiting room." Alan just managed to curb his sarcasm in the last few syllables; it felt like swerving from the edge of a cliff.

"This place is a horror show, Alan." Roger met the doorway and braced his arms against its edges.

"It's just cramped. But she only needs one clear space; I vacuumed. And your ashtray is clean."

"Can't we do this at Arden's house?"

"There's no one to let us in."

Roger made a sound. He pushed his fingers through his hair. "How long will she be in here?"

"Ninety minutes each." Alan stretched. "I'm gunna bake, Roger. She can eat cookies and she'll feel welcome. It will smell pretty great."

"But she's here any minute."

"Go first." Alan stood. "Take the couch. Relax, you see her all the time. You're just panicked about the fifteenth—,"

Roger moaned.

"—and you'll get a chance to tell her about it," Alan continued. In the kitchen, he searched cabinets. "You're going to tell her the truth." He peeked into the living room. "Right?"

Roger gripped the couch and sat on the armrest. "I'll try." He sank back onto the cushions. "I just don't want...her to think...I'm crazy."

The first thing Leena asked her patient about was the front door.

"Four locks, Roger? That's excessive."

"I'm sorry."

Alan measured flour. He poked it. "Yeah, it's excessive," he muttered. He gently set the measuring cups back on the table.

"...when I called you, Roger, where were you?"

"On the kitchen floor. It was the first time my legs went out in at least two months."

"What triggered it?"

Alan bit his lip. He opened a bag of sugar.

"I'm, I mean, what I said on the phone. It was about that."

"Your birthday? We can talk about that, but are you still driving?"

"My legs don't go out when I'm driving, believe me. Driving is chill."

Alan slowly stirred. He squinted when Roger started talking about his memoir.

"If I meet my deadline, then they're going to publish this thing. And if they publish it, then I'm really going to sound crazy. A TV interview is one thing, you know, but reading about Luna, it'll make people nuts. They'll laugh. They'll take Alan away."

"I seriously doubt that, Roger. You're young and likable and it'll probably be well-received."

"But the thing."

"What thing?"

"Cope Syndrome. It's going to make me look *incompetent.*" There's a beat. "I'm learning a lot of new words."

Alan opened a drawer and picked up a spoon between thumb and forefinger.

"Roger, you're the first person to have it. I've heard you tell me about Luna for a long time, and it doesn't make you incompetent."

"But that's easy for you to say. You invented the syndrome."

"I didn't invent it, alright? I just called it something on TV."

"Well that's what I'm saying, TV is different."

It took awhile for Leena to answer. "It's just a defense mechanism."

"But I'm the least defensive person I know." Roger sighed. "I like the name, by the way. I like it when you use my name."

Alan's elbow knocked a cup of flour off the table and he rushed to clean it, straining his ears. By the time he'd gotten done whipping things into dough, they were talking about Luna. Alan softly set the mixer on the table.

"I don't know what to tell you about missing Micah, Roger, I really need more details."

"Why?"

"Well I need to know a lot if I'm going to decode the meaning of a fictional person."

A pressure—huge pressure—compressed the side of Alan's head. He fell sideways into a chair to steady himself. He shook his head to clear the dizziness, then squinted at the ceiling, trying to remember who Micah was. Roger mentioned the name in some of his old anecdotes, as a man who had saved him, or sold him, or both—Alan could not recall. Micah had an estate, he knew, and a gardener. Roger called for his brother. Alan jumped and ran into the living room.

"Are the cookies baking?"

"I just need to put them in oven. I mean the oven."

Leena angled her face into Alan's periphery. "Hello. You're making cookies?"

"Yes, ma'am."

"Can you hear us in there, Alan?"

"A little bit. I'm sorry."

Roger's leg bounced. "It's okay. Just put them in the oven and read in your room so Leena can do her job."

Alan read until he heard Leena call his name. She stood by the foot of the stairs. Alan sat on a warm couch. "Were the cookies good?"

"So good." Leena handed a plate to Alan. "We saved some for you."

Alan slowly chewed. "Where's Roger?"

"He said he was going to smoke outside. Honestly, Alan, are you uncomfortable about this?"

Alan shrugged. "I think I'm always uncomfortable."

"I helped Arden pick out those new clothes. Do you like them?"

"Yes. Thank you." Alan felt hot. Leena asked about school. Alan blinked. "Aren't you supposed to ask me about rough topics?"

"So school isn't rough, then?"

"It's dull. I want to learn things."

"So you don't learn from school."

Alan tried to suppress a smile. He shook his head. "You don't have to ask me about school."

"Okay...I heard about your mother."

Alan took a deep breath. He wanted to spit out the cookie.

"Roger thinks you're a little worried about it."

Alan swallowed. "I shouldn't be."

"What would happen if you met her again? Have you thought about it?"

A pause happened. "If she finds me, she'll try to kill me. Unless she, like, stopped drinking. Which I doubt." He rubbed his right eye. "I sound like a teenager."

"But you are."

Alan gripped the cuffs of his jacket.

"Alan, you said 'if she finds me…' do you think she's looking?"

"I worry that she is."

"Have you tried writing a letter to her? Sometimes it helps to put your thoughts on paper."

Alan swallowed and nodded. Leena took notes. He rubbed his knees.

"Roger told me to tell you he's worried about your phobia."

"What phobia?"

"You don't like to be touched."

"Oh," Alan said, "right. I don't."

"What are your thoughts when someone touches you?"

Alan squinted. "There's no thoughts. It's just like needles."

"Is it worse if you don't know the person very well?"

"I don't know."

"Does it matter if they're a boy or girl?"

Alan fell on his side and rolled on the couch. "I don't know. Women don't touch me anyway." He scratched the back of his neck. "Did Arden say why she gave me an appointment with you?"

"You talk about kidnapping and it scares her."

Alan lay down and crossed his arms. "That's not fair."

"She says you're spending too much time with Roger."

"He's my brother. He's my friend."

"Yes, but you should have some healthier friends." Something changed in Leena's voice. "He loves you a lot, Alan. It makes him anxious around you. Volatile."

"He's like that about everything." Alan rubbed his stomach while Leena took notes. She said: "Do you think there is cause to be anxious about you?"

"No. I take care of myself."

Leena tapped a pen against her lips. "But when Roger refused to move to the new house at the last minute, you stayed with him. And you're still here."

"I thought I could convince him to move out but I couldn't and now I'm deciding where to go."

"Do you think he's your responsibility?"

"He is."

"Why?"

"Just...because."

"You didn't kidnap Roger."

"But it's my fault." Alan sat up. "It was supposed to be me."

If we were watching this from one side of the room, it is at this point that we would pivot to the other:

"Who told you that?"

Alan shook his head. "What do you mean?"

"Did someone tell you that you should have been taken instead of your brother?"

Alan cracked knuckles. "Why would you ask that? Of course someone told me that."

Leena flinched. She wrote notes. Alan put his arms around his knees. "Did Roger tell you anything about his birthday?"

"I can't say."

"Are you not allowed to?"

"I can only advise you, Alan. If you are uncomfortable around him on then you should go to your cousin's house."

"I'm never comfortable. I feel guilty." *Stop it, stop talking,* Alan thought to himself with rising panic. "I mean, it's fine. I'm fine."

Leena sighed. "Would you feel less guilty if you were kidnapped? You haven't done anything wrong."

Alan coughed. "I want to go to the bathroom."

For the next seven days, Roger did not leave his room. Alan brought him meals. "It's lasagna, Roger, come on. It's your favorite. Here's only a little bit. Eat while it's hot." Roger took a couple small bites. Alan dumped cold food in the trash and took his bike to school. Plates collected in the sink.

On the eighth day, Alan did not bring a meal. "I knew you wouldn't eat breakfast, so I didn't bother to make it. But you've got to get up by tonight. Arden and Jenna are coming." Roger did not speak. His brother picked up a plate from the bed and left. Alan dropped the dish in the sink. He grabbed a sponge. "She'll probably bring something expensive."

He plugged the drain and turned on the faucet. "A new TV or computer or something else you'll never use because you're too lazy or too afraid." Alan shook the soap bottle and squeezed it. He scrubbed hard. "But don't bother to get up, no. Just keep wallowing."

Roger left his room. He went downstairs.

Alan shook the bottle again. He knocked it against the edge of the sink. "Yeah, we're all very sorry for you. Poor little Roger got taken away from his batshit mommy. Maybe you should grab a bottle of vodka and join her."

Roger had entered the kitchen. He stood behind his brother.

The sink was filled to capacity. Alan shut off the faucet. "Wish I could go to Luna. At least I'd be away from here. At least a kidnapper would give a shit about whether I lived or died."

Roger flexed his fingers.

"We're sure sorry, Roger. Too sorry to say happy birthday to your face. Well, happy birthday, Roger! Happy fucking—,"

Roger pushed his brother's head into the sink. Bubbles rose through the water. He took Alan's right wrist and held it still. "Don't say that." Alan's left hand pushed the rim of the sink. It searched for Roger's arm and pulled on his sleeve. Roger lifted his brother's head from the water. Alan spat and coughed. He said Roger's name. Roger pushed him under again.

Water roared. It was burning Alan's throat. When Roger's arms relaxed, Alan emerged. He ran into the garage and lifted the kickstand on his bike. The door strained open.

Alan's fingers trembled on the brakes. He pumped his legs past burning. Wind dried Alan's face and hair. His chattering teeth was as loud as his pulse. He rode into a park and stopped near a lake. Alan threw rocks at it. He sat and hugged his own knees. He sat still for so long that a hare approached and sniffed his shoes.

An unknown man paced alone on the lake shore. Alan stood; the hare disappeared. He watched the man's progress, then turned away and walked. Alan stopped at a weeping willow. He sat under it. He looked left. The man was much closer to him. He had his hands in his pockets. Their eyes met and the man smiled. Alan looked at the birds. He clenched his fists. The man kept walking and stopped in front of the willow tree. "It's pretty cold for April."

"Yes, sir."

"Are you here by yourself?"

Alan looked at the man. "No," he whispered.

Wind pushed the man's hair. He crouched. "Can't hear you, son."

"Yes...yeah, I am alone. I'm by myself."

"Nature walks are good. Especially alone. I like your jacket." They locked eyes. "Are you alright?"

Alan shook his head. "I don't know."

"How old are you?"

"Fifteen." Then, when he saw that the man wasn't buying it: "Thirteen."

"Do you have anyone to talk to? Someone you can call?"

"No, I don't have a...I should go," Alan said. But he did not move.

"You don't have to leave." The man stood. He motioned sideways. "Take a walk with me."

Alan blinked. "I think I know you," he said flatly, then crawled around the tree and got to his feet. He walked up a slope. The man followed him. "Where are you going?"

"Home."

"Why? It's a nice day."

"No."

"Just take a walk—,"

"I said no."

"No to what? I just wanna walk."

Alan ran. The man sprinted after him. Alan tripped; a rock split his bottom lip. The man landed on him and failed to stifle Alan's scream with a hand—Alan shouted and shouted.

"Take it easy—no one's gunna miss you."

Alan's skin burned. The man reached into his pocket. Alan thrashed like a fish out of water. He kicked the man off of him and ran for the bike. Alan picked it up off the grass, swung his leg over and pedaled. He did not touch the brakes. The bike strained under his weight. The chain snapped. Wires popped. The front wheel bent into an arch. Spokes fractured. The bike flipped. Alan's body tumbled until he lost impulsion.

Alan could not breathe for several seconds. He opened his eyes. Branches danced above his head. When he tried to stand, his left ankle collapsed. Alan landed on his hands and knees. He looked upwards.

The bike was dark against a pale sky. "No..." Alan gasped and kept gasping. He crawled towards the wreckage. "No, bike...my...broken..." He stared at the handles which were once intimate with his palms. His hands hovered above the ruins. The gasping grew loud. It halted. Alan angled his neck away from a knife.

"The person who can spin a fantasy out of an
oppressive reality has access to untold power."
—*Robert Greene*

II

Alan's Wake

Water dripped.

Roger shook two pills from a bottle. He chewed them and swallowed. He did not look at the kitchen table; it carried Alan's messenger bag, the one that Alan was so rarely without. Roger picked out a third pill. The couch creaked under his weight. He rested an arm over his eyes, and within minutes his breathing was deep and even. Five hours later, he woke up in his bed without knowing how he got there. Roger rubbed his face and frowned. He picked up his alarm clock. A pencil and notebook sat on his bedside table. He opened the notebook and wrote: *Sleep walking: April. Couch to my bed.*

Roger looked around the room. He stretched his legs and his foot brushed something cold. Roger lifted the blanket. *Digital camera in bed with me,* he wrote, *the door is closed and locked. I don't know where the kid is.*

Roger turned on the camera. On the tiny screen he found pictures of himself with tired eyes. He found pictures of his younger brother's empty mattress. Pictures of the boy asleep. On his stomach, on his back, on his side. Backwards in time.

Sleeping with his arms exposed, sleeping and breathing clouds. Roger thought of the empty mattress and called Alan's name with a dry mouth. The house was empty.

Alan Cope wore heavy goggles with opaque lenses. He struggled under tight ropes and layered duct tape. His body shook at the joints. Alan Cope was a terrified boy.

Alan was tied to four bed posts. A dog licked his left ankle. Tape sealed Alan's mouth like a second skin. He thought of his bike. When the knife had met his neck, Alan had thought—had thought—had thought. The dog raised its head. A door creaked open and the man entered the room. A flash of light happened and a photograph landed on Alan's chest. The man picked it up and shook it.

"You tire me out," he said.

Alan sneezed and sniffed. The man stared at him for a long time. "I think I have a son your age," he said, and stroked the dog. "Your hair is still wet, you're probably gonna get sick." He pulled a string from the tear in Alan's pants that originated from their struggle in the park. "I'm going to the hardware store, I won't be gone long."

Alan was alone in the room. The dog returned to licking Alan's shoe. Alan sneezed again and tried to rub his nose on his shoulder. Hot, moist breath accompanied the dog's chewing as it worked through the rope on Alan's ankle. Alan wanted to speak to the animal. He waited. When his leg was free, Alan flexed it. The knee popped. The ankle throbbed. Alan's chest was heaving. He wanted to let his mouth breathe open.

When the man returned, he pushed Alan's freed leg against the mattress and sat on it. He peeled duct tape off of his captive's mouth. Alan licked his lips. "I don't think you should kill me," he said.

"You're jumping to conclusions, son." The man lifted Alan's t-shirt with something cold.

"What is that?!" Alan demanded, and then an intense pressure cut into his side and he screamed. Time slowed. Blood warmed the sheets underneath him and it made the room feel cooler and he wondered if anyone could hear him. His scream stopped abruptly and he said in a sober voice: "Do not kill me. My cousin is rich. I can do things."

The man lifted the goggles off Alan's face. "You can *do things?*"

It was as if another force was running Alan's thoughts. He could shock the man into another course of action, one that could take the length of precious seconds or minutes. "I can swallow a gallon of bleach," he said, staring at the ceiling, willing it to absorb fear.

A bloody knife cut the bonds on Alan's wrists. The man lifted him by slow degrees and Alan felt his head spinning. He thought of women telling stories—campfires, long skirts, the smell of smoke—he locked eyes with his assailant. "I like drinking bleach," he said, "it reminds me of my mother."

The man picked up Alan's chin. "You have a rich cousin?"

"Yes." Alan resisted the urge to blink, the urge to swallow.

"Old money or new money?"

"New...money." Alan blinked. The man was spreading blood across Alan's forehead like butter, and Alan was memorizing him, the shade of his eyes, the shape of his face and his mouth.

"Are you an immigrant?"

"W-What?"

"Tell them," the man said, and he pointed across the room at something.

It was a camera, perched on three legs, watching the two of them with a singular glistening eye. Alan could see his body distorted in it, his eyes blending in with its depths, a single leg still tethered out beside him like a dancer.

The man leaned forward to examine something and then stood up. He clapped Alan's shoulder. "Tell them about yourself," he said, "and make it good." He left the room.

Alan looked into the lens. Coherence fled from him. He screamed like a broken violin and promptly fell forward, fainting a little.

The man reentered the room with an open bottle of bleach and shook the boy awake. "They wanna see you drink bleach like you said."

Alan could barely make out the bottle. He reached for it, looking up at the man. The smell of the bleach woke him up a bit. He started to tilt the bottle, then flung bleach into the man's face.

The dog leapt on the bed next to Alan while his assailant roared and rushed to a sink. Alan honed in on his tethered ankle, transformed by adrenaline into a master of knots. After freeing himself he stumbled to the window; he was at least twelve feet away from a landing. Still gripping the rope, he darted out of the room on his toes, hardly breathing. Alan barely registered the man washing bleach out of his face before kicking open a screen door and launching himself over a splintered wooden balcony.

By some blessing he hit the topmost part of a slope just six feet down. He rolled, he launched into a sprint over grass and then rocks and then asphalt.

The man heard his dog and followed a trail of blood at a run. He spotted the boy, called him a terrible name and started gaining on him.

Alan heard a highway. He shouted that there was a fire.

He knew from Roger's repeated ramblings against society that screaming "fire" was the best way to get help, but the sound of running behind him was closer than that of the highway. As quick as it had arrived, Alan's adrenaline evaporated. He felt the gash in his side, the cracks in the pavement beneath him, and, oddly, he smelled ash. He caught a glimpse of himself in an abandoned pane of glass.

A whistling pierced the space with the precision and depth of silence itself. Then it stopped and Alan lost consciousness. When he woke up, he was under water.

"If you don't call the police, then you're not my sister."

"Calm down, Jenna. Alan's not stupid." Arden opened her phone. "He just wanted to get out of the house and away from this guy." She nodded at the couch. Roger was lying on it. His legs had given out hours ago. He held Alan's messenger bag against his chest.

Jenna said: "He never goes out without his bag."

"If you want to call the police, by all means do it yourself. Tell them that a thirteen year old boy decided to go out for a bike ride. Tell them to deploy their forces immediately."

"No," Roger's voice was stale from lack of use. "If the cops go looking, then whoever has—whoever has...." He shook his head. "Whoever has the kid is going to get angry and he'll hurt him. We have to look for Alan ourselves and not tell anyone."

"Nobody *has* Alan. Do you know the statistical likelihood of both of you being kidnapped? It won't happen. It hasn't happened."

Roger laughed mirthlessly. Jenna picked the phone off of his lap. "I'm calling."

"No...I'll fucking do it." Arden grabbed the phone from her sister and took it to the kitchen. "My cousin's missing," she said a moment later. "He's thirteen and doesn't have his phone with him and no one knows where he's been since this morning." Her voice cracked.

Jenna sat next to Roger. "The police can help," she said. "They can do things that we can't."

"You're a better person than me."

"Would you stop saying that? Why do you do that?"

Roger's lips were as pale as his hands. "Will you get me something to throw up in?" When he retched into the trash bin his cousin offered, nothing came out. "I knew he might not come back...as soon as he ran out the door, I'd never been so, so scared about him."

"What did you do?" Jenna put the bin on the floor.

"I yelled at him. About, um..." the man pinched his brow. "about our mom."

"You can't do that, Roger!"

"I know, I know..."

Arden stepped back into the living room with the phone pressed against her shoulder. "Roger—do you have a recent picture of him?"

"No."

"Class picture?"

"He's not allowed to do pictures." Roger thought of his digital camera and Alan's empty mattress. "I don't have anything we can use."

Arden spoke fast. "I'm going home to look for pictures, Jenna. You stay here. And Roger...your *birthday present* is in the driveway. So that you know."

Roger held the messenger bag. Jenna's eyes were saturated. She rapidly pressed buttons on her cellphone. "Leena texted me. She wants me to tell you that she's out looking for Alan right now." Roger closed his eyes. He waited for his legs to start hurting.

When Arden returned, she was cursing herself. "They found his bike," she yelled from the kitchen. "It's in pieces. He needed a goddamn new bike!"

Jenna rubbed her eyes. "How do they know it's his bike?"

Tingling pain blossomed around Roger's knees. "Because I labeled it so," he said. "I took a marker and I labeled it like ALAN'S BIKE because I didn't want it to be take, I mean stolen." Roger buried his face in the messenger bag and wailed.

Chords anchored Alan's legs to the bottom of a pool. He wore a mask. All he saw was paleness. He remembered the smell of ash and wondered if he was in a hospital.

And then, as if in slow motion, a figure descended in the water in front of him. Someone with stems rising out of their hair like symmetrical branches. But before realizing that he was looking at a person with antlers, Alan was startled by the features of their face: they were thrown in a dynamic relief such as he had never seen. As the figure swam closer, Alan reached forward and found the same variation in his own hand. He wasn't sure what he was seeing, but he knew it was the visual quality Roger told him about.

The figure was a teenaged boy, older than Alan and darker than him, with eyes that looked like the sound of wind. He fiddled with the cord around Alan's legs and it came free. Alan had a thousand questions, but when he hit the water's surface he felt himself losing consciousness again.

"Are you awake?"

Alan could not tell if the voice belonged to a man or a woman. He opened his eyes and discovered that the person looked as androgynous as they sounded.

"My name is Rusha," they said. "Where are you from?"

Alan's teeth chattered. "Court, Cortland."

"On Earth?"

"What?"

"You're from Earth."

Alan tried to lift his head. "Where am I?"

"You're in Luna. How young are you?"

"Thirteen." Alan's eyes darted. "Let me back in the water." His ears popped.

"We can't afford to keep you in subaqueous pressure anymore, I'm sorry. We need your consent to move forward."

"Why is...what's that? Why am I?"

"What you're seeing is called color. There is more than just darkness and paleness in Luna."

Alan's head pounded. "I can't be, can't breathe."

Rusha touched Alan's face and he flinched. Rusha said: "listen to me, child. You're in Luna now. This can be fatal for you."

"I want to go home."

"No one can take you home. But I can give you Larque."

"What?"

"Larque will preserve your sense of balance and help you breathe."

"What is it?"

"It's a body casting method based on the principles of weight and magnetism." Rusha's eyes looked pale, but they were not. They sounded as though they were reading fine print. "I just need your consent and then I'll take a fingerprint."

Alan shut his eyes. In a flash, he remembered waking in the dead of night to hear his brother screaming.

"You'll die without Larque. The shock will kill you in a few hours, at best."

"Kay. Take my fingerprint."

A moment later, Rusha backed away from Alan's table and spoke at the ceiling. "This is Rusha, I have a consenting thirteen year old in pod five who lost subaqueous pressure."

Just like that—two women came in and started pushing Alan's table down a hall. A dull humming rose and fell as he passed under squares of fluorescent light.

"We're going to a pressurized chamber," said the woman with paler hair. "It will help you control the tremors while we apply Larque."

Alan heard her words before he understood them. He felt as though his brain were running in slow motion. He noticed a small microphone attached to the woman's pale shirt and fixed his gaze on the colorless image. The woman frowned. "Marilyn. Does he look young enough to you?"

"We'll find out. Someone will, anyway."

Alan would never have thought that wearing magnets could help him breathe, but it did. His teeth stopped chattering but his head was sore. He stared at Marilyn's hair. "Where does color come from?"

She shook her head. "I don't know, dear. It's just something your eyes do." She pulled a tape measure across Alan's foot. "Jace, do you need help?"

"Nope." Jace stood behind Alan and pulled the cords on his magnetic vest. Alan watched his waist shrink. "It must be very tight," he said.

"It is."

"Doesn't feel as tight as it looks."

"Sit up a little more."

Alan obeyed. Marilyn tsked. "You're hurt."

Alan looked at his swollen ankle. It was smothered with hues he had never seen. "I am hurt. It looks like—like the sound of a bass drum."

"Larque will fix it. What's your name?"

"Alan Cope."

"Can you point your toes, Alan?"

Alan pointed as far as he could. Marilyn slipped metal tubes around Alan's feet. Each one had a knob that clicked when she turned it. The tubes tightened with each click. "How does that feel?"

"A little tighter, please." He could feel it working.

"Do you remember how you got to Luna?"

"I don't know, I...I smelled smoke, and there was whistling." Pain shot up Alan's neck. "It hurts to remember."

"Don't try too hard. Had you heard about Luna before?"

"Yes. My brother was here. He said it was a world with three moons."

Jace paused in the act of opening a drawer. "You say he was here? So he got back? To Earth?"

"Yeah. He says he was in Luna for...for, ah..." Alan's eyes closed. Marilyn's hand was cupped around his calf. His skin tingled like a dry tongue meeting water; there was a tension in his body that he realized upon its release. She lifted his leg onto a pillow.

Jace broke Alan from his reverie. "For what?"

"Oh...I forgot..." He did indeed.

The women flooded him with questions about Roger and life in Cortland. Marilyn placed magnets on the metal around Alan's lower legs. After removing the metal casts, she told him to keep his toes pointed. Alan could not have disobeyed her; his feet were stiff and a bit numb. The women tied boots around Alan's legs. The boots held pointed feet. The bottoms were heavy and magnetic. Jace tied a thick pelt around Alan's shoulders. It reached his collarbone and magnets clung to its leathery underside. They gave him headphones that alleviated his headache.

Alan lifted one leg. "How am I gonna walk?"

Jace smiled. "Slowly." She helped Alan off the table and he leaned against her, arms tingling. "How will I run?" He asked. Marilyn laughed.

The women led Alan down a narrow hallway. The walls were carpeted, but the floor was not. Alan felt sweat blossom over his collarbone as they passed numbered doors. "Where are we going?"

"You're going to take Mycholia."

"What does that—what is it?"

"It's an ingredient in Kisslic."

Alan lost track of who was speaking to him. "What is that?"

"Rusha sells it. It prevents aging and heals almost every sickness; not for people from Earth, but for us. We can't make it without people like you. You'll be saving a lot of lives."

"People like me...will it make me sick?"

"You're obligated to take Mycholia. It's a condition of having Larque." One of the numbered doors opened onto a small room. A man stood in a corner next a machine that Alan did not understand and had never seen. The man was wiping his hands on a rag. The women left them alone. Alan nodded at the machine. "What does that do?"

The man looked at him. "Did you say something?"

"I just...I want to know how this works."

The man cocked his head and then shrugged. He pulled a pouch out from under the machine; it looked like a bag of coffee. "This is Mycholia concentrate." He tilted the bag over a tube. Dark pebbles flowed into it. "When I turn the machine on, the rocks are ground with water, and then the steam fills this tube, which is connected to your mask."

He held up the thing and Alan flinched. "It looked like a snout."

The man fed the ribbed tube through the mask. "When you exhale, your breath comes into this dome," he said, tapping it. "And it drips out the bottom as *essentia osculum*, which is Kisslic. Now lay down."

More fine print. Alan couldn't relinquish the feeling that something about these people felt scripted, as if they were adhering to contracts unbeknownst to him.

Alan looked at the table on his left. "Why are there straps on the table?"

"In case you don't cooperate."

Alan sat slowly, and was glad to take the weight off his toes. He closed his eyes and took a deep breath. "Do I have to do this?"

"It's in your contract. Now open your mouth."

Alan stared at the man. "What?"

"The tube goes in your mouth. Over your tongue."

"Oh, I'm sorry, I, I can't do that."

"You have to."

Alan pulled his lips in and gave his head a small shake. A flicker of tension passed between them; a moment of searching eyes and pleading brows.

Alan tried to roll off the table. When the man grabbed him, Alan kicked his legs like a dying insect. Some heated instinct governed his struggle. Three more men crowded the room to restrain him. Alan would not cry out because he was fighting to keep his mouth shut. They tightened straps across his body.

"That's enough, back off." The man holding the mask pinched Alan's nose shut. "Open your mouth. It only hurts for a second."

Alan grinned and breathed through his teeth. The man cursed and thrust the mask at someone across the table. He slid his thumb and forefinger over Alan's teeth.

Put a square around the subject. Put a circle around the object. His mouth opened.

The tube made him gag and the mask made his face feel tight. He wanted to beg them to take it off, take it out, it was choking him...

...and then the Mycholia boiled, percolated, steamed up and up, Alan breathed it in...

His muscles relaxed and his pupils gleamed enormous. One of the men scratched the top of Alan's head. "Nice and docile now, aren't you?"

The men filed out of the room. Alan felt his aspect expand beyond the limits of his body. He floated as a wispy thought: *bad, bad bike broke beneath boy body.*

Leena sat in Roger's living room. She took notes and drank water. Next to her laptop was a headshot of Alan Cope, drawn with charcoal by his older brother. When Roger shared his drawing, she honestly announced that it captured Alan's poise better than any photograph could.

Leena gave Roger's basement door soft knocks. "Would you like some coffee?"

"Come in."

Roger sat under the window. A telescope stood next to him. His hands were dark from charcoal. "I'm drawing more Alan," he said. The drawing on his lap looked exactly like the original.

"It's great, Roger. Did you trace it?"

"I didn't have to." Roger's voice was light and frail. The darkness around his eyes predated Alan's disappearance. Leena held Roger's hands still with her own. "That's great," she said, "but you don't have to make copies yourself. Arden is going to do it."

"Oh, it's not an exact copy. In this one I'm adding duct tape. The pictures must be accurate, so that he can be recognized."

"I think you need a break."

Roger had a frayed laugh.

Leena stroked the telescope. "I wonder when you got this..." she looked out the window.

"I never used it until now. Leena, listen: when you make the lost boy posters, please make them say 'where is Alan Cope,' and not 'where is this boy,' so that everyone will know what the kid is called. They might want to walk along the highway, say, and call his name."

"Okay, Roger, I'll do that."

"Just make sure."

"Alan will be fine.."

Roger nodded. "Yes, Micah will take care of him."

Leena gripped the end of the telescope. She looked at him. "What did you say?"

"Micah will take care of my little brother until I find a way back to Luna."

Leena shivered. "Micah's not real."

Roger took a deep breath and bent low over his drawing.

"Roger, Luna isn't real."

He set his drawing on the floor and stood over her. "Just because you have the power to convince me that I'm wrong doesn't mean you should."

Leena could not take her hand off the telescope. "Luna is not real. It's *not.*"

"It is real. I saw red on his bag, and you..." Roger left a charcoal smudge where he touched her face. "You have color all over your face, Leena. You just can't see it."

Her fingers closed around his wrists. She pushed herself away. "I really can't stand when you touch me like that."

"Sure, sure." He winked at her.

Leena looked away from his face—she clocked his forearm, how it was longer than his waist. Her eyes watered.

"I won't let you convince me that I'm wrong anymore," Roger went on. "I say, some days: I'm sick. But other days, I know that I'm right. I'm right about Luna, I'm right about love and I'm right about me and you." His lips stayed puckered on the last word.

"I will find help you find Alan, Roger, but you can't honestly believe in Luna, you're fragile and it's killing me."

Roger pointed a smudged finger at the door. "Then you can leave."

Leena used the stair railing. She leaned over the kitchen sink to wash charcoal off her face—cold water. She splashed it on her neck, too. Arden entered the house. Leena gave her the drawing. "We're using this for the posters. Roger's in the basement and I sent Jenna upstairs to sleep, if she can. I'm assuming you still want to send her to school tomorrow."

"It will do more harm than good if she stays home."

Leena looked at her friend. "You've been out all night."

Arden nodded. "Thanks for being here."

"I'll stay until we find him—, I'll stay as long as you need."

Arden sat on the couch. She rubbed her face. "It's five AM now...so it's been..."

"About ten hours."

"I was just at the police station. They were questioning a man about some, you know, breaking and entering...and arson, I think. And they found some photographs in his coat."

"Arden, they found a video."

Arden fisted her hands. "I know."

"Don't watch it."

"I already did. He runs off. At the end of it. Gets free."

"Okay." Leena bit her thumbnail. "I'm sorry, Arden."

"I'm fine."

"No, you're not." Leena put an arm around her friend. "I wish you could just let this take its course."

"You can't. You can't wait this kind of thing out, Leena."

"I know, but I'm here for you. We'll come up with a plan."

Arden straightened her back. She looked the woman beside her. "Listen to me. *We can not let Roger find out about that video.*"

Her friend nodded. "I know." Arden rubbed her face and rubbed her face. Leena left the couch and poured coffee. "You don't think Roger suspects anything?"

"He knows Alan's gone."

"No, not that. I meant about me."

Arden looked at the ceiling. "Not again, Leena. He doesn't know. He's very trusting."

"I'm lying to him, Arden."

"No, you're not." Arden looked at Leena. "You are a doctor."

"I'm not a therapist," Leena whispered.

"Well, what's the difference? What's the difference as long as he thinks you are? I told you he won't listen to anyone else. He won't see anyone else."

Leena passed a mug to her friend. "I know, but he's not a kid anymore, and he thinks he's in love with me, and now he has to cope with something that's beyond what I know how to help with, Arden. I didn't think I'd be in this position."

"What is wrong with you?" Arden stood. "You just said you'd be here for me, and you're bringing this up now?"

"Arden, please..."

"Don't beg me. Just don't."

Leena nodded. "Okay. I'm sorry, you're right."

Micah Larque approached Rusha's building. He held a jacket in both hands. Rusha's receptionist, Candy, opened the door for him. "Well if it isn't Mr. Larque himself!" She retreated to her desk chair. "Rusha has really missed you. Are you here to supervise Larque application?"

"Not today, though I will soon. Rusha tells me that some of the boys need adjustments."

"Yes, Mr. Larque, some of them do." Candy nodded at the jacket. "I trust the clothes are helping you in your research?"

"Yes, thank you for sending them. I wonder if you could scan this jacket for me, I'd like to see the boy to whom it belonged."

"Of course. Would you like some Kisslic while you wait? Water? Coffee?"

"No, thank you." Micah sat on a leather couch and rested his hands on crossed knees. He only needed Kisslic every few hours and rarely exceeded that amount. He looked up at a corner of the room and watched the progress of a tiny spider. Micah took a deep breath. When he first examined the words inside the jacket now in Candy's hands, the handwriting he saw had made his eyes water.

"Mr. Larque, I've found him. His number is 1507 and he's in Pod 31, taking Mycholia right now. Do you still have a master key?"

"Yes, Candy, thank you."

Something hard was in Alan's mouth. He did slow blinking. He did not realize he was grinding his teeth on a tube. He was aware of shrinking into an aching body and a self called Alan Cope. Micah slowly walked around Alan's table. His hands descended around the boy's face. He pulled up the mask. Micah examined the broken tube.

Alan licked his teeth, they were oddly rubbery. "Will you let me up?"

Micah unbuckled straps. Alan pushed himself onto his elbows. His nose started bleeding.

Micah adjusted a knob on Alan's headphones. "That's better for you."

Blood reached Alan's chin. Drops tapped his midriff and he twitched like a prey animal. "I want to be at home."

Micah's eyes flicked between Alan's. "I know."

Alan stared at the man beside him. "I'm sick. I need a map. You have furs on, too. Is it cold on Luna?"

"Yes."

"You're aristocracy," Alan said. "I dunno, I dunno why I'm talking so much..."

"It's a side effect."

Alan ignored him. "I know you're aristocracy because you're wearing a crest." He poked the pin on Micah's cloak. His finger remained poised in the air for a moment, half raised. "I know that letter L...I saw it before."

Micah watched the subtle fault lines in the boy's brow, his pouting mouth. Roger's lips always puckered when he was thinking.

"It was on Roger's leg." Alan's hand dropped. "He has that tattooed on his leg."

Micah nodded. He set the jacket on Alan's lap. "This is yours, Alan."

"Oh." Alan clutched the thing. "That's so peculiar." He fell back on the table. "I feel awful."

Micah checked his pocket watch. "Can you do arithmetic?" Alan rubbed his face. Micah went on: "Try adding in your head—,"

"In my head?"

"—and keep your eyes closed. I'll be back soon."

Alan chased floating thoughts. He nodded once and said: "He knows my name I think."

Rusha's office was windowless. Micah sat beside an oil lamp. "Alright, you win. There's someone I want to buy from you."

Rusha had been sipping Kisslic from a wine class and they suddenly coughed, spraying dark flecks all over their documents.

"You? You, sanctimonious Micah, want a child in-house?"

Micah sighed. "Yes. I need to raise my dosage anyway. And you're always complaining about how hard it is to send Kisslic all the way over to my estate, aren't you?"

"No, Micah, you know I'm fine with that, hmm? Old friends."

Micah shrugged. "Still, it'll make it easier for you. And I can test the magnets on him."

"You have one in mind?"

"1507. He's in pod 31."

Rusha opened a drawer. "1507 is new. Very new. I only let out boys who are close to retirement, Micah, and this kid is nowhere near that. His yield is incredible." The drawer shut. "Why don't you come to the next auction?"

"Oh, please." Micah pulled off his gloves. "This room is always too hot. Listen, Rusha, the boy damaged your equipment already. He bit through the tube."

Rusha nodded and scribbled something on a notepad. "Thanks for the head up, I'll get him a mouth guard. Maybe have his teeth removed."

"Rusha!"

"What?" Rusha held their palms out, blinking. Micah just stared at them until Rusha dropped their hands. "Listen, Micah, I'm in hot water, here. Boiling water. I had no way of knowing that people would need more, or that they'd get dependent on it, alright, but it heals!" Rusha lifted the wine glass. "This stuff saves lives, and our supply is in danger."

"I know."

"It saved *your* life, Micah."

"I *know.*"

"I can't afford to lose inventory because some kid has a teething problem. And I can't afford to give him away."

"How much do you want?"

Rusha gave him a pained expression. "You're my best friend."

"I know you're not running a charity."

They rubbed their fingers together. "How's life treating you?"

"Fine. It's nice being far away. I'm sick of the city. Did you get my letter about the tide?"

"I don't want to talk about that today."

Micah sighed and looked at the envelopes and notes scattered across Rusha's desk. It reminded him of the days when they were still neighbors, when Micah was struggling to recover from illness and false accusations... Rusha had spent those days holed up in lab, looking for a cure until they accidentally discovered Kisslic when a child from Earth smoked Mycholia in Micah's front room, eliminating the man's lung problems overnight.

Micah took a deep breath. "Let me take him home."

"Can't you work your savior complex with something else, Micah? Adopt a kitten? Or take another one? 1322 needs a home...."

"Rusha...."

"...His antlers are ten inches high! What?"

"I want 1507. He can take Mycholia at my estate. I won't need it all, you can come pick up inventory every once in awhile if you're fearful about it." Rusha frowned. There was a pause. "I know what people will say about me," Micah went on, reining the elephant in the room. "I know some people still think I'm a monster, but I did nothing wrong, Rusha."

"I know."

"I never hurt any one of those kids. I just don't want to be seen at an auction. And I know you don't put up anyone with a good yield."

Rusha made an exasperated sound. "So I come to your estate, take my share of Kisslic, and he gets the comfort and privacy of your home. Why?"

"I'm nostalgic."

"Then take a different one. An older one."

"I want *that one!*" A pause happened.

Rusha's eyes narrowed. "Why?"

Micah stared at his friend, trying to deduce whether they knew that 1507 was Roger Cope's brother. Could that be why they was so reluctant to let him go? "If I tell you, Rusha, you have to promise you'll let me take him home. Promise that you're not going to make a scene. You're not going to tell a soul."

"Okay...."

"I think 1507 is Roger's brother. Roger Cope."

"...Are you sure?"

"I'm almost positive."

"You know what people will think."

"I know what they'll think. I don't care."

"Micah, you can't have him."

"A promise is a promise."

Rusha cursed and downed the last of his Kisslic. "Take him quietly. You're sentimentality is destroying me, Micah."

The man was out of his chair already. "I know. Thank you."

"Set him up in your basement."

"I will."

Rusha rubbed their face. "A liter to six ounces, Micah...a liter to just six ounces! You'd better keep his yield, you'd really better keep his yield."

Micah hesitated. "I don't want him to feel sick all the time."

Rusha pointed a pen at the man. "If I don't get enough, you will compensate me. One way or another."

Luna's sky had sharp, sweeping colors. Alan stared at it. He connected three moons with his vision until fog obstructed it. He rubbed his hands over the dark leather seats of Micah's car. "Clouds descend," he said. "Micah?"

"Yes, Alan?"

"Roger says that you took care of him." Alan pressed his forehead against the cold car window. "Did you kidnap him?"

"No."

"Do you know who kidnapped my brother?"

"Someone from your world must have done it, Alan. I try not to think about those things." Micah turned on his radio.

After a moment, Alan grinned. "I like this song."

"It's Vivaldi."

"What?"

"You don't know Vivaldi?"

"No, sir, I don't. And it makes like, like when you play it, I'm floating."

Micah sighed. "Do you play?"

"Play what?"

"Never mind. I'll teach you later."

The song ended, the car hummed at Alan's ears. "I am drowsy, that's what I am."

"No, Alan, you're not. You just feel drowsiness. There's a difference."

"OkaythenI *feel* drowsy."

"Much better."

Alan stared at his hands and flexed them. "Wow," he said, "there's a difference."

As they neared Micah's property, Alan felt recognition like a blaze; a familiarity of being locked in an unfamiliar car with an unfamiliar man. He stared at his jacket and had a vision of layered duct tape. "I want you to tell me about my brother please," he said.

"I want you to tell me about him, too. Over dinner."

Alan felt weakness like a tremor in his sternum. "Are you going to hurt me? When?"

The man made a sound and shook his head. "No, no, no. Shush."

Mist shrouded Micah's estate. Upon entering the manor, Alan paused to admire colored furniture. Marble gleamed under his boots. Micah waved at the room. "Do you like it?"

"It's posh, alright," Alan said.

Micah pointed at a wall. "That's a portrait of your brother."

Alan saw it and shivered. His eyes fixated on the painting even as he tried to turn his head. The boy in the portrait bore Roger's distinctive qualities: squinty eyes, a peckish, freckled face and hair that grew forward in brief, aggressive strokes. His posture suggested the same precocious tendency of his younger brother. Alan said: "That's not my brother."

"Yes it is."

"But my brother doesn't have antlers!" Alan cried. He looked at the man.

Micah said: "they were added for effect."

"Why, though? Sir," Alan added when Micah looked at him.

"Antlers are a symptom of Mycholia. If you take it for years, and you become too old to produce Kisslic, it happens. Usually around fifteen or sixteen. Roger wanted to look more like a traditional Larque boy."

"But he never grew antlers!"

"No, he didn't...he just never lost it..."

"Never lost what?"

Micah shrugged. "The thing that dies when you get older. And I'll tell you, all men get antlers here."

Alan stared at him.

Micah went on: "We just cut them down."

"No..." already on his toes, Alan peered at Micah's head. The man suddenly took his hand—

—lifted it—

and in Micah's hair, Alan felt a rough, bony nub. He ripped his hand away like it was on fire.

"What's wrong?"

"That can't be real."

"When you're older, Alan, you will learn that nothing is real."

Alan leaned against the papered wall. "How do you find people from Earth? How do they get here?"

"No one knows how they get here, but we know when they arrive. Rusha designed a system of seismographic bells, like chimes, and they vibrate when someone from Earth enters Luna. They're stationed all over the island; this island, the one we're on, it's the only land that Luna has. Most of Luna is ocean."

Alan blinked and looked away from the painting. "Have you ever heard the bells ring?"

Micah's eyebrows raised by a fraction and he shook his head. "Only wolves can hear them. Rusha keeps a wolf by all of the bell stations and they howl when their bell rings."

"How can Rusha tell between those howls and regular howls?"

"What do you mean?"

"Like, apart from the trained wolves. What about the wild wolves?"

Micah smiled a bit. "There are no wild wolves, here. All of them belong to a bell station, with a Wolf Keeper. There's some controversy about that, but..." he took a deep breath. "It's not the kind that you'd be familiar with."

Alan swallowed. He rubbed his hand, trying to erase the sensation of the chopped antler. "May I use your bathroom?"

Alan vomited hard. It was very dark and that made him worry. The floor was cold on his knees. The faucet was fashioned to look like a snake. Alan remembered Roger's hands in his hair. He froze mid-step when he saw Micah waiting outside the bathroom.

The man studied his nails. "I did wonder when you would get sick."

"Was that—, am I supposed to get sick?"

"It's another side effect. Do you know how long you were taking Mycholia?"

"No, sir."

Micah frowned at him. His voice seemed to be coming from far away. "Do you want to eat?"

"Not often," Alan admitted.

The man smiled. "How about now?"

Alan could not tell if he was feeling fear or curiosity. "Sure."

Micah ate with his left hand resting beside the plate. A cloth napkin met his lips between small bites. Alan watched. "You eat like Roger," he said.

"Hm. It's your brother who eats like me."

"Roger's left handed but he eats with the right one."

Micah nodded. He chewed slow.

"Which color does our hair have?" Alan asked.

"That's black."

"What about the tablecloth?" Alan pushed it with a finger. "'There's pictures of leaves on it. They're real-looking."

"That's a photographic print. Terribly expensive to make, though. The couch has clouds on it, if you look close. Those are blue and white. And I've got a chair upholstered with a supernova."

"A supernova? Like, from a galaxy? Roger loves space stuff."

"Don't mumble so, Alan, it's impolite." Forks clicked. "I'll show you the color spectrum later."

Alan nibbled a buttery shrimp. Micah took a deep breath. His hands fell onto his lap. "How is Roger?"

"He's functioning."

"Oh, good...he's not blind, or anything?"

"Oh, no! No, sir. He's okay. I mean his legs get paralyzed sometimes. And there's the anxiety, but he has meds for that."

"Meds?"

"Yes, sir. Medicine."

"Do the leeches still help him?"

Alan rubbed his arm. "Leeches? We don't—, no sir, we don't use leeches in Cortland, I mean, not to heal people. Not anymore."

Micah raised an eyebrow. "We don't either. Leeches were a matter of preference for your brother."

Alan suddenly froze, he was filled with the image of his brother applying leeches to his own neck, his own arms. He felt Micah staring at him.

"Have you lost your appetite?"

"I'm afraid so, sir."

Wind pushed branches against a nearby window. Micah muttered something about a tide. Then his voice rang out: "where did you say you were from?"

"Cortland."

"What happened to Tioga?"

"Nothing." Alan leaned back in his chair. "Everyone left, so Arden took me to Cortland." Silence happened. Alan scratched the back of his neck. "I guess that doesn't make a lot of sense. Roger was gone, right? And Diane, my mother, she kept wandering off with her vodka, she said she was looking for him. But she...well, everyone was saying, it's her fault Roger was...she knew the guy. Who kidnapped him. Like apparently she took money from him or something. And then eventually, she went out and didn't come back. And my dad had a...had a stroke, you know what that is? I called 911, but it took too long. We lived in the country." Alan closed his eyes. He leaned his head against a fist. A rancid taste crept up his tongue and he thought of Mycholia.

"Arden is your cousin, I think? Or your aunt?"

"My cousin. She picked me up from a police station." The taste evaporated.

Micah took a sip of wine and licked his lips. "And Roger came back awhile after that?"

"Yes, sir." Alan opened his eyes.

Micah squinted and leaned forward. "It must have been hard on you."

"No." Alan coughed hard. "Don't say that, it's fine at home. Really. In fact, I'd like to go back now." He shot up from the chair.

"Alan, you can't go back right now. I think you know that."

Alan put down his fork and stared at his plate. He felt like there was a vice tightening around his neck.

Micah said, "I'm sorry."

The boy lifted the pelt off his shoulders and rubbed his eyes with it.

"I'm so sorry."

It wasn't long before flames licked Alan's throat, he wanted another Mycholia dose so bad. For whatever reason, Micah was reluctant to administer it. He instead opted to show Alan his brother's old room:

It put Alan's gaze to work. The ceiling was covered in hand drawn stick figures. The carpeted walls held feathers, wooden clocks, patches of furry hide, marionettes, ribbons, jewelry and a fishing net—all with sparkling pushpins. A paper banner said THIS ROOM. It looked like a hybrid abode of a creative child and a lonely specter. Alan sat on the bed and hugged his knees. He took the tea that Micah offered but did not drink it. The man carried a long necked bottle. He sat on the end of the bed. Clocks ticked at them. "Please don't cry, Alan. Don't make me see you cry."

"I'm not." Alan took a sip of tea and swallowed with difficulty. He nodded at the bottle. "What's that?"

Micah lifted his fingers off the logo. "It's Kisslic. It prevents aging, I've been drinking it since I was in my thirties...long time. It can make you live forever," he added with a chuckle. "But don't try it. It's poisonous to you. Anyway, it's like drinking sweat." He took a gulp and grimaced. "Do you know, Alan, how long it takes for one Larque boy to make this much Kisslic?" He waved the bottle.

"No, sir."

"Forty-eight hours, usually. But only about an hour for you."

"Why?"

Micah shrugged. "Do not wander alone," he said suddenly, "you will always be vulnerable in Luna."

Alan stretched out his legs. "I guess I'm pretty easy to recognize. On account of the clothes."

"No, it isn't that." Micah waved a hand. "Lots of people wear my clothes now. I'm afraid the whole 'Larque look' has caught on." Micah scratched his nose.

Alan's tea smelled like earth. He stopped mid-sip. "Why do you think that?"

The man shook his head. He stood and paced the room. "Something political but...I'm not political. Not anymore." He fingered the fishnet. "Your brother put all these things on the wall; this was his room. He spent a lot of time here."

Alan closed his eyes and nodded. After a pause, he asked: "how did you find me? Where did you get my jacket?"

"I like to collect clothes from earth. I recognized the jacket. And the handwriting in it."

"It was Roger's jacket before. That's why it says THIS JACKET and then it says ALAN'S JACKET underneath that. Do you have the rest of my clothes? My shoes?"

"They might be in my workroom. You should take a look, when you feel better."

Alan did not think that he could feel better. Rest and clarifying tea made his memories rush like a maddening current. His hands met the blanket beside him and he pulled it up to his face.

"Don't be sad, Alan." Micah pushed a hand through his own hair. "What can I do? I've spent years trying to find a way for you to get home." He circled the bed and knelt beside Alan. "What should I do when you're upset?"

"Please go away. Leave me alone."

Micah stood and rubbed his chest. "I'm sorry, I know you want to go home. If you come downstairs, be careful of the hallway. There is no banister." He left the door ajar.

Alan kept still until he was certain that Micah was out of earshot. He made himself as small as possible under the blanket.

Micah would spend hours in his studio. Alan peered in from time to time to watch the man work. There was a lightness to him, a sense of peace in his moving around sewing tables that Alan had never witnessed before and he longed to be nearer to such a gravitational energy. Micah didn't appear to notice Alan's surveillance until they made eye contact one day. Alan jumped and ran to the end of the hall. He heard Micah's voice behind him.

"It's alright, Alan, you can come in if you like."

The studio doorway was a white light breaking into the hall. Alan slowly walked up to it and stood with his hands braced against its edges. He watched Micah's sewing movements. The man wasn't looking at him. He pulled up a stool. "Come in, have a seat."

When Alan entered he pressed his back against the wall and looked at a scrap of cotton on the floor. Micah unravelled a measuring tape. "If I wanted to hurt you, Alan, I would have done it by now."

Alan approached the stool. Micah handed him a needle and asked him to string it. It took the whole of Alan's attention. It had been so long since he felt this close to safe that it was like a muscle un-flexing. He handed the needle to Micah and Micah thanked him.

"I'm making a seam," he said, "it's like the spot in your jacket where I found your name."

"Is that why you wanted me?" Alan said bitterly, the words fleeing his mouth before he thought about them. "Because of my name?"

Micah laughed lightly. "I was just curious about Roger. I miss him very much...curious enough to take on some risk...." No words were exchanged as the man stood and crossed the room to a shelf full of fabrics.

Alan fixed his gaze on a magnetic strip on the table. He started to straighten the needles on it. "How much?" he asked in as casual a tone as he could manage. They made eye contact. "I think a person ought to know how much they fetch for, that's all."

Micah was shaking his head. "You misunderstood me. I didn't buy you." He stopped there.

Alan shrugged and scratched his arm. "What was he like? When he was my age?"

"Your brother?

Alan nodded and Micah smiled. "He was petty. And performative, and loud. Came to all my functions with me. Always tried to get into the wine. Roger is incredibly sweet when he wants to be. He talked someone out of suicide. It was all over the papers."

"Oh." Alan stared at his lap.

"You sound surprised."

"Naw. Roger can be nice. He takes in a lot of women."

Micah laughed and returned to the table. "I'll bet he's enjoying his twenties."

Alan sighed. "He dates a lot of people at the same time. When they yell at him he gets small and sad and they can't stay angry. They feel bad for us. Sometimes they bring me stuff." He could sense that Micah's eyes were on him, but in the act of attentive listening. "I don't know how he can do it when he doesn't even care that much. He's in love with Leena."

"Do you like Leena, too?"

"Not like that. She's like our social worker, sort of. She's a family friend." Alan's palms were moist. "Sorry."

"Why are you sorry?"

Alan rubbed his neck and slunk out of the studio.

Over the next several weeks, Alan tried to stay active against periodic spells of malaise. Hours in Micah's library taught him about the origins of Kisslic, among other things. He found colored paints under his bed and memorized their names. He cooked his own meals. While pondering Micah's warnings about venturing far by himself, it occurred to him that the man might be taking advantage of his ignorance.

But to what end? Alan wondered this as he tiptoed along Micah's garden wall. He held a paintball gun that he would not use because he didn't want to scare off the fox that had been following him. Micah offered luxuries that Alan politely declined. He had a sense that Mycholia was available, but Micah told him it was dangerous, so he did not press the issue. Alan stopped to rub the silky petals of a red flower. Most of the time, the man locked himself in his workroom, and Alan did not himself feel captive. In fact, it was the paralysis of unfamiliar freedom which trapped Alan more than the confines of the estate. He felt like a costly painting or an exotic pet; precious and superfluous at once. Nether of these qualities were consistent with his life in Cortland.

Part of him wondered why he couldn't fit under convention; he thought of falling to his knees and crying for home. But that would only be expressing a pre-existing ache for something that he had never had. Guilt flashed through Alan whenever he realized that he missed a man who had tried to drown him.

Alan sat on the garden wall. He sullenly scratched around the fox's ears. Attempts to recall the events which led up to his arrival at Micah's estate made Alan sick with fright. The moons confused him. He lacked a sense of time.

Alan approached Micah's pond. He could watch forever that world defined by water's surface, its movement by waves responding to the golden animals that swirled galactic in its depth. They were unlike any fish Alan had seen before.

The gardener, Quinn, came out with a bucket and Alan froze. Quinn was a big man with muscles that worked under tanned skin. Alan was nervous of him. The man fed the pond, spotted Alan with a shaded gaze and beckoned. "Come over, boy, come see the fish."

Alan sat at the edge of the pond. Quinn netted a fish and lifted it from the water. It put up no resistance. "You can touch it."

Alan glanced at the man's face. He stroked the fish. "It's real smooth."

"It can live up to two hours outside of water." Quinn lowered the fish back into the pond. It danced out of the net. He took large breaths. "You look anemic."

"I try to eat," Alan said. "I'm just not good at it."

"Hmm. You're on Mycholia?"

"Yes, sir, every day." Alan obediently lied, putting the paintball gun on his lap.

By angles and heft and projection the man lifted the net and set it on the garden wall. "You don't look like it." He waiting in silence for Alan to respond.

"I'm not, really. But I'm not supposed to tell anyone that. Micah says I don't have to take it."

Quinn put his hands on hips. "Withdrawal can be dangerous."

"Am I going to die of withdrawal?"

Quinn smiled. "No, I don't think so. You could overdose, though. Roger came close all the time. Micah never...said no to him." He put a tube in the pond and sifted it around the bottom.

"Could I ask you something, sir? Do you drink Kisslic?"

"Not yet. Micah's offered it to me, but once you start you're on it for life. I thought I'd wait until I'm fifty, at least. That's assuming my wife can accept it...."

"You have a wife?"

"A wife and a son. But they don't live around here, they live in the mist. In the center of Luna," Quinn added upon seeing Alan squint. "It's safer there." He gave Alan a significant look as he said this.

Alan looked at his reflection in the water. "I don't really look like Roger. Even when he was my age."

The man studied the boy with his eyes. "You take the sky light better than he did. He was always burning and freckling. But you'd better go inside, anyway. Micah will worry after you."

In the house, Micah paused in the act of closing his jacket. "Alan, where did that animal come from?"

"It found me outside, sir."

"And it followed you?"

"Yes, sir, it follows me."

"Well, then..." Micah adjusted his collar. "If it makes you happy. Did you try the gun?"

"I didn't want to scare the fox away."

Micah shrugged. "So much for painting the roses red. Are you going to name it?"

Alan blinked at him. "It's a fox."

"That's not a name."

"Okay, she can be red, then. Little Red."

Micah shook his head, but he was smiling. "It's orange."

Alan scratched his collarbone. The fox followed him to an armchair. Alan stared at his knees. "I have a question."

"Yes, Alan?"

"Why is there no banister?"

Micah's voice echoed from behind the armchair. "It broke when your brother leaned on it."

"Why was he leaning on it?"

"Your brother was hallucinating and thought the balcony would swallow him, and he had to use its teeth to get across safely."

"And he thought that the banister rungs were teeth?"

"Evidently." Micah sat on his cloudy couch.

Alan pulled the fox onto his lap. "Did he break any bones?"

Micah shook his head. "Only balcony bones. But he fell—I think eight feet. It was the first time that he couldn't feel his legs." Alan pushed a hand back and forth over the fox's back. Micah said: "That animal is very tolerant of you."

"Most are." Alan touched the fur which hung over his collarbone. The fox was softer. "I've been in your library."

"Do you enjoy it?"

Alan felt an enormous pressure on the back of his head. "I enjoy it," he said, but he did not. He normally loved reading, but every book in the library seemed to slowly descend into something violent and upsetting the longer he read it. It made his head reel. Silence happened.

The fox sneezed. Alan pushed its tail off the armrest. "I can...I'll put her back in the garden."

"No, sit." Micah rubbed his face.

More silence. Alan lifted the fox's forelegs. "Should I name it Socks?"

Micah slowly blinked. "Little Red is fine." He watched Alan fiddle with the fox's ears. "I'm glad you're here."

Alan nodded. "Thanks. I mean. Thanks for the, you know, the helping me."

"You take nothing for granted. You're easy to help." Their eyes met. The fox leaped off Alan's lap.

Alan watched the animal snuffle around the room. Some part of him seemed to announce dimly that he was lost in a trance. He was compelled to ask questions not for the answers, but for second truths that the answers might contain. He thought there was a name for this but he couldn't remember it. "I have another question. I can't wear normal clothes here?"

"No. It would kill you. Larque is a science."

"I know." Subtext, that was the word for it. Alan looked down at his legs and saw hooves. He shook his head to clear this vision as the fox slinked under the coffee table.

He felt oddly sleepy. "I don't like going so deep underwater every time I want a bath."

Micah stretched his arms and stood. "I'm going to dinner with a few friends. You may join."

Alan did not want to leave the fox, but he was eager to see more of Luna and could not remember his last visit to a restaurant. Micah took the boy into one of his brightly lit workrooms. Alan lingered near the entrance and watched Micah navigate between long white tables, running his hands over stretches of silk and canvas. He stopped at a clothing rack.

"I only hoped this would fit you, Alan, I had no measurements...is it warm?"

"Yes, sir...I like these buttons."

"I cut those from antlers."

Alan stopped fingering them. "Whose antlers?"

Micah smiled. "Human antlers are no good for that." He finished buttoning Alan's coat. These buttons are from a stag."

In the car, Alan clutched the sides of his seat. Micah gave him instructions on conduct: "Keep both hands in full view at all times. Maintain your unassuming nature, keep your eyes as you do, nice and big. No no, don't squint."

"It happens when I listen."

"Then try to stop it. It makes you look thoughtful."

"But I'm thinking."

"Oh, I know. Just try not to let on that you're anything but a typical Larque boy on Mycholia."

"Oh..."

"You're making Kisslic, Alan, as far as anybody knows. And I'm in serious trouble if someone finds out that you're a wasted resource."

Alan frowned. "I don't like that."

"That's just how it is. Don't worry, don't worry."

Green and white dominated the place. Alan had never seen colors so carefully juxtaposed; it excited him much more than the prospect of a meal. When Alan's steak arrived, Micah pulled it to his side of the table to cut it. One of his friends tsked.

"Micah, why bring him to a place like this?"

"He's been depressed."

To validate the claim, Alan sighed.

"They're all depressed. Until they're manic. I think it's too much trouble, to keep one in the house. But that's me."

While eating, Alan found a vein in the meat. It looked like a winter tree. He shifted the branches with a fork and wondered if he had such plant-like veins in his own body.

"Diane said that she would join us."

Someone laughed. "I guess we should hold off on the wine, then?"

"It won't make a difference, you know her. Who invited her?"

"She invited herself," Micah said, and there was a collective groan.

Alan put the vein in a napkin and set down his fork. It can't be her, he thought, don't be absurd.

Alan did not see the woman join the table; his gaze was averted to his plate. But his breath stopped when he recognized his mother's voice: "Another pet, Micah?"

"It's nice to see you too, Diane."

Her laugh pierced the surrounding tables.

Spots blossomed in Alan's vision. He glanced up and saw the woman's eyes, which were as enormous and dark as his own. He remembered breath and took one. He bounced one knee and then the other. Diane draped a coat around her chair. "I'm need the bathroom. Get me a steak if I'm not back."

The succotash made Alan suddenly nauseous; but it had the desired effect. His eyes were glossy and listless. His very lips were pale. Micah told his friends he had an early morning, and they left.

On the way home, Alan rubbed and rubbed his neck. Micah gave him uneasy glances. "You look tired...are you tired, Alan?" A pause. "Hmm? You look sleepy. Did you like the food okay?" Micah licked his lips. He chuckled. "I think we had them fooled. You can say whatever's on your mind now...Alan?'

Alan parted dry lips. "How is my mom here?"

The car rumbled in solitude for a bit. "So, that was your mother."

"Why didn't you say?"

Micah shook his head. "I wasn't sure. I didn't know."

There was but one question on Alan's mind about this: "if she's here, though, she can't go back to Earth, right?"

Micah shook his head. "No, she can't."

A storm started. Black gates opened and Micah pulled into his driveway. Alan retreated to his room. The fox yipped and Alan whistled. "Here, Little Red." The fox crossed the bannister-bereft balcony and leaped onto Alan's bed. Alan stroked the thing. "It's only lightning. Bet you're glad that you're inside, now." His voice lowered to a whisper. "My mother doesn't recognize me, Little Red...I thought I would want to see her again, if I was allowed." He took a shuddering breath. "But I didn't want her to see her again. I don't. She put—she put..." Alan breathed deep again and pulled the fox onto his lap. He cupped a hand around its ear. "She put a plastic bag on my head." He covered his mouth after saying it, then wrung his hands.

He had heard why Diane wasn't allowed near him. He knew. But before that night, he didn't *know*.

He used to see young Roger in his mind's eye, a child but still the big brother, standing by himself at the end of a long driveway. That was how It Happened, he imagined, it was a collage of what he learned at school: Roger standing alone in the driveway, a Stranger driving up, grabbing him, and then he was capital K *Kidnapped*.

That vision seemed tame, now—his childhood ideation felt so silly, such an ineffectual facsimile in the face of his own tumble, the broken bike, the sharp huge knife under his chin.

Micah's silhouette slipped into Alan's doorframe. He knocked on it with two knuckles.

"Come in," Alan said.

Micah sat next to him. "I love the rain."

"Me too."

"Are you alright?"

Alan sniffed. "I think so." He held his own elbows, then looked squarely at the man beside him. "What, you wanna hug me or something?"

Micah made a non-commital noise and rubbed his forehead. Alan sighed. "Roger always looks at me so, when he's wanting to hug me."

"I'm sorry, Alan."

"I know. I mean, don't be."

Thunder and lightening shared a moment. In its aftermath, Micah frowned. "Did you hear a knocking?"

Alan shook his head.

"Hm...I heard a knocking. Have you been to the coast, Alan?"

"No, sir."

"I think you would love it. You should see it, before the big tide comes in—"

"Doesn't the tide come in every day?"

Puzzled, Micah shook his head. "I'm going to check the door. You just stay here."

The fox yipped again and Alan stroked it. He stared at the storm stricken window in front of him. The fox trembled in his arms. Alan heard several voices; loud ones that accelerated into an argument. He heard Micah yell his name. Heart pounding, Alan pulled a jeweled letter opener out of the wall and crossed the hallway with the fox in his wake. At the foot of the staircase, he froze. Micah was caught beside a rifle and bleeding from the mouth. The man holding the gun nodded at Alan's hand. "Drop that...drop it." The letter opener hit marble. "Laurent, the boy's here. Come check him."

A white coated man appeared from behind Alan. He had a black zippered case under one arm. Roger's portrait dwarfed the room's inhabitants. The fox's ears flattened. Laurent circled Alan until his shadow fell over the boy. He took a small flashlight out of the case. "Look at me." Light met Alan's eyes direct. He perceived a pattern of veins and the sting of urgency. The fox made a soft growl and it seemed to Alan that the animal was attached to him by invisible nerves. He wanted to lock it away from the man and his prying light. Laurent grabbed Alan's face and pulled his lips away from his teeth. "I might do a blood test." The fox snarled and clamped its jaws over the white coat. Laurent kicked the animal across the room. It hit the opposite wall and collapsed, twitching, on the floor.

Alan kneeled beside it. "Why—why would you do that?"

Laurent lifted Alan by his scruff. "You'll learn pretty quick not to argue, where you're going."

"Leave him alone." Micah's voice was louder and deeper than Alan had ever heard it. "It's my fault."

"We know," said the man with the rifle. "Why not put the kid on Mycholia?"

"Because it's not right."

The man laughed and laughed. He turned to Alan. "This man doesn't care about you, make no mistake. He's the one who started this. Everything we're going do to you, you can blame him—"

Micah kicked the man's gut and seized Alan. "You will do nothing."

Laurent seemed unaffected. "Why the concern? You experimented with Roger. And you still came running to us for help when they had him in the underground circuit. He'd covered himself in leeches, now, where do you think he got an idea like that?"

Micah seethed. "Shut up. You've no right coming into my home like this."

Laurent turned. "Rusha will need the book, Micah."

"What book?"

The doctor narrowed his eyes and slowly spoke: "The one Roger toted around. About lobotomies."

"No," Micah said without blinking. "I don't have it so there's no point taking any collateral."

"Okay, okay," the doctor was lending Micah tiny little nods.

The armed man straightened up and—BANG— shot Micah.

Alan screamed and felt something hot spreading over his side. It was Micah's blood. Hotter than that was the man's breath in his ear: "I'm sorry. Tell Roger I'm sorry." They peeled Alan away from him and dragged him outside.

When Alan was thrown in their van, he stopped resisting. The armed man hit him with the back of his gun and then with a closed fist. Alan didn't move and said "okay, *okay.*"

Someone applied cords to his wrists and ankles. A cloth pulled at the corners of his mouth. It tasted like a rotten apple.

Back at Rusha's facility, though, it took three people to strap Alan to a table. He wasn't sure what a lobotomy was but was afraid they would try it. They didn't.

The tube was down his throat in less than a minute, followed by Mycholia.

Sleep happened often. Thoughts accumulated, each one a grain of sand in the silt of Alan's conscience. The monotony of his Mycholia intake met occasional bouts of anxiety that made his body tense and sore. And then, after time and time, he owned moments of near clarity; an awareness of being underwater, of being without clothes, of food coming through his Mycholia tube, of being back on the table and wondering whether any of it had really happened.

Alan Cope produced Kisslic. Abundantly, then moderately, then sparsely. Then he was at an auction. He could not remember how he arrived there and he didn't know how he could sense that it was an auction. His head dropped forward from the weight of a vapor mask. He felt hands, one after another after another, feeling the top of his head. Someone announced numbers. Alan craved glistening Mycholia rocks, the sound and smell of them. Someone led him to a car.

Much later, Alan managed to lift his knees. He was on a table without any straps. He tried waggling them: no straps at all. He shifted weight and shifted again. He landed on linoleum.

Alan pulled the tube from his mouth by degrees, the crease between his eyes deepening as he did so. When the tube left his body, he stared with horror at its length.

Movement made aches. Alan knew that he was dragging himself over the floor by the sound of his palms slapping it. *Contact,* he thought, *and impulsion.* The scent of Mycholia made him stop and look left. A ribbed tube connected another boy to a domed Kisslic harvester, but this boy wasn't on a table. He hung upside down from the ceiling. Alan made a strangled noise and lifted himself to crawl. A breeze led him to a door left ajar.

Snow reflected on the black of his eyes. Tears cut the cold on his face. "I'm outside. I am outside." Impulsion made steps. Alan heard a car door shut, and someone calling at him. Then, as a sound so internal and shocking as to make Alan clap his hands over his headphones,

Roger's voice spoke: *Escape, kid. That's what this is! You can escape!*

Alan could not run. There wasn't any place to hide. He spotted a hill and climbed. Someone yelled after him. Alan picked his way over rocks, then boulders. Snow covered everything. He climbed until he was beyond reach.

Alan stepped and stepped. A bear trap snapped over his left leg and he collapsed. Alan lay still. His breath could be detected only by faint wisps of vapor. Snow settled on his hair. A gray wolf wandered up to him, crying in whistles. Larque boots conquered Alan's vision, and he turned his gaze upwards. A man with four-pronged antlers stared back at him. He pulled a revolver from his belt.

"Please," Alan said, "please, please...." He did not know for what he was pleading. The antlered man put away his revolved and picked up Alan's ankle's, dragging him. The snow seemed to smooth out under him, harder but grittier. The wolf followed. Alan thought that he felt like raw meat on crushed ice, and the arrival of such a metaphor refreshed him. He had broken through a cerebral staleness. Dark blood gushed into snow. At least I got outside, Alan thought. At least I managed to climb this far.

And he was suddenly freezing, unable to breathe, when the nose of a huge animal slipped under his chin....

In New York, New York, a twelve year old girl roamed a zoo. She froze in front of a polar bear tank. "Someone's in the water," she cried, "there's a boy in the water!"

"Now if, during this brief period, Oliver had been surrounded by careful grandmothers, anxious aunts, experienced nurses, and doctors of profound wisdom, he would most inevitably and indubitably have been killed in no time. There being nobody by, however...Oliver and Nature fought out the point between them."
—*Charles Dickens*

III

Alan's Body

A lan Cope was pale with dark bruises. He moaned
often on a hospital bed, which was quickly wet from
nervous sweat. He refused to swallow anything, he refused
needles. Someone told him that he couldn't make the pain
go away by any other means, and Alan said: "GO away, I
want a girl doctor."

He rubbed his face again and again on a pillow. A
nurse brought him a phone. "It's your cousin," she said.

"What?"

"It's your cousin, she wants to talk to you."

Alan's eyes roved the hospital room. He took the
phone. "Hello? It's me." Arden could hardly finish a
sentence. Alan's vision blurred. "Just hurry," he said,
"please hurry."

The nurse told Alan that hours separated him from
Cortland. She brought him hot packs for his ankles. While
applying them, Alan saw his medical bracelet: *Cope,
Alan...July thirty-first, two thousand and nine...*he had
turned fifteen. He had been fifteen for three and a half

days. Alan stared at the colorless hot pack. It had tiny hearts on it.

When his family arrived, they smothered Alan like a fever. They crowded his bed, crying all at once. "Don't you ever do that to me again," Roger repeated in hoarse cries, "don't you ever, ever do that again." He held Alan, who, in a glittering moment, found that he was able to relax in his brother's arms. Arden said that they could not go home until Alan had undergone a variety of tests. Needles slid into veins. Alan bit his knuckles.

The drive back to Cortland had a misty quality; Alan was safe but he could not believe it. He ached for another instance of affection, but he would not ask for it. He kept flinching.

"What wrong?" Roger asked him again and again, and Alan told him he was fine, but he kept flinching. Finally Roger put a hand across his eyes: "The streetlights are bothering you." It was true. Alan tried to cover his own eyes, but he soon fell asleep.

When the car first stopped, Roger kissed his brother's forehead and the boy jerked awake. "It's okay, kid, cool it. You're with us."

"Where'm I?"

"Pit stop. Do you want anything?"

"Me?"

Jenna nudged him. "Yeah, you, Alan. What do you want?" They gave him expectant stares. Alan looked at each of them in turn and shrugged.

Roger opened the door. Alan grabbed his brother's arm.

"It's okay, I'm coming right back. You stay here, Alan, stay in the car." The door shut loud. A stream of light struck half of Alan's bruised face.

"Are you okay?" Jenna whispered.

Alan nodded. "You guys look different." He watched Roger disappear into the store.

"Yeah." Jenna craned her neck and saw Arden waiting by the gas pump. "Listen, Alan," she said, "they won't want to tell you but you're better off hearing it from me."

Alan shook his head a little. "What?"

"We didn't have a photo of you..." Alan looked at Jenna. She had gotten a pale streak in her hair. "Some people thought you weren't really missing, Alan. Some people thought you weren't real at all. That it was fake."

"They think I'm fake."

"No fake, just…that you're not real. I know that's *crazy.*" A pause happened. "I'm really sorry."

Alan didn't know what to say. The door opened and Roger passed him a soda-pop. Alan took it from him and lifted it up to his eyes, watching the bubbles race upward.

When Arden pulled into her driveway, Leena ran out the front door. She lifted Alan and spun him. His face went into her shoulder. He slept with a full stomach and the dog slept beside him. He had undressed in the dark and refused to look at the mirror that faced his bed.

Sun made morning. Alan rubbed his face on the pillow—it was warm—it was the dog. He lifted his head and stroked the coarse hairs on Butter's stomach. Alan slowly sat up, forgetting the mirror. He froze mid-stretch. Bruises corresponded to physical aches. Hands slowly descended around a hollow face.

The door opened. Bony arms dropped to Alan's sides. "What's wrong with me, Arden?"

"Nothing, nothing. I'm glad you're awake."

"What's that in your hand?"

"These are for your pain." She held out a bottle. "Two in the morning…"

"I can't swallow pills."

"...two at night...you're okay, Alan. You're just, you know, you need some time to recover."

Alan could not swallow the pills. Attempts made spitting and coughs. Aches throbbed harder, then become sharp pains with the movement of his wakefulness. For some moments, Alan thought he had managed to take a pill properly before finding the thing under his tongue.

Alan did not know that he was grinding his teeth. A pill popped. Alan pushed his tongue against its bitter remnants. A second pill cracked and dissolved as dust.

In the kitchen, Alan stared at his brother's arms. "You're huge."

Leena smiled at him. "I told you a wheelchair would give you strong arms."

"A wheelchair? What happened?"

Roger scratched his elbow. "My legs were gone a lot. While you were away."

Leena patted the seat next to her. "Come sit with us, Alan. Do you want some coffee?"

Roger shook his head. "He can't have anything that will block ingredients."

"Nutrients," Alan corrected. He took comfort in the familiarity of Roger's semantical confusion.

"Did Arden give you the vitamins I bought?" Leena asked. She brushed a hand over Alan's hair; his scalp trembled. He shook his head.

While Leena searched the pantry, Alan counted the bones in his hands. Roger watched him.

"I think they're still in my car," Leena said. She left the brothers alone.

"Are you okay, kid?" Roger said. "Would you look at me?" Alan picked at a hangnail. Roger lowered his voice. "Alan, please be honest with me, are you—,"

"Nothing happened, okay?"

"I don't believe you."

"I don't wanna talk."

A rustling grocery bag marked Leena's return. She set bottles on the table: vitamin C, vitamin A, iron and vitamin K. "You usually cut your own hair, Alan, don't you?"

"Yes, Dr. Strang."

Silence happened. "She's not my doctor," Roger said.

Alan cocked his eyebrows. "Oh?"

Roger leaned his head against a fist. Leena said nothing. "Alan cuts his own hair."

"I used to cut my dad's hair all the time," Leena uttered. "I could cut yours at my place, if you want."

Alan looked at the table. "It is awfully long."

Roger pinched his brother's cheek. "Don't be shy."

Dark hair fell in clumps. Fingers brushed Alan's ear. On his lap, Leena's cat purred.

"How short do you want it?"

"Like Roger's, I guess."

"Short in the back?"

"Long in the front." It was barely a mumble.

"You seem tired, Alan."

Scissors cut with soft scrapes. Leena slipped her hand under Alan's chin. "Keep your head up. So, you're fifteen now; we've got a couple of birthdays to make up for and the rest of the summer to celebrate. Roger kept going on about what he would do when you came home. He's dying to take you for a ride on his moped."

"He's got a moped?"

"Arden bought it for his 22nd birthday. He hasn't used it very much. Especially over the last few months...oh, I'm so glad you're home."

Alan remembered the sound of his own un-fractured voice on the day he was kidnapped: *she'll probably bring something expensive...something else you'll never use because you're too lazy or too afraid.*

An electric razor hummed. "Have you had any other patients who were kidnapped?" Alan asked, "besides Roger."

Leena stopped moving for a long moment, while the razor hummed and hummed. "Not really. Not like this. What happened with Roger is pretty unusual."

"It's unusual because he was found, right?"

"It's not really that. I've met more people who were kidnapped by someone in their family. Like an estranged parent, or a relative having a psychotic break."

The humming stopped. "Do I have to answer questions about it? Roger said that he was questioned a lot."

"If people know who you are, they'll probably ask you things. But you don't have to say anything if you don't want to."

"I don't mean people, I mean like the cops or something."

"I'm not sure. Arden is better qualified to answer that. Did I mess up your hair?"

Alan shook it out. "No, it's tops. Really cool."

The cat stood and arched its back. "You'll be fine, Alan," Leena said, "just try to stay home for awhile, avoid the press and spend time with your family. I'm certain you're not in trouble. But if someone hurts you—,"

"I didn't say that anyone hurt me."

"I know, Alan, I know. I just want to say that if you ask me, you should assess your responsibility."

"I shouldn't have to say anything." Alan scratched one knee with the other. He wondered how thoughts could leave a body so unchecked. "What if I can't remember, anyway? I don't know how I ended up in a damn zoo."

"I believe you, Alan." And then: "All we care about —we don't care, we just want you to be safe."

"You say that." Alan rubbed his eyes. "You say you believe me, but what if I said I was in Luna the whole time? Would you believe me or would you say that I had Cope Syndrome?"

Leena paused in the act of putting scissors in a drawer. "Do not joke about that."

"What if I'm not joking?"

"Your brother's in serious trouble, if you're not joking."

"What kind of trouble?"

"If Roger is messing with your understanding of things. That would be a problem. For me."

Alan spun around, ready to argue at her, but suddenly grabbed his head. "Did you feel anything!? In my hair?"

When Alan got home, Roger snapped a chocolate bar into pieces. "Do you want some, kid?"

"Naw, I'm alright." Alan put his hands in his pockets. "Where's your ashtray?"

"Oh, it's...I'm trying not to smoke anymore. Sit, I've got to talk to you."

"Am I in trouble?"

"Hell, no. Don't look at me that way."

"Okay but why are you looking at *me* that way?"

Roger waved an arm at the couch. "Would you sit?"

Alan leaned against the wall behind him and folded his arms. "I don't want to sit."

Roger stepped backwards. He sat on the armrest of the couch. "What happened to your jacket?"

"You said that I wasn't in trouble."

"I'm not mad at you," Roger said through a mouthful of chocolate. "I'm just curious about where it went." But Alan could tell, from the way Roger said it, the way he waggled his hand, the way that the skinny bone in his forearm flickered, that he was maybe a bit angry.

"I dunno where it went."

"Did someone take it from you?"

Alan shuffled his feet. "Yeah."

"Do you know who took it?"

Alan shrugged. "Why would that matter?"

"It matters because I'm asking."

"Leena said that I don't have to tell you anything about anything."

"So no one's making you talk?"

Alan shook his head. Roger scoffed and shook his head. "Okay. Lucky bastard." Alan shrugged at him. They stared at each other for a long time.

"Okay." Roger nodded. He put a finger to his lips; very angry. "So, technically speaking, it's no one's business what happened to you. And it's not mine."

"That's right."

"Well that's great, kid. That's fucking great, because if you did happen to tell anyone that you were in Luna, they wouldn't let us keep having these precious moments."

Alan waited for his brother to say something else. He heard Roger take another bite of chocolate. "I don't know what happened to your stupid jacket."

"This is not about the jacket, Alan. Look at me."

Alan's eyes rolled up to meet his brother. "What?"

"You cannot have Cope Syndrome." Roger stood and slowly approached the boy. "I got the diagnosis. It's mine. So how do you think it sounds if you tell her you've been to Luna?"

"It doesn't sound good."

Roger nodded. "So, if you're not gonna talk—*you're not gonna talk*. Fine. But don't leave me in the dark."

Alan drew a hand across his own forehead. "I don't know where the jacket is...I think Micah's still got it. I'm sorry, I'm real sorry."

Roger picked at his teeth. "This sucks." He sat on the couch. "I'm not—this isn't better."

"What do you mean?"

"I thought if you ended up in Luna—and you believed me, I would feel better."

"I always believed you, Roger."

"I feel worse, now." He glared at Alan. "At least I was important before. I was like a fairytale." He grabbed the front of Alan's shirt and tugged him close. "Now we're two of a kind."

Alan didn't know how to answer this. He suddenly felt very dizzy. "They put me on Mycholia for a long time."

"Tell me about it." Roger walked towards a trash can with the chocolate wrapper in his hands.

"No...listen." Rasping made Alan's voice. He tried to follow his brother into the kitchen.

"You'll be fine. You're stronger than I am."

Dark spots danced in Alan's peripheral vision. "Roger. I'm sick."

"You are fine!" Roger threw out the wrapper and crunched the trash with his foot. Alan came up behind him and tugged his shirt. "I think I'm going to pass out."

Roger turned; Alan collapsed.

"It's okay!" Roger's voice broke when he caught the boy. "Sorry! Fuck, I'm sorry. I just needed to smoke."

Fever conquered Alan's body. He chewed pills in the morning and pills in the night. They lived in his pockets. Prescription bottles rattled all the time, rattle rattle. Alan rarely slept for more than an hour at a time, as he was often woken by a recurring dream which he could not remember until he was in it again. He woke gasping like "okay, kay, kay." He cooked far more than he ate. Vomiting, though practiced, was no longer voluntary.

Alan broke the can opener. They got hard raw beans and he soaked them in huge batches and it took a long time to cook them. He stirred pot after pot and ripped stalks of romaine off their firm round centers and this is what they ate most nights. Eventually, Alan dropped his stirring spoon and examined his hands. "They're like shadows. My nails. Roger. Look, black."

"I don't know that word if you don't know that word."

"They're *shadowy.*"

Roger did not look up from the catalogue on his lap. "That's from Mycholia withdrawal. It's benign, like the nosebleeds. It'll go away." Alan stirred. A police siren rose and fell. Roger flipped a page. "What kind of jacket did you want again?"

"We're not getting anything."

"Yeah but what did you want?"

"The black one with the white stripes on the sleeves."

"Again with the language—"

"I don't care, I like the white stripes." Alan tapped the spoon against the pot. "Dinner's near ready."

Roger turned the TV on. Alan turned it off. At the kitchen table he took a knife to hot cornbread and made thick slices. "Do you want butter?"

"I'll get it." Roger opened the fridge.

Alan paused mid-slice. "Mom was in Luna."

Roger turned. "What?"

"Mom was in Luna." Alan rubbed his palms on his jeans. "Shut the fridge."

"How could she be in Luna? Was she wearing Larque?"

"No, I don't...know."

"You don't know as in you don't know or no as in no?"

"I don't know. Shut the fridge." Chili flooded bowls. "I'm going with Jenna to the thing tomorrow."

"What thing?"

"The art fair thing. In town, like."

Corn bread split under Roger's fingers. "Do you need me to drive you?"

"Her friend is going to. The one with the legs all day."

"Don't talk about girls like that, it's purgatory."

Alan blew at a spoonful of chili. "I think you mean derogatory."

"Fine. You should go out. Would you just ask me next time? Not tell me like it's last thing."

"I did tell you before, you just never listen."

Roger dropped his spoon and rubbed his temples. "I don't know if I can go out tomorrow and I don't want you to go without me."

Alan shook his head. "Why? Why? I have been kidnapped. The thing has happened, you think it's going to happen again?"

"What if someone recognizes you?"

"I'll wear a damn hat."

Roger picked up his bowl and left the table—but the way he did it, the obtuse angle of his arm that held the bowl lower than his chest—from this, Alan gleaned that Roger was in a soft mood, and he though to take advantage of it before sunrise. A moment later, the television made noise.

Alan tried to sleep in tight, twisted sheets. Roger lay on the couch downstairs. The television flashed light at him. At 4 AM, he saw Alan's movement by peripheral vision. "You're awake," Roger said.

"Yeah."

"It's 4 AM. What are you doing up?"

Stair rung shadows sliced Alan's body at an angle. "What are *you doing* up?"

"I'm watching the television." Roger shifted his legs. "You can sit."

Alan approached the couch. He sat with his knees against his chest and rubbed his feet. "What show are you looking at?"

"It's a film." Commercials spoke. Roger silenced it with a button.

"A movie. Okay." Alan's ankle popped and he flinched. "Roger, do you think I ought to see a doctor?"

"No."

A pause happened. "Okay." Alan counted several breaths, then said: "I think maybe I need to see a doctor." Roger groaned.

"Never mind," Alan said, "forget it."

Commercials came and went: just try this vacuum; you won't regret it. We value our customers, unlike our competitor. My wardrobe has never been better, or more affordable.

"Roger. I think you know what I'm worried about."

"I don't."

"You do." Roger tried to pick up the remote—Alan snatched it. "You got the same problem, that's why you're not fucking anybody—"

Roger lunged at Alan and tried to wrest the remote from Alan, who threw it into the kitchen.

"Watch your language!"

"It's the color—"

"Who *cares* what color it is?"

"That what I'm *asking if that is normal.*"

Roger sat up. "Go get the remote and I'll tell you."

"Tell me and I'll get it."

"Why do you want to know?"

"Because you made me skip sex ed so now you gotta tell me. Sorry not sorry."

Roger folded himself forward and crushed his fingers under his own feet. "No. It's not normal. We are not normal. Happy?"

Alan pulled on a loose string from his sweater.

Roger left the couch. The fridge opened.

"I'm worried about it," Alan said in a loud voice.

"Doesn't matter," Roger called back at him. He opened a drawer and slammed it shut. "No one has to know." His hand closed over a cup of yogurt.

Alan pushed his sleeves away from his hands. Roger returned to the couch. "It doesn't matter."

"You said it wasn't normal."

"It's fine as long as everything's...working properly. Would you let it go?" Roger tore foil off the yogurt cup and flicked it at the coffee table.

"It bothers me."

"Then bleach your sheets and don't think about it."

"But, Roger..." Alan stood. Commercials returned. "Roger, it bothers me—,"

"OH MY GOD I want a cigarette so bad."

Alan stared at his brother, who stared at the television. He muted the television again. Roger spooned yogurt into his mouth, then finally said. "Are you gonna come out or something?"

"No." Alan kept staring.

Roger sighed. "Then what *is it?*"

"Don't freak out but I'm saying, for the future, what do I do when a girl wants to have sex on me?"

"No one is going to have sex *on* you because you don't have to. You don't have to have sex with anyone. Congratulations and you're welcome."

"Okay. Okay." More quiet. "Roger."

"*What?*"

"I'm wondering how long—well, if you're a girl, let's say, how long do you think you want to wait before doing it?" And then: "Why are you smiling?"

Roger shrugged. "You don't have to have sex at all. Ever. I would...I would've given my left arm to be a virgin at your age." The smile faded. And then he gave Alan a look.

In his whole life Alan never imagined his brother would think something like this, let alone say it out loud—and then to punctuate it with this peculiar look: Not angry, not with any conviction at all. It was as if, for the first time, Roger was curious about him.

And that's when Alan knew that the next question he had wanted to ask *(but then how do you know if someone loves you)?* was already answered by this look.

"Maybe we're not as much the same as you think."

Roger turned back to the television. "I hope not."

Alan opened his mouth again; Roger stopped him with a hand.

"You really want to go out with the girls tomorrow, is that it?"

Alan nodded.

The next morning, Alan frowned at a mirror. "These sunglasses are too big."

"Your eyes are too big."

"I guess."

"Okay." Roger rubbed his eyes. He searched two drawers for a wallet. "Help me give you money."

"It's in your black jeans pocket," Alan said. He would not look at his brother.

"You said it was in the dresser."

"So it is."

Roger slammed two drawers; one open and one shut. Alan jumped and Roger cursed under his breath. "I'm not gunna slug you, get back here. What kind of money do you need?"

"I dunno. A ten and a five."

"All of mine have twenty on them."

"That's fine. One of those is fine."

"Get yourself a wallet. And here's quarters. Bring home some gum balls."

Alan rolled his eyes. "Gum balls, right." He took the twenty dollar bill and left the room.

"Wait," Roger said, "make sure you take your secular phone!" He looked at the mirror and lifted his shirt. His once concave stomach was now sublimely flat. "Oh my God, I'm gaining weight…"

When they got to the art fair, the girls crowded Alan and spoke in questions. He forwarded the inquiries to his cousin and, when he could, spoke to her under his breath: "why are they laughing at everything?"

"I can't imagine," Jenna said in a loud voice, "but it's getting annoying, don't you think?"

"They used to ignore me and now they won't leave me alone." Alan sighed. "It's because I went missing, right? Now I'm all interesting."

Jenna laughed. "Naw, that's not it." And then, lower: "better not be it."

They passed some tents and entered others. One of the girls said, "there's a lot of naked women around here."

"Those are pictures of naked women," Alan said, "not actually naked women."

The girls stared at him. Alan left the tent and walked alone. He stopped at a tent that sold things he could understand: watches, wallets, enamel flowers on chains. "How much is this?"

"That's eighteen dollars. And if you put it around your neck, it becomes jewelry. That's the idea."

"Gee." Alan touched the thing. "I don't have anyone to give this to."

When he left the tent with a wallet, rain fell. Alan squinted in search of the girls. He saw them approach a nearby cafe and ran towards it. Alan ordered hot tea and sat still while it steamed at his face. People flooded the place as rain fell and some of them were men with hands in their pockets. Alan did not touch his tea. Time stopped the progress of steam. Rain halted and the cafe emptied around Alan and the chattering girls. He did, indeed, spot a gum ball machine.

Black, white and gray. Alan wondered what colored gum balls were like. Maybe he would have wanted one, then. He took a sip of tea and then rubbed his hands on his jeans. "I'm forgetting something," he uttered, but no one seemed to hear. "I've forgotten something."

When the girls got up to leave, Alan stood and then sat. "I don't feel right."

Jenna frowned. "Don't you wanna leave?"

"Yeah, I...no." Alan gritted his teeth against an internal shriek. "I feel like I'm falling." Pressure clouded his head. The girls stared at him; he stared at the trembling hands in his lap.

Roger had a phone in one hand and cigarette in the other. His shoulders slumped. "He's fine, Jenna. Tell him he's okay. It's just a panic attack. Can you bring him home?" Roger pushed the cigarette into the couch and watched smoke rise.

When he got home, Alan threw the hat and sunglasses on the floor. The brothers sat on the couch. Roger put a hand on the boy's shoulder and Alan sobbed on contact. Roger put his face in the boy's hair and said "I know." Alan cried against him for nearly an hour, and then the tears came to a sudden stop. Alan head lifted. "Is the front door all locked?"

"Of course it is."

"I've gotta tell, Roger. Like about the man what kidnapped me."

Roger flinched and sighed through his teeth. "God, Alan."

"They'll get him, right? Like if I go to the cops and tell?"

Roger closed a hand around Alan's upper arm. He rubbed his thumb on a bruise.

Alan sniffed. "Stop that."

"I'm trying to rub it out."

"Well you can't, it's not marker. Stop it."

Roger's hand rested. Alan's head fell to one side. "You're smoking again."

"I'm not."

"But I smell it."

"Well I have to or I'll get fat."

"But Roger—"

"I'm sorry." Roger pushed his brother away from him. "I don't think you should got to the cops."

"Why not?"

"I can tell you what's going to happen." Roger leaned forward and stared at the reflective coffee table. "You give them a description and and they keep it in a file and you call them the next time he tries to hurt you. Unless you know his name?"

"I don't."

"That's right, you don't. So *nothing doing.* Unless. Unless you really think you can remember."

This made Alan pause. "I should have talked to them from the start."

"But can you remember?"

Alan went to the local police station with Arden and returned home hours later with a surging pain in his head.

He stared at the kitchen table. Roger flipped a chair around and straddled it. "Well?"

Alan's eyes shut. "They have him already for arson and robbery. He had like a photograph of me."

"A photograph?"

"Yeah." Alan's eyes opened. "The kind that comes out of the camera. I forgot what they're called. But the thing is, you were right."

"About what?"

"I couldn't really remember. They found him in the house he broke into—my DNA was there. But I don't remember."

Roger reached forward and rubbed his brother's shoulder. "They're watching him. That's what matters."

Alan coughed. He stood and approached the sliding glass door. His breath fogged it. "It's too cold for your garden."

"It's August."

"It is August." Alan looked over his shoulder at Roger. "And it's very cold out."

"You've got a fever. Zip up your jacket." Alan didn't move. Roger stood. "You look like bones. I wish you would eat."

"I eat my medicine."

Roger let out one of his loose, nervous chuckles. "I'll—I'll make you a lunch."

Alan swallowed. "Can I ask you something?"

"Yeah, if you eat lunch."

"Can I have your mace?"

Roger lets out a deep sigh, the sigh of centuries.

Alan gave him a doleful look. "I'll try to eat my lunch."

Roger shut the fridge. "You said that mace was for girls."

"I know. It was an awful thing to say." Alan put a finger in his mouth.

Roger grabbed Alan's hand. "Stop that."

"I have to count my teeth to know if I'm dreaming." Alan rubbed his wrists.

"You're not dreaming."

"I feel like I must be."

"No!" Roger dropped a bag of apples. They both bent down to gather them up. "You're not—try not to think that way, you have to try."

Books surrounded Alan's mattress. He stacked titles onto titles around the place where he slept. Alan spent long hours in his room.

In the kitchen pantry, Roger's pill bottles sat empty. Roger stared at them. A moment later, Alan's bedroom door opened. Roger nodded at the book in Alan's lap. "What's the book about?"

Alan looked away from it. "What's the book about?"

"Yeah."

"A boy. The book is about a boy."

Roger put a hand on his head. His elbow came to rest against the doorframe. "Why do I have a feeling this is going to make me uneasy?"

"Well..." Alan stared at the triangle of space framed by his brother's crooked, leaning arm. He felt trapped in it. "Well, I don't know, it's not real."

Roger stepped in and seized the book. He flicked through it, frowning. "How did you get this smut?"

"It is not smut." Alan watched his brother scan the back cover. He stood. "There, you see? It's just about a boy."

Roger handed back the book with his finger in it. Alan folded a page. Roger put his hands on his hips. "Have you seen my pills?"

Alan's head dipped. "What?"

"My medicine is all gone."

Alan quailed. "Oh…I ate it," he mouthed.

Roger blinked. "You did what?"

"I ate the pills. I ate them all."

"Ate them?" Roger threw his hands into the air. His expression struggled through a web of incoherence. "You took my pills? What the hell, kid! Those are for anxiety."

"Well…I was very anxious."

A vein jumped in Roger's temple. He smacked Alan's face, started to walk away, then spun around and smacked it again. "What the hell were you thinking, huh? Tell me, I wanna know, what the hell were you thinking?"

Alan held his stinging face. "I—I ran out my medicine so I took summa yours."

"You don't know what you're doing," Roger hissed, "you can't just take any medication that you want. Look at me! Don't do that again. You can't take anything without a subscription."

"Prescription," Alan said, and acute regret flooded his system.

Roger frowned. "You think you're smarter than me," he whispered.

"No, no, I didn't mean it like that."

Roger grabbed his brother's hair. "You think you're smarter than me?" He dragged Alan into the bathroom.

"You think you're real grown up, taking my medication like that?"

"No, I'm sorry, I didn't know!"

"That's right, you didn't know!" Roger slammed the door behind him.

Alan flinched. "Cut it out, I get it."

"You are not sick!" Roger shouted. Tiles echoed his voice.

Alan backed against the wall. "Okay, okay. Yeah, it's yours. You're sick and I'm not."

"Even if you remembered what happened to you, no one would believe you. Be glad you don't remember."

Roger was examining the shower, his eyes grazed the spout, the edges, the drain. He pulled the knob. The walls groaned and water arrived in seconds.

Alan held a defensive hand out in front of him. "Roger, please, cool it." His eyes were shut. He perceived his own aversive stance, the freezing water falling, his brother's shouting face and the mirror that reflected them all.

Roger's body shook. "What the hell is wrong with you, chucking back pills like a neurotic? I bet you're making half this shit up."

Alan didn't know what he was referring to, and then suddenly had the very upsetting sense that Roger wasn't really talking to him at all, but rather to himself.

"St-stop it, stop. Would you put that thing down?"

Roger grabbed the shower head and pointed it at his brother. Put a square around the subject. Put a circle around the object. He laughed a little. Alan shrieked. Roger dropped the shower head and covered his ears. Fault-lines split the mirror into reflective regions. Roger ran out of the bathroom. He tripped over a pile of books and landed on Alan's mattress, then cursed loudly. Alan stopped screaming.

Roger slowly approached the bathroom. Alan was curled into a corner of the room. Water sprayed the walls and floor. Roger shut it off, grabbed a towel and descended around his younger brother. Water climbed over his left pant leg. "Stop crying. Stop that, okay?"

Alan's eyes opened. Roger pushed the towel across the boy's face. "Are you okay?"

Alan creased his brow. He grabbed the front of Roger's shirt with both hands. "Is mom in the house?" His voice was barely above a whisper.

"No, Alan, no...why do you think she's in the house?"

Alan turned to look at the shower head and slowly straightened his limbs. Roger followed his gaze.

"What just happened?"

"Someone sprayed the water at me."

"I'm sorry!" Roger's voice broke. "I know it was cold, I forgot she use to do that, I'm..." He looked at his brother. "I'm terrible. I'm sorry." Alan did not look at Roger. "We'll have your birthday this weekend, okay?"

"Roger...shut up."

"Okay."

Alan did not speak. He took the towel and left the bathroom. Roger followed him to the doorway. "Where are you going?"

"Basement."

"But the basement's for emergencies." Roger rubbed his forehead with the heel of one hand. "Okay, kid. Okay. I set up the telescope..." Alan was out of earshot.

Then Alan was in the basement without really being sure how he got there. It smelled like paper. Charcoal drawings covered the floor. Alan saw them and retched. When nothing came up he seized a stick of charcoal and pushed it down his throat. He coughed black dust.

Alan pulled a cellphone from his pocket. "Jenna hi can you come over? Okay. I'm okay, everything's fine." He took a deep breath. "I just don't wanna be alone." He waited silently for his cousin. He lay on concrete and rested a hand on charcoal pieces. He rolled one under his palm and it snapped. Alan broke it and broke it. He rubbed dark grit between his fingertips.

Jenna arrived wearing a backpack. "Roger wouldn't say why you were down here. What happened to your face?"

Alan waved a hand. "Charcoal."

Jenna laughed. "It looks like you were trying to eat it."

Alan opened his mouth and coughed. Jenna sat in front of him. "Oh my God...you tried to eat the charcoal."

Alan looked away from her and shrugged. "Did you bring something to do?"

"I brought a board game." Jenna didn't move. "You can't eat charcoal. That's dangerous."

Alan huffed. "What is it with everyone telling me what to do? It's just charcoal. It's a rock. Calm down."

Jenna opened her backpack. She took out a board game and stacked cards while her cousin sorted plastic pieces by shape. "It's not food," she finally said, "you shouldn't eat something if it isn't food."

"I like the texture," Alan admitted, studying the dice in his hand. He shook the dice and Jenna grabbed his wrist. "Promise you won't eat charcoal again."

"I promise."

"And nothing else weird, either. Like rocks or soap or something."

"Why would I eat soap?" Alan said, although his mind flew back to long moments of brushing his fingers through powdered detergent.

"I'm serious, Alan! There was a girl at school who ate body scrub and she had to go to the hospital."

"Okay. I promise."

"She almost died."

"Okay, alright. Let me roll the dice."

Jenna examined the ends of her hair. "Why are you wet?"

"I took a cold shower. Your turn."

"Do you normally shower with your clothes on?"

Alan frowned. "I guess not. I mean, no. But I made a mistake."

Jenna paused in the act of lifting a card. "What happened?"

Alan rested his chin on his hand. "Nothing. What's your card say?"

"Move back three spaces. Alan, you can still tell me something. If you want."

Alan moved Jenna's piece. He picked up the dice. "If something bad happens to you, how do you know if it's your fault?"

"What are you....saying?"

Alan squinted. He bit his lip. "I think it's my fault I was kidnapped."

Jenna shook her head. "How?"

"Because...because." Alan shrugged and rubbed his jaw. He heard the man's footsteps, he smelled the lake. "Because I was being stupid." He blinked. "I keep thinking—,"

"Yeah, you keep thinking. Stop it, Alan. No, don't look at me like that, I'm serious. You think too much."

Alan rolled the dice and moved his piece.

"You have to get out more." Jenna took the dice. "We should double date."

Alan imagined himself kissing a girl outside of a cinema. It was like imagining what it would be like to ride a tiger. He blinked and saw Jenna's plastic beaded bracelet. "We're only fifteen," he said.

"Not for *long,* though."

And like that, it was Alan's birthday. Roger opened the front door. "Good afternoon, Leena."

"You're so formal." She clacked in, looking at the streamers curled around the banister. "I like the decorations."

"Thank you, I did it myself. That's a lovely cake."

"It's for Alan. Where is he?"

"I made him go play in the yard. You're the first to arrive."

Leena felt hot. She followed Roger into the living room and paused at the sight of a fish bowl. "That's beautiful," she said.

Roger put his hands in his pockets. "That's my present for Alan."

Leena put the cake on the coffee table and sat on the floor to look at the fish. "It's blowing bubbles."

"Yeah, he's a plakat."

"Plakat?" Leena smiled and looked up at him.

Roger sat next to her. "A plakat is a fish."

Leena looked back at the bowl. "Plakats blow bubbles?"

"The boys do. They make a nest of bubbles for their babies. But this one is alone, he's not going to have any. He just doesn't know that."

"That's cute. And it...wow. It's so pretty. It's like..." She saw color for an instant—then it faded. Leena cocked her head and an earring dropped to the floor. Roger picked up the glittering thing. Leena rubbed her eyes. "I'm seeing things."

"I get that."

"Yeah...it's gone now." Leena touched her neck. "Where's my...oh."

Roger held the earring by its wire. Leena felt it gently probe the lower part of her ear. Her collarbone itched. Roger's face froze in concentration. When the wire slipped through Leena's ear, he drew back an inch. "Does that hurt?" She shook her head. Roger stroked the earring with a finger. "Careful you don't lose them." He felt a hand on his knee.

"Are your legs okay?" Leena asked.

"I think so."

"They're trembling." Leena's jeweled necklace reflected the sun; she watched tiny flecks of light swarm Roger's face. They shifted with her breath.

"I'm always trembling." Roger leaned forward. His mouth was no longer a mouth, but a throbbing wound.

Leena turned away from him and moved to sit on the couch. Her hands were in her hair. "I'm so stupid."

"You're not stupid."

"I *can not.*'

Roger rubbed his mouth with the back of his hand. He slowly stood.

"Don't, don't start," Leena said. "You were Alan's age when I met you."

Roger kept rubbing his mouth. His body leaned into itself; his shoulders hunched tense as if shards formed his spine.

"I don't want another lecture," Leena continued in a low voice.

"I wasn't going to lecture you." Roger's voice was faint. The woman looked away from him. His hand dropped to his side. She must have forgotten that the earrings had been a gift from him. Roger left the room.

Alan sat in the yard. A squirrel crawled over his knee. A bird landed on his shoulder. Roger approached him from behind. "Alan! I've been calling you." The animals dispersed.

Alan blinked and looked over his shoulder. "Hi."

"Hi, yeah, hi. You can come inside now. Come on." Roger held out a hand and Alan stroked it with a finger. "Are you okay?"

"Of course, I'm fine." Roger gave him a tight smile. "There's a cake for you."

Alan watched his brother's face. "Leena's here, isn't she?" He entered the house and smiled at the decorations, then at Leena. "Hello, Miss Strang. Have you seen the weather? There's a tornado coming."

"Woah, kid." Roger pulled a caterpillar out of Alan's hair. "He's got an imagination."

When his cousins arrived, Alan was carefully slicing cake. He had a keen awareness that everyone had gathered at the house for his sake, and he lacked a natural response to this. Jenna waved an envelope under Alan's nose. "Happy birthday, this is for you."

"Thanks very much," Alan muttered. He put it next to the fish bowl. Arden set a box on the table.

"Alan, are you sure you want to stay here?" Arden asked, "you don't want to go to a bowling alley, or something?" She looked at her phone as she spoke.

"I'd like to stay here."

"We could go to a park."

"Quit already," Roger cut in, "he doesn't want to leave the house."

The coffee maker beeped and Alan ran to get it. He opened gifts while those around him nursed steaming mugs. Roger watched Leena fasten a watch around Alan's slender wrist. She had taken it out of a soft, little box that she had taken out of her black, little purse that she had probably taken out of a large, bright store while thinking of Alan, who smiled. "You didn't have to get me something."

"Every young man needs a watch."

"I like it," Alan said, "I like the weight of it." Alan read the letter from his cousins and rubbed his eyes. "I'm glad you're glad I'm back."

Arden nodded at the box on the table. "Open that."

Alan peeled back the wrappings and grinned. "Roger! I've got my own stereo."

"It's even better than mine," Jenna said. "You can record with it. And it has radio, see?" She pointed at it. "Plug it in and I'll show you."

Roger ate cake with a spoon and licked frosting off his lips. He paced while swallowing and stopped beside a kitchen window. Clouds gathered.

Alan split cake with a fork and pushed it around his plate. He sat while the stereo emitted white noise. "There's a tornado coming."

Sirens played distant, and then with immediate closeness. Alan looked at the fast forward button on the stereo. Plates were lifted by quick movements.

"What is that?" Jenna asked.

Alan knew. "That's a tornado siren."

Everyone moved into the basement while the sirens echoed. "We really can't go out now," Arden said over the aria. "Have we—have we ever had a tornado?"

"Not in Cortland," Alan said, and blood rivered from his nose.

Roger unbuttoned his shirt and pressed it on Alan's face.

Arden set down her purse. "Roger, that's disgusting."

"It's a shirt, Arden, okay? It's a *shirt*. Put your head back, kid."

Wind compelled the trees to bowing, and Jenna looked up through the window at them; their character had changed by this foreign dance. Jenna approached her bleeding cousin. "How do you know it's a tornado?"

"He doesn't know," Roger said, "he's just anxious."

"I want my medicine," Alan said.

"There's no more of it."

Alan's joints were cold and his bleeding was hot. Roger and Arden bickered above him. He looked at Leena. "I feel like I can't breathe."

She took Alan's hand and rubbed it between her palms.

"Why are you doing that?"

"Roger said you've been having panic attacks."

"My whole body hurts."

Roger turned away from his cousin. He saw Leena rub Alan's hand. The house shook from the force of the storm; Alan sat down and absorbed it. He felt his brother's gaze and pulled his hand away from Leena.

"You alright, kid?" Roger asked through a tense jaw. "You've hardly eaten."

Jenna spoke before Alan could. "What's in those?"

"What's in what," Roger said.

"Those backpacks." She directed her gaze towards a corner of the room.

Roger crossed his arms. "Nothing. It's for emergencies."

Alan whined. He lifted the bloody shirt from his face and looked at it. It had an oblong stain that looked like the head of a dark dog. Leena looked at the backpacks. "Roger, do you have any of your meds in those bags?"

"Yeah, one of the front pockets." He watched the woman bend over them. "But it's very old."

Leena ignored him. She searched pockets. Roger stood next to her. "I'm alright, Leena. Really."

She pulled out a sandwich bag with pills in it. "It's not for you, it's for your brother."

"No!" Roger grabbed her arms. "You can't do that!"

"Do not grab me."

"They're mine! You know they're mine, you got them for me!"

"Let me go."

Roger's hand fell to his sides and he shook his head. "You can't, he's had too many."

"What do you mean?" Leena's lips hardly moved. Arden looked up from her phone.

"He took a bunch of them," Roger said, "last week he took five or seven, I don't know. He did it behind my back."

"It's okay." Leena's words hid under breath.

"No, it's not okay," Roger reached for the pills and Leena snatched it back. She leaned towards his ear; he felt faint. "For God's sake, they're sugar pills."

Roger stood still while thunder cracked. He heard Leena behind him.

"Take these, Alan. Swallow them."

Alan coughed. "I'll be in trouble."

"No, I'm a doctor. It's okay."

Roger's eyes were hot and watering. Dust covered the backpacks at his feet. He had packed those when he was much younger, just in case.

"I'm selling this old house," Arden said, and Roger blinked. Shingles slid off the roof and landed at the level of their ears. Arden shook her head. She looked at Roger, who took a deep, shuddering breath.

"I think everyone should leave," he said, "before the storm gets any worse."

"Fine." Arden dropped her phone into her purse. "There's a TV in our basement. Come on, kids."

"He's staying." Roger pointed at Alan.

"No, he's not. He's not staying here. I don't know why I ever leave him with you."

Roger faced his cousin. "It's not you leaving him with me, I'm the one letting him go with you, understand?" He pointed at himself. "He's in my care."

"Sure."

Leena shot a glance at her friend. "Arden, come on. Please."

Alan's nose had stopped bleeding. Jenna fisted her hands.

Roger stepped sideways. "I sure as hell take care of him. I'm there for him."

"Whatever makes you feel better, Thumper."

Leena moaned. "Oh don't *call* him that, Arden!" Alan's belly stiffened. He pressed the heels of his hands against his ears.

Roger pointed at his own temples. "Are you delusional? You saw me sign the damn papers. I took custody because I was sick of your complaining."

"Fake papers. I faked the whole thing, okay? How's that for being there for him?"

"You—you're nasty—l" Roger shut his eyes for a moment, his face went blank, and then, in a tone that didn't entirely belong to him: *"bitch lawyer!"*

Arden crossed her arms. "I didn't have to be a lawyer to convince you, you'll believe anything."

Leena touched Roger's arm. Softly, she said: "Thumper—"

He shook her off. "We read parenting books and got a real job and I was working!"

"Yeah, and you were fired for sexual harassment."

Roger kicked a wall; his younger brother backed against the water heater. *"I did not harass that woman!"*

Arden pointed at the water heater. "You see why I did it? What's Alan supposed to do when you decide to kick something?" Roger stretched into his natural height. Arden backed away from him. "You weren't stable. You tried to kill yourself. You were nailing your clothes to the wall!"

Roger's voice dropped back to its typical octave. "Don't pretend. If you really cared about us, you would have let us live with your mom."

Arden's mouth dropped open. She struck Roger's face.

"Shut up, shut up, shut up!" Alan stood. "Your mom's alive? What the hell!" His family stared at him. "I didn't ask to be everyone's problem, alright? I can take care of myself!" He gasped for air. He threw the bloodied shirt at them and went upstairs.

"So," Roger seethed. "I don't have custody of the kid and I've been taking placebos for seven years. Anything else you ladies would care to share with me?"

None answered. Jenna wept, her eyes fixed on the shirt on the floor. Roger crossed over to the backpacks and swung one onto each shoulder. Leena tried to call him back on his way up the stairs.

"Don't, Leena!" Roger's voice shattered. "Don't say my name!"

Alan stood against the wind. A garage opened behind him. He watched a doe cross the street with flinging movements. A loaded backpack landed at his feet. Alan looked up to see his brother. He shook his head. "No!"

Roger stared back. He went into his car and backed it out, and it rolled to a stop beside Alan, who felt that some aspect of himself extended beyond the limits of his body. He harbored an awareness of the storm as it was in that moment, how it was before, and how it could be after. He knew that his body had gone from standing against the wind to leaning into it, though there was no visible evidence of this transition.

He saw the boy standing beside the backpack, not wanting to get in the car but having nowhere to run and hearing in his own head the voice of a woman who spoke of more typical abductions while trimming the hair above his ears. Alan threw the backpack in the car, and his body in after it.

Roger leaned forward when he drove. He turned on the radio, heard static, and turned it off. The car yielded before a highway. Roger looked over his shoulder. "I don't wanna hate women. I don't want to."

Hail pelted the car. Alan rubbed his neck so hard it made him see specks. He watched the progress of a raindrop on his window, tapping it until Roger told him to stop. He turned to him.

"Why did Arden call you Thumper?"

Roger glanced at him, again with that new curiosity. "Who?"

Lightning cracked the sky. Alan felt suddenly frightened, and decided he would never ask about Thumper again—and he wouldn't.The car stopped in front of a motel.

Roger stared at a piano in its lobby. He pushed a pouch into his brother's chest. "Find eighty dollars." They checked into a room, and it smelled wet. Alan lay in the bed and faced the wall. Behind him, Roger stretched. "I can't drive through a storm." He dropped a backpack. "It's not bad in here. They've got cable. Are you hungry? There's food across the street." Roger stared at the body breathing under sheets. "You want a cheeseburger?"

"I hate you."

Roger's heart stung like an infection. He reached for the bathroom door. Alan slept through the night. Roger showered and lay awake. His head dampened the pillow beneath him.

Mist shrouded morning. Roger drank black coffee and wrapped bagels in plastic. "Do you think Arden's called the fuzz yet?"

"I dunno."

"You were right about the cold. It's too cold for August." The brothers packed in shuffling movements, mutually fearful of eye contact. They left the motel while the sun rose. Alan walked with his head down against extreme pressure; whether it came from his brother's long legged presence or the mist that clouded them both he could not tell. Roger's eyes darted. He put a hand on his brother's upper back and unlocked a car.

Alan adjusted his seat. "We can't drive through mist."

"What mist?"

"Where can we go?"

"I know where we're going." Roger froze with his hand on the gearshift. "Why do you hate me?"

"We can't drive through mist."

"Alan, when I came home you ran up the street to see me. A car almost hit you, you were so damn excited."

"I was seven." Alan crossed his arms and pressed his forehead against the window.

The car drifted. "I know it's early," Roger said, "you can take a nap."

Alan was rising out of his doze when the sudden image of handwritten confessions flashed his eyes open. He sat forward. "Turn around!"

"What?"

"I forgot something important. Turn around."

"What did you forget? I'll call the motel."

"It's at home, turn around!"

"I *can't* just turn around we've already left New York."

Alan's heart changed rhythm. "Roger, where are we going?"

"Somewhere. I'm deciding. Put your seat belt on."

Alan stared out a window for several minutes, saw the street signs and shook his head. "I don't want to be in Pennsylvania. I don't want to be here."

"Why not? Mom's not going to pop out from a bush; no, no, I didn't mean it—calm down, I'm sorry."

The view in the windshield rushed at Alan. His palms pressed against the dashboard and he bowed his head. He tried to pull breath in by sharp thrusts. "This is...your big plan? Go back to that shit house..."

"It's still our house." Roger's hand drifted, wrist up, to the stop of the steering wheel. "I thought you missed the farm." Alan's elbow struck glass.

"Don't break the window, kid, take it easy!"

"DON'T TELL ME TO TAKE IT EASY!" Alan threw his bag into the backseat and launched his body after it.

Roger pressed a button. The car clicked and slowed. Alan pulled his jacket closed. The car stopped and he heard a door open and shut, open and shut.

Roger was sitting beside him. "What else?"

"What do you mean, what else?"

"What else can't I say or do?"

Alan looked at his brother: raised eyebrows, his typical squint: no alarm bells there. "I was being serious."

Roger nodded. "I didn't know. That you didn't want to hear that." Their eyes contacted.

"You can't tell me to take it easy."

"Okay....What else?"

Silence happened. Alan swallowed. "You can't grab me." His brother nodded again. "And don't take pictures of me without asking and don't keep your hands in your pockets."

Roger shut his eyes and rubbed his forehead. "Okay." He wiped a tear off Alan's face. "Anything else?"

Alan looked at his hands. "Don't grab me."

"I won't grab you."

"I don't hate you." Alan exhaled.

Sirens swelled. The brothers watched speeding police cars. Roger's breath misted. "Alan...I'm terrible at being an adult, I know. But you have to listen to me." He looked away from the window. "Okay? You have to trust me."

They drove. Their car passed between pine trees and over gravel. Roger hit the brakes. "That's where it happened."

Alan blinked. "What?"

Roger pointed. Alan looked out the window. "Did he take the dog?"

Roger blinked. "What?"

"We never found the dog."

"Right...we took the dog, too."

"What happened to her?"

Roger shook his head. "I don't remember." The car rolled forward. "Are you okay?"

"Sure, I'm okay."

Grass rippled at the level of their arms. The house watched their approach and mirrored their gaunt, abandoned affect.

Alan's eyes flicked between the windows and caught a flash of color. "Someone's in the house!" His knees buckled and Roger caught him.

"Nonono, no one's in the house, kid."

"I saw little red—"

"You didn't. It's Mycholia, okay? Just walk behind me."

The ceilings of the house swelled over Alan's vision. Alan sat on a couch and dust rose in swirls.

"Stay there, kid. I'm going to check the place out."

"You said there was no one."

Roger lifted his voice. "There could be an animal. Don't worry, you're safe with me. I'm not going to let anything touch you." He entered a dark hallway and pulled a handgun out of his backpack.

Roger entered rooms sideways. He held the weapon at his chest and thrust it out with his arms in the slender V-shape like he had seen at the cinema. He smelled his mother and then stepped in the fragments of a perfume bottle: and this gave him a vision of his mother holding Alan as a baby, too close to the stove.

He got down to his belly on the rug, swept aside the glass and felt for the edges of the perfume spill. A slight stiffness in the carpet gave it away, and he was overcome with the need to clean it.

When Roger entered his childhood room he stared, open mouthed, at its bed. It was unmade as it had been on the morning of his tenth birthday. He looked at a mirror. "Don't lose it," he whispered. The gun met its reflection. "Keep it together. Don't. Lose. It."

Several mice crowded the couch where Alan sat. He opened a hand to one of them. Roger saw it and made a disgusted noise. "That's a rodent. Don't touch rodents, that's the first rule." He pushed things off shelves. Dust formed indoor clouds.

Alan nudged the mice off of the couch. "What are you doing?"

"I'm trying, kid, to make a clear space."

Alan watched a plush tiger hit the floor. Stuffing and stitches took the place of where its tail ought to have been. He could not take his eyes off the thing. "Roger, is Arden's mom really alive?"

"I don't care." Roger kicked the toy, it slid under the couch.

Alan pulled his collar away from his neck. "Roger, please take your medicine."

The man stopped moving. "Every woman's a liar. And I thought that women were good, I really did."

Alan was shaking his head. "That's impossible, Roger, no one's a liar."

"Drop the tone, drop it. I have enough to contend with. Get off the floor!"

Alan's arm was beneath the couch. Something skittered over his wrist. He emerged with the tiger, which Roger grabbed from him.

"Parasites, kid, don't touch that!"

Alan looked at his brother's hand. "Are you hungry?"

"Are you? Do you want food?"

Alan sighed. "I don't know. Should I go shopping now?"

Roger was shaking his head. "No, no, I do that. You stay here and I'll go do that. Okay?"

"You're going to go alone?"

Roger nodded. "I go alone, you stay in the house. That's rule number two. Okay?"

"Okay."

"Alright."

Alan was alone in the house. He pressed the heels of his hands into his eyes and heard a dog whine. He looked around and then upwards.

Alan searched for the crying dog. He checked rooms and then closets and then cabinets. He sat tense behind a front window until his brother returned. "Roger, did you see it outside?"

"See what?"

"The dog! Listen for it." The animal howled. "It's stuck somewhere," Alan said. "I couldn't find it in the house."

"Would you stop this, kid?"

"It's making me nervous."

"I can't even hear it."

"How?" They stared at each other; wide eyes and narrow ones.

"Alan..."

"It's loud. There! Can't you hear that?"

Roger shook his head. "I don't hear it, Alan." The man had chattering teeth. A train whistle echoed. "That's a real sound, the train," Roger said. "You can look for that."

Alan sat among plastic bags. "Did you get toothbrushes?"

"There's one in your backpack."

"Oh." Alan stared into one of the bags. He bit his lip. "I'm on the milk."

Roger had a smoking cigarette. He rubbed his forehead.

Alan nudged his brother. "Roger, did you see? I'm on the milk carton."

Roger took it from him, stared at it. Looked at his brother, then back at the carton. "Please eat something. Rule number three is you have to try and eat something."

"But I'm not hungry."

"Yes, you are. You are hungry, you're just not paying attention."

Roger watched his brother eat two crackers. "Put on the coat I bought."

"Why?"

"Because it's freezing, Alan. There's snow. It's snowing."

Alan put on the coat. He saw his brother's shivering form. "Hot air rises," he said.

They went upstairs. "This is different from your other room." Alan settled on the bed.

Roger cornered himself. "What other room?"

"Your room at Micah's place. It was full of things. It had a big sign that said THIS ROOM on it."

"Yeah. I liked labeling things back then. I labeled everything. Aren't you cold?"

"It is, but I'm not."

Roger dropped his cigarette. He pushed it with his shoe. "We have to get out of here."

"Why?"

"Because I'm stupid, Alan. I'm dumb. They'll find us here."

Alan studied the stillness of his own hands. "So what? So what if they find us?"

"I'm in deep. They won't let us see each other again."

"No, they can't do that!" Alan threw his legs over the side of the bed. "Why would they do that?"

"Because I've kidnapped you."

Alan shook his head. "No, don't say that. This doesn't count. You're my brother"

"I'm an adult and you're—,"

"No!" Alan took off the coat. "I'm not kidnapped. I will say if I'm kidnapped or not. It's not the same thing. Kidnapping is bondage."

Roger hissed between his teeth. He pinched his nose. "For God's sake stop talking." The window over his left shoulder cracked under frost. "I could set a false trail..." He rubbed his arm. "Move over, my legs are going out."

The bed was full. The brothers slept. Alan said "flood" and turned his head. He kicked. His head lifted and sank. Roger grunted and rubbed his face. He watched Alan breathe clouds and then stop. Roger nudged him, then shook him. "Get up." Alan's eyes opened.

Roger leaned over him. "Breathe, for God's sake. You're not breathing!" Roger had such a hard grip on the boy he could feel blood beating in his own thumbs.

Alan saw mist flow from Roger's mouth. Panic was a prickling heat in his shoulders and chest. He pushed his brother off him and spots ran in his vision until air rushed, unbidden, and he was breathing again with his fist against the side of his head. "I had no breath," Alan realized aloud.

"I know!" Roger squeezed him. "Don't do that again. And take the blanket."

"I'm not cold."

"You are! Pay attention." Roger pulled the blanket around his brother. "Rule number four: don't scare me. Okay?"

"Okay."

"Alright."

Roger found the source of the train whistle and stood by its track while Alan lay in the house, convinced of an approaching flood. He could not trace the source of his conviction any farther than a vague sense of pressure and blueness, and did not voice his fear. It was no more real than the hallucinatory dog whining; that is, Alan could clearly sense it but was isolated in his perception. And when he was alone in the house, every sensation plateaued in its authenticity. He had never felt so alone, not even when he woke up tethered to a stranger's bed.

Roger became the barometer for telling which senses were shared and which were not. The shared senses,

Alan determined, were the real ones. So he listened to the train whistle with wide eyes.

The sky issued pressure that compelled Alan to sleep again and again. Roger woke him once in the kitchen and twice by the front door. In the kitchen, Alan had been holding a knife over his own hand.

"You're sleepwalking, kid," Roger said. "It's dangerous. You have to stay awake when I'm not here, okay? Rule number seven."

Occasionally, the dog's whine conquered Roger's speech. Roger often repeated himself. He watched Alan sleep. One morning they found themselves again in the kitchen. Roger held a spoon in front of his brother's mouth. "Come on. One bite, okay? Just one. Just this spoon."

"There's cereal on it."

Roger pushed a hand through his hair and shook off the loose strands. "Open your mouth."

Alan shook his head. Something moved in the corner of his vision. He glanced at it. "Roger, is that my hand on the table?"

"Yes."

"Is the faucet dripping behind you?"

Roger glanced at it. "No, it's not."

Alan stared at the sink. It dripped loud. He sighed and looked back the shaking spoon. "You're feeling cold, Roger. You should button your collar."

"It doesn't button."

Alan frowned. "You have a bruise on your neck. Where is that from?"

"I'll tell you if you take one bite. I'll tell you and I'll button my collar."

Alan's left wrist twisted against metal. "Will you uncuff me from the table?"

Roger nodded. "Yes. Please, Alan, I just want you to eat something."

"You grabbed me."

"What?"

"You promised that you wouldn't grab me but you did."

"Damn it, Alan!" Roger dropped the spoon. "I'm trying. Look at me. I'm trying. Now eat."

Alan looked at the spoon.

"You have to trust me," Roger said. "Rule number five."

Alan opened his mouth. A cold spoon entered.

"See? You're fine. It'll be okay...Alan. You have to swallow."

Alan swallowed. His eyes watered. Roger knelt between table legs and unlocked handcuffs. "Hey," he looked at Alan, "hey, you're not breathing."

Alan breathed in and promptly vomited. Roger groaned and helped him out of the chair. "Are you dizzy?"

Alan shook his head. "What's wrong with me?"

"I don't know. I think nothing. Do you want any of my pills?"

"Do I have to swallow them?"

"You have to swallow them."

"No thanks, then. You need them." Ice hit the window. "You said you'd tell me what happened to your neck if I ate the spoon."

Roger stroked the boy's hair. "You didn't eat the spoon."

Alan blinked. "Did someone bite on you?

Roger popped his collar and put a hand on his brother's shoulder. "Let's play cards"

Alan did not look at the hand on his shoulder. The man's eyebrow twitched and twitched. "You should relax, Roger."

"I can't relax." Their voices had gone down to whispers.

"No one's going to find me."

Roger's breath stopped. He looked where Alan's jaw might be. "What?"

Alan sighed. "There's too much snow for someone to find us." He made a pinched expression. "I think you should relax."

Mist rushed out of Roger's mouth. His hand dropped. He left the kitchen and the floor shook under him. The front door opened and shut. When Alan heard the car, he took off his coat and took off his jacket. He stood, breathing, and then water busted out of the faucet. Alan jumped and ran upstairs.

Alan was again in Roger's childhood bed. He rolled onto his back and breathed into his stomach. A sudden sheet of water fell over the window and sunlight shot severe through its frame. Water flowed over the whole house. Alan curled into a fetal position and retched. He punched his navel. He tried to sit. The house cracked at its joints. Alan fell off the bed and stood with the sheets around him. Snow kept melting in flashes. Teeth scraped Alan's bottom lip. Breath no longer misted. "Pay attention," Alan said aloud, "if I'm talking, then I'm breathing." He put a finger in his mouth and counted his teeth.

Alan walked on quivering joints. He peeled off his shirt. "I hate clothes. They sweat on me and it makes them heavier than my body altogether." Alan's eyes squinted—he was growing into them. The dog whined. "Roger will come back, now. He'll have to."

But the sun rose and fell and rose and fell and Roger was not in the house. Alan drank water. His pants became heavy. They fell off while Alan was climbing stairs. His legs were bones. He searched Roger's closet for a belt.

The faucet sometimes dripped. Alan lay down against the sound of the dog, and then there were scrapes to hear. He perceived them as pale, rough streaks over darkness. They clouded his vision, released, clouded and released. Alan rolled over and pressed his ears. He pulled a pillow over his head. A child screamed. Water rushed.

Alan paced from room to room. He said that the sounds were not real and he felt it in his throat but could not hear his own speech. The house groaned. Sound echoed on its walls. Alan kicked at the front door. He twisted the knob in a flash and then his hand was back on his ear and he was running. The groans and echoes followed. Grass whipped his elbows.

Then Alan was still. The grass flowed in soundless waves. Alan panted. His arms slowly dropped away from his head. He blinked and lay in the grass. Alan settled against the gentle silence.

Nearby, a girl sat on the back of an animal. Her balance was an intimate rhythm that she knew by pressure and contact. The animal moved forward.

The girl took a deep breath "The warm is back, Pony-Horse." She sent a flicker of tension through her legs and clucked. The animal hit a two beat gait. Then the animal halted and she lurched. The animal started approaching the old house. The girl astride it watched its ears until he stopped beside a boy in the grass. The girl stared at a long time at the boy. His eyes were closed. He hummed and touched his throat while he did it.

The animal lowered its neck. It was a horse. Alan knew it by the heavy head and belted mouth. The girl sat the horse and the horse settled in the grass, though she did not ask it to.

The girl was called Nala. Alan's eyes opened and they were huge. Nala's hair was red.

"You look like Alan Cope," she said.

Alan breathed. He saw Nala's lips move and shook his head like he wasn't sure. He wished he'd kept his shirt.

Nala bit her lip. "Have you had anything to eat?"

Alan shook his head again. He wanted to understand what she was saying. Nala's legs moved and under them the horse's hide was dark with sweat. Alan sighed. Nala smacked her horse. "Get up." Alan started to take off his belt and she hit the horse again. "Get up, Pony-Horse!"

Alan tapped the animal with his belt. Nala's hands knotted in the horse's mane while it found its feet. Then she went back up and her knees were next to Alan's throat. He held the belt up to her with one hand and he was holding his pants up with the other. His palms felt itchy.

"I don't need that," Nala said, and Alan just blinked at her. She took the belt. "You look a lot like Alan Cope...." She stared at him and scratched her collarbone. Then she said to him, "you've got a tick on you."

Nala's hand crashed against Alan's ear. Sound returned so violently, he gasped with shock. She pinched the tick out of the boy's hairline. The animal turned around with the girl on its back.

Sweat coated Alan's body wet. He let his pants drop and threw them over one shoulder. He heard again and again the crash of the girl's hand as he took heavy steps back to the house. Once there, he ran to the kitchen. Alan ate crackers and opened a pack of jerky.

Alan opened doors and windows. He slept to the sound of animals what had woken up in the heat. They drifted in and out of the house while he slept. There was food in Alan's belly and he breathed into it. The train whistle blew.

And then Alan heard the front door open. He sat up in bed. "Roger?" The front door shut. Alan pulled clothes onto himself. A roach crawled over his foot. He put on shoes. "Roger! Why did you take so long?" Alan froze on the last stair. Blood trickled in his nose. "That's lemon vodka..."

Roger stood in the kitchen. "Did you make something to eat?"

"No." Alan looked around at his brother with one hand gripping the banister. "There's hardly any food left. Why are you standing like that?" He glanced at the bottle on the table. "You can't drink. You promised you wouldn't drink."

Roger yawned. Alan stomped over creaking wood. He felt for a flashlight on the counter and turned it on. "Are you listening to me?"

"Stop telling me what to do."

Alan breathed. "Jeez, Roger, I'll stop telling you what to do when you get some sense!"

Roger pushed him. "Shush, shut up. What have you been doing? I have a lot of sense. I've been out working. I'm the one with sense."

Alan shook. "I'm calling the fuzz and I'm telling them where I am, I'm telling, I swear to God..." The dog cried in swollen whistles. Alan blinked against a swoon.

"Like hell you are. I'm your only family. Look at me. No one else loves you, understand? I cleaned mom's perfume off the floor for you. Me, I did it. You wanna live with women the rest of your life? You think they're gunna take care of you?"

"No, I don't...know."

"No as in no or no as in you dunno?"

Alan could not hear his brother over the dog. He set the flashlight on the table and walked back to the staircase.

Roger grabbed him and pushed him against its rungs. "How much Mycholia did you have?"

"I...I don't know." Distress caught Alan's face. "I swear I don't."

"Come on, how much? How much did you make for those bastards, huh?" Roger shook him.

Alan lifted his chin. He squared his shoulders. "I fucking don't know. I'm going upstairs."

"How much? I know. I know Micah pumped you full of it." Roger pinched the boy's face. "What the hell is this, are you eating at all?"

Blood sprayed from Alan's nose. He flicked his head away from the hand. He climbed a step and climbed a step.

Roger seized the back of Alan's shirt. Alan felt it tear above his clavicle. He heard the fibers separate, and then he was against the rungs again. He took a gasp. His neck hurt.

Roger's breath was sour. "Don't walk away from me."

Alan pushed his unmoving brother. "Micah didn't give me any, okay? He didn't do anything weird, you need to cool it." Hoarseness took his voice. "Get away from me, you're drunk."

"Like hell he didn't!"

"...no. He didn't."

"You are a lying whore." Roger had a fistful of the shirt. His wrist pressed into Alan's side. Put a square around the subject. Put a circle around the object. "What happened here?"

"Stop it, Thumper. Stop."

It almost worked. Roger hesitated for a beat, then said: "Leave him out of this."

"Then *you stop!*"

"Answer me."

Alan turned his head away from his brother. "I don't know what you mean!"

"Did you do this yourself? You're cutting yourself?"

Alan looked at the ceiling. "I did not cut myself!"

"Then what the hell is it?"

"Get your hands off me!"

Roger's voice dropped an octave. "What makes you think you can say that?"

Alan punched Roger's chest. He twisted and spat. "I didn't cut myself, okay? It wasn't me." The dog howled.

Roger shook him again. "Then why'd you let anyone do that to you? You stupid kid, can't you scream?"

"Yes!" Alan shouted at the ceiling. "Yes, I screamed, I swear to God I screamed, Roger, please!"

"Stop crying! What are you crying for?"

"Roger," Alan said between sobs, "Roger, you're scaring me..."

"Fine." Roger released the boy. "That's fine, if you're such a pussy." He stepped off the staircase.

Alan rubbed his side. "Asshole," he muttered.

Roger whirled and struck Alan's head. Alan grabbed a stair rung. It broke when he fell. His head hit the floor.

"That's what you get." Roger picked the bottle off the table. "That's what you get for mouthing off at the only person who loves you. Sense, my ass." Then: "This is fucking delicious. I don't know what it is, but it's fucking *delicious.*"

Moonlight flooded the ceiling. Alan heard the front door shut. It was hard to breathe. He tasted blood and tried to lift his head. He saw his shoes. They were black shoes with white laces. Alan passed out of wakefulness.

Roger drove out what gas was left in his car. He walked on train tracks and slipped many times on wet rocks. He did not realize he was on a bridge until he saw the water over a hundred feet below him. In Roger's brow were subtle fault lines. His lips puckered. Wind came from above and around, it greeted him alone and fluttered his clothes. The water rippled.

"He hadn't prepared for this, he had no plan, but
some hidden, fiery part of him had, it seemed, been
making observations as the rest of his mind stayed
cocooned in its thick, cottony slumber."
—*Hanya Yanagihara*

IV

Alan's Apocalypse

In Luna, Roger Cope broke water's surface. Blood curled out of his nose and floated like the tendrils of a sea animal. A net cocooned him and pulled. He met terra firma. He thrashed in the net and cried, "Larque!" with the same fervor one would use for words like "stop!" or "wait!" or "run!"

Let's meet Catarina: she had a long neck and a thick yellow fringe. On her lap was an intestinal mass of fibers that she pulled and knotted and repeated. She wore the kinetic affect of a swan. What met her ears in that moment was heavy steps of someone dragging someone else. Catarina looked up from her work. She ran outside. "Not another one, Kris."

Kris held wet blankets around a boy, dripping wet. "He's special, Catarina, he's the one I seen before in the snow. The one who got himself in the bear trap."

Catarina nodded at the pond. "Go on, then, you should put him back in."

Moons lit water ethereal as Kris made his way back to the pond and threw in the soaked and shaking body of Alan Cope. Alan met awareness underwater. Everything was blue. The water was a warmth that loosened his eyes while above him an antlered man pulled membrane in masses over water's surface. It floated like seaweed.

Alan had no knowledge of swimming. His arms danced upwards like he had seen on television. Pointed feet took the action of minnows. Alan met the membrane and gulped the air of an updraft. He heard a voice.

"Stay under that fiber. Can you hear us?"

"Yes!"

From above was a feathered laugh of relief. "That's awesome, just keep breathing. We'll pull you out."

After a few minutes, Kris and Catarina took Alan out with the fiber and told him to roll on the ground. Alan wormed natal-like in the soft wet masses until Catarina stopped him with placating hands and pulled the membrane off. Alan's head was freezing. He looked into the woman's face.

"You are okay?" She asked.

Alan nodded. "I'm okay."

"Okay."

"Alright!" A new voice soared over the pond. A man stepped into light. His coat was enormous and lined with fur, the spiked shadow of which cast over Alan's chin like a sea urchin. "We've got ourselves another one, aye? Bring him in, miss, it's going arctic out here."

Catarina helped Alan rise. "Not so loud, Tuck. Isn't your sister sleeping?"

"Not anymore."

Warmth had a front of piled logs. A steepled ceiling made Alan's head reel: An auburn haired girl emerged with a plush horse. It had ribbons for a mane and tail. Tuck picked the girl up and held her against his chest. He pointed at Alan. "You see, Tabitha, I told you." The girl gasped and her brother chuckled.

Catarina tsked. "Put her in bed, Tuck. The boy has to adjust." Alan sat on a nearby chair. The woman's hands descended around his face. "What happened?" she asked.

Alan blinked hard. "I got hit," he mouthed.

Catarina held a honeycomb over the injury and said that that would prevent scarring. Alan doubted it. "I'm fine," he said, "it's just I'm tired." The antlered man moved in his peripheral vision.

"I can't let you sleep yet," Kris said. "I've got to check your eyes and everything." He was in front of Alan and touching him and asking what he could feel. "I'm not sure," Alan kept saying, "have you got your hand on me?"

"I'm only checkin' your reflex," Kris said. He was grinning. "You're the fifth person from Earth that won't need Larque."

Tabitha's eyes glistened at Alan. "What hit your face?" Her head cocked like an animal. Alan sensed from her a unified will that he had long ago lost or perhaps never achieved.

"It was a man," he said. "It must have been my brother."

Roger sat in Rusha's hot office. He had just had an altercation in a pressurized chamber wherein he had explained, with perfect clarity and violent gestures, that he had been to Luna before and would not take any Mycholia unless he could speak to Micah first. Roger rested an ankle on a knee and slipped an elbow over the back of his chair. He stared sidelong at Rusha's computer. It floated by means that were invisible; or perhaps it only seemed that way to him because he could never understand things like computers and the difference between secular and cellular and other details that seemed to come naturally to everyone else.

Roger heard the door open behind him. Rusha walked to his desk chair but did not sit. "You look comfortable."

Roger's chin lifted. "I am comfortable."

"You said that you've been here before?"

"I'm Roger Cope."

Rusha nodded. "I want to check your fingerprint."

Roger laughed. "You remember me, Rusha. I was your best advocate."

"Yes, yes, the Lucid Larque Boy. You were quite the mascot at conferences. My entire business might have crumbled without you."

"It might have!"

Rusha relaxed into an s-shaped posture. "There's always a market for immortality, Roger. Don't try to exercise leverage you don't have."

A bottle of ink sat open on the desk. Roger's hand hovered above it for a moment. He slipped each finger in by turns and then stretched his arm across the desk. Ink dripped over a bowl of candy. Rusha replaced the bowl with off-white paper. He flipped Roger's hand by the wrist and pushed it down, smiling.

"That's enough." Roger pulled his hand back. He felt himself adopt the posture he had witnessed women wear when they knew they were being watched. Rusha held the paper against the glow of an oil lamp.

Roger saw them study the fingerprints. "I'm not of any use to you, Rusha."

"How did you get here?"

"I don't know."

Rusha looked at him. They lowered the paper. "Did you fall, or did you jump?"

"What do you mean?" A quake ran through Roger's neck. He gripped the right side of his head and left ink stains there. "There was a bridge...why do you want to know?"

"You are of great use to me, Mr. Cope."

"No, I won't make Kisslic. It's too late for me."

"That's only beside the point."

Roger's voice hardened. "I drowned my little brother."

"Not to death." Rusha started tapping the computer monitor. "He gave us a full account of it during a bath. Quite the babbler when he thinks no one's watching. He couldn't remember how he got here either, though. Something about being tied in a bed."

Desperation tensed the muscles of Roger's throat. "No one can remember."

Rusha pressed the paper against a plate of glass. "No one who's been here only once." He pressed a button and looked at Roger. "You're right about one thing: you'd be a waste of Mycholia. Your brother, on the other hand, had an excellent yield." Roger heard buzzing and the dial of a coil-wired phone. He heard Rusha's voice: "He is who he says he is. You can take him to see Micah, if that's what he wants."

Roger stood to meet white coated men. They wore vapor masks and handed him one.

"What's this for?"

"We're going outside," said one.

"The air is bad," said the other. Their voices were fuzzily muffled.

Roger followed them into a second building. He stepped over its threshold and into a bout of weak kneed remembrance. They passed pods of silent, breathing boys. A white coated woman stepped into the hall and ran her hands through her hair. "I'm dead. We lost another one."

The men stopped. "What happened?"

"It wasn't my fault, I just came on duty and someone forgot to change the tubes."

Masks were removed. "So?"

"So, toxic shock. The pod's gone dry and he's going to see it with that damn computer. Can I grab him? Please?" She seized Roger's wrist and one of the men shook his head.

"We're supposed to get him out of here."

The woman narrowed her eyes. "Where?"

The men looked at each other. "It's Rusha's business," one of them said, and an argument opened. Roger watched three faces look at each other and at him, one confused one frustrated and one coveting, and he thought it's been so long since a woman looked at him coveting, if at all, and it quite excited him but no, you imbecile, she doesn't want you to have sex with her and that can't be the source of that intolerable heat, it's not her, it's the damn—

"Carpeted walls?!" Roger blurted, and they looked at him. "You have floating computers and colors and things I don't understand, but you're still using carpet?"

In the mornings, Alan strained against muscular limitation while his new friends formed graceful arcs with their backs. Kris led stretching exercises that he said were necessary to help one acclimate to Luna's atmosphere, and indeed, dizziness took Alan entirely by noon on the days when he did not join them.

Alan rarely spoke to Catarina for fear of catching jealous eyes. He knew she was much older than him but could not guess her age. She said the same of him. Alan often wondered if she was really from Earth after all and whether she could read minds, but he was significantly calmed by the realization that he had wondered this about most women. After that, he wanted to write down his thoughts to prevent further confusion. Tabitha shared paper with him. She followed Alan everywhere. So did the wolf.

Alan had asked Kris about the wolf, and, of course, he could not provide an answer without working in a long story about Catarina.

"I couldn't let her die," he said for the dozenth time, "and I know Rusha's team won't take any ladies on account of them not making Kisslic, you know, so all I could think of was to put her in my pond and try to help her breathe. It hadn't happened to me before, running into a female on duty. Next thing you know she's pulling blankets under water and training me out of Larque. She understands the science. She catches on to those things, Cat does. The kinds of things you don't see. She figured a way to apply the pressure."

Alan straddled a chair. "How long was she in the water?"

"She was in and out for days. I prayed the whole time Rusha's team wouldn't be coming in to check on me..."

Like a mermaid, Alan thought. "So they would check on you to make sure you're keeping this wolf, right?"

"Right, and they'll come if I'm not close to quota. The wolf is supposed to show me where people from Earth show up. Leads me there, like, if he hears some whistling. There's a lot of false alarms. Poor old dog, they won't even let me name him. I'd get in trouble."

Alan sighed. "Wolf is a fine name."

"He is mighty attached to you." Kris rubbed his chin. "Matter of fact, I think he recognizes you from when you were in the snow. What was that about?"

"What was what about?"

"What is it about you going to Earth and coming back again?"

Alan shrugged. "I don't know, I woke up with a polar bear. How did you get here?"

"I was in my parent's trailer, waiting on them to come back from something, and it started to snow. Or maybe it didn't, it was hot when they left. But I seem to remember it snowed and snowed and I waited on them...and I was in Luna a little after that." Kris rubbed his neck. "I get this awful pain sometimes..."

Catarina appeared in the doorway. "It's your antlers. I told you to wear the neck brace when you sleep."

Kris said something about the relief found in her massages. Alan did not notice when they left the room. The wolf sniffed his mouth and then made its way to the window. They both listened to the distant sound of water. "I know," Alan said to the wolf. He looked at his thigh because he felt an uncomfortable, probing warmth there and he wanted to move away from it but his leg was too heavy, so he looked out the window. "I know."

No one explained the carpeted walls to Roger. He was led into semi-darkness and heard a door close and lock behind him.

"Rusha said I could see Micah."

"You will."

Roger slipped his hands into pockets and watched a memory of Micah sewing in his studio, saying *look, little faun, consider the hand. Consider the stitches of the pocket and what they must carry.*

A lamp went on and revealed a table and one chair in the center of the room. One of the men pointed at it. "Have a seat."

Roger sat and tried to turn the lamp away from his face, but it wouldn't budge. He could barely see the men in front of him. A sigh came out of darkness. "Alright, we're going to show you some old footage, and then you need to answer some questions."

"Sure," Roger said, "I might do that." A soft square of light defined the left side of the room. In it was a film projected of Roger as a child, with Micah next to him. Roger recalled that moment to the quick; the sweet-smelling cold in the room and the excitement of being shown off at Micah's conference and the man sitting in front of a microphone, the peculiar kinship between the device and his name. The room was full of people, many of them with their heads bent over notes, others looking forward at Micah and rubbing their faces in variations of pensive stillness. One of them stood and asked what would happen to "the kid" if he stopped taking Mycholia.

Micah spoke in mic: "Firstly, his name is Roger and I call him by his name. If he stops taking Mycholia, he has withdrawal symptoms like anyone else. It's very distressing. He takes a lot of Mycholia, and very regularly. But he has a lovely temperament, and I think that's easy to see."

Roger kicked his legs in response. He was grinning. Someone else stood up in the audience. "I'm wondering," she said, "What are your thoughts about that? How do you contribute to his temperament, as you put it? Do you have any recommendations?"

Young Roger seized the mic. "It's easy, I just go to a different place in my head. And I really want to try a lobotomy, and that's where you—,"

Micah chuckled. "He's full of earthly ideas like that."

"And leeches are good," young Roger leaned into the mic and Micah. "I like leeches for muscle aches. I have a jar of them at home. They all have the same name."

Micah began an awkward attempt to explain bloodletting when young Roger suddenly collapsed. The mic hit the floor with an apocalyptic boom.

The film stopped. Roger felt frustration flare as if he was eleven again, stomping the floor and screaming at Micah to *give back the icepick*. The boy in the projection was fuzzy maybe from pixels but no, it was the fibers of the carpeted wall. His eyelids were dark from dependence on Mycholia and Micah both. The projection vanished and Roger lost the first half of a question:

"...tell us about what that did for you?"

Roger stared into darkness. "He was so worried about me."

"What about the lobotomy?

"What about it, why?"

"Did you get one? Why did you want one?"

"No I didn't get a lobotomy, are you crazy? What do you care?" A moment passed and Roger jerked in response to a sudden pain in his ears.

One of the men slid a device across the table's surface. "You see this knob? It's a portable knob. It controls the electromagnetic field of this facility and all its branches."

Roger felt the heavy weight of dread. "So it's...so it controls...."

The anonymous man turned the knob again and Roger yelped over the similar cries of a thousand children.

He sat panting with his palm pressing his head and the other on his navel.

One of the men said: "Do you know how Larque works?"

Roger swallowed. "Yes."

"And you know that you're not the only one getting hurt?"

Roger's wrists burned in bated stillness. "I'm not so sure. You have to regulate the magnetic field, not abuse it. Otherwise the Larque boys would die, and then who would make the Kisslic? So I'm not so sure." He saw the two men look at each other and then remembered it was too dark and no, you imbecile, you just saw the afterimage of the lamp and you're flicking your eyes.

Alan thought of the girl with the red hair. He missed her, and every time he saw red came the crash against his ear. It was only one of many sounds that happened to him when he saw color but he chased it anyway, finding Little Red in flowers and berries with Tabitha.

"Are you sure you want to follow me, Tabby? Your big brother might get jealous."

"Why?"

"I don't know," Alan said, "I don't know why anyone gets jealous. I've never had it...well, maybe sometimes," he amended, recalling an image of Roger flirting at a check-out counter with that tired, leaning way of his.

Tuck had been envious, though. Alan wore a beaded necklace that Tabitha made him and Tuck had asked about it at the dinner table, wondering aloud why he didn't have one, and with more humor in his voice than was natural for him. Anxiety visited Alan like a periodic draught and when it did, he counted the beads with his eyes shut and it soothed him. He cooked more often than anyone and handled the food with gentle, sedate fingers. Catarina watched Alan cook one day and asked him whether he preferred the cooking or the eating.

"I like making things," Alan responded. "And I'm not very good at eating. I try, but it gets the best of me. I used to be okay at it."

"How do you mean, gets the best of you?"

"I dunno. It feels like chewing carpet or shoes. I could do it, but I don't know, it's like...it's cumbersome, is what it is." Alan sliced a tomato and spooned out the aspic.

"So," Catarina picked up the knife and washed it, "what happened to you?"

"What do you mean?"

"You don't want to eat. Tuck says you have flat affect. You do not want to eat. Did we do something wrong?"

"No, I'm sorry." Alan shrank from her. "I've been here too long, I'll go now."

Alan abandoned the food. Catarina followed him out of the kitchen and into the storage closet where he'd been sleeping. He took personal items off a shelf and put them in a pillowcase: rocks, beads, a notebook full of thoughts and dead flowers.

Catarina threw up her arms. "What are you doing?"

"I'll leave—out of your way."

"What way? You're not in the way."

"Miss Catarina, if Kris sees you here he might get mad."

"But you're just a boy!"

Alan suddenly couldn't move and he stared at the piece of wood in his hand that he'd tried to carve into a horse, but it looked more like a dog, but then why should it look like anything but a piece of wood? He put the wood back on the shelf—slow, careful, automaton.

Catarina swallowed. "Do you want to go for a walk?" She tugged on his hand and he didn't move. He thought of the fibers on his jeans, if you felt them they went in ridges up and down like hills, like an enormous blue landscape he could crawl into and no one would see him....

"Tabby?" Catarina released Alan and walked about the cabin. "Tabby, can you come here? Alan is sad again."

Tabitha found Alan in a corner with his arms around his legs. She talked to him about something called Hard Times, and how it made him a hero. Alan heard her voice on the wind around him; everything was blue. He followed the voice over a hill of cotton and looked down into a closet where he saw his own body sitting. He kept watch for awhile, then reentered the body and lifted his head.

Tabitha was next to him. Alan looked at her. "Have I finished making dinner?"

"I dunno."

"Hm." Alan counted beads. "Did I clock out for a bit?"

"What?"

"Was I quiet? For a while?"

The girl huffed. "You're always quiet for a while."

Alan stretched. "I'm sorry, Tabby, I didn't mean it. I'm not used to being around other people."

"Why not?"

"Well," Alan crossed his legs and stretched forward, "my brother kept me inside all the time, because he was nervous. And it made me nervous, too, I dunno." He stood. "Let's go to the kitchen."

"I want a snack before dinner."

Alan washed berries in a bowl. This is it, came the sound of thought, it's coming and you know it. *Enough water to swallow it all.* He gave the bowl to Tabitha and leaned against the sink, shaking his head. It was neurosis, Roger had said. Just neurosis. A clean, clinical thing.

But it had a whisper of knowledge behind it, a little knowledge of how things would happen just the instant before they did. The sight of the drain and then looking at the drain. The echo of Tabitha's scraping chair and then the chair scraping. The water coming at the window—

Alan threw Tabitha to the floor and himself over her. The bowl fell; Alan heard a crash and braced for water.

Tuck followed his sister's scream. He grabbed Alan with one fistful of shirt and one fistful of hair and pulled him off of her. The floor under Alan's hands ebbed and flowed until he realized there was no water around him at all. He braved a series of flinching apologies to Tabitha's brother and, in the black of night, he left like a boy in a story.

Alan lifted himself from blankets on the floor and took everything except the wooden figure that was maybe an animal, which he left beside Tabitha's sleeping form.

He stepped outside and looked up into altostratus. His pillowcase glowed and was heavy. He threw it over his shoulder and walked. The longer Alan walked, the more certain he became about his decision to leave. He had started to become useless, Catarina could not understand that. Tuck and Kris were more useful than him in every regard. Anyway, by forcing him out of Larque they had granted Alan freedom. If he didn't wear Larque, if he kept his mouth silent, no one would suspect that he had arrived in Luna by an abuse on earth, by a knife and a kidnapper, or a fight with a brother, or a slip of paper that said *Rx Cope Syndrome.*

Micah twisted on a bed. The room was too hot, the room was too cold. Quinn stood in the doorway with a carafe. "Please have water."

"I won't have water." Micah cast an arm over his face, then at the pillow beside him. "Let me die."

"I will let you die," Quinn said, "but I won't let you suffer." It was over a year now since he had stood safely behind a third floor window to watch as Rusha's men came up the drive and exited moments later with a screaming Alan Cope. He wanted to leap through the frame of his vision to stop them, and indeed he had shattered window when they drove away.

Micah was suddenly still. "Where's Alan?"

Quinn paused in the act of pouring water. "He's playing safely in the garden."

The bed ridden man turned his sagging face to the water. "My papers, Quinn."

"You've put everything in order," Quinn reminded him, "you can rest."

"It's for your son, all of it." Micah nudged him. "You're so much a better father than I." His hand, bruised from bite marks, took the glass of water, then dropped it at the sound of knocking. "Don't let them in."

"I have to, Micah, they'll force it. Don't worry, there's no more wrong they can do to you."

Micah grit his teeth. "Then get a rifle. Do some wrong to them." He tried to sit up while Quinn left the room.

The front entrance was a double door; Quinn held one of them open at the width of his hips. He was looking at a Larque boy—no, a Larque *man,* standing at the threshold with white coats on either side. "Who are you?"

"I'm Roger Cope."

Quinn swallowed. "You can't see him, he's not himself."

Roger opened his mouth but the man on his left interrupted. "We have a permit to inspect this property. Let us in. And get my partner a cup of coffee." Roger locked eyes with Quinn, who slowly opened the door.

The white coats sat on Micah's cloud couch, Quinn nodded at the Larque man between them. "I want him to make the coffee. So I know who he is."

Roger's boots were so loud in the kitchen—Micah used to tell him you're shameless to stomp around so, I'm making you a healthy lunch, and himself whining: no Micah, I wanted cake and you never let me have what I want, and Micah cutting him generous slices of such.

Here are the spoons again, little L and little L like my tattoo, I wonder where the man is and will he remember me, I want to see him before they kill me, lobotomy, Quinn's watching. Lobotomy, with what? Celery sticks? They'll notice.

"Hurry up." Roger heard the voice behind him, he passed coffee grinds over the sink, spilled some, then in went his finger spelling L-O-B

"Roger," Quinn said, "I have moved the sugar." The words were slow and significant.

O-T

"We don't take sugar in our coffee."

Quinn turned. "What a shock. Do you always speak for your partner?"

"You know it's Roger Cope, this is a waste of time," the other man said, "bring him back in here."

O-M-Y. Lobotomy, come and get me, read it quickly. Quinn tugged Roger out of the kitchen.

Here we come to the point wherein Alan was pursued by a beast: a bear.

Alan did not want to have a dialogue with the bear. It had been following him, and was the largest animal yet to do so. He wanted to collapse, and pictured it over and over, the crush of falling knees and leaves under them, resting his face on that tired tree, or that one. But the bear was behind him.

It wasn't chasing him quickly, but it wouldn't let him alone. He tried walking slower and then faster again to lose track of its misting breath. He looked back and saw wet, uneven teeth. Alan thought of his own teeth and counted them, and tripped and cursed his mother.

He cursed, and he felt frustration in his body, yet he couldn't shake a sense of assurance that he was on the correct path. He had long abandoned the pillowcase; had hurled it in a fit of nervousness to try and distract the bear away from him, yet he didn't think about Ration, or what he would do for food. He passed shattered seashells, deposits of sand, carrion. Nothing was living except the bear and himself. It hurt to swallow. He took off his jacket.

"Alright, bear," Alan finally said, "the heat has been pumping all day. It's hot, and then cold and then hot. Like Roger's attitude." He laughed and then nearly tripped when he felt the bear's nose on his hand; it was enormous and wet. Alan kept walking, he feared running, his legs shook with the effort against it, running meant a race that the bear could win. He remembered that there were toys of this animal on Earth, button eyes and plastic noses, safe and dry and it may have been easier to remember if he had ever had one.

"I had a tiger." Alan's voice had gone viral-dry. "I'll bet you have more teeth than I. It really isn't fair." He put his jacket on again. "Don't you have anything else...to do?" He was panting. "Can't you...leave a boy alone?" There was a steep mound ahead of them. Alan had been regarding it, keenly searching for a way around, but there was no clear path, and he started to climb and hope that the bear would not follow.

"I should tell you how I lost my lower left incisor," Alan said. He leaned on a dark black rock for balance. "Or my front baby teeth, how did I first lose those? I should tell you, bear." He climbed forward. "It would scare you off." Alan heard the animal grunting behind him and his eyes burned. I'm going to be eaten, he thought, I'll be swallowed whole by the maw of a bear, consumed like Roger says a woman consumes. I think I'm scared. I must be scared, it's the only way to account for this intolerable heat—,

Alan found his feet on flat ground, he turned around to face the bear and back himself against a tree—something circled in his head, blood pressure it must be, come and take me. He couldn't remember if the jacket was still on him. His arms had white stripes but it seemed that they were always a part of him the way his shoes were a part of him, the way a bicycle clicking had been him breathing, its metal shattering akin to someone binding him—

"...in the back of a van," Alan said. The bear was coming towards him. The leaves watched, the sky watched, and it was better, he thought, than the glistening eye of a camera with people on the other end. There was something he ought to say, something about country, or not a country.

The bear's head lowered. The ground shivered under its steps, and then the jaws of a dark black trap snapped into its front paw.

Alan jerked his own legs towards him when he saw it, then he crawled around the tree and ran. He slipped and went down a slope, the landing was a shivering concuss, as if his body had hit the surface of a drum. He picked up his feet and ankles, moving them, checking them, and then saw a house on the horizon. He walked towards it.

Approaching the front door it occurred to Alan that it could be a man on the other end, or a woman, and what would Roger say, how would he seduce himself in? And when the door opened by a woman Alan said, "I can drink a gallon of water."

The water was a little sweet; he vibrated with thirst. The woman watched.

"You look familiar," she said.

Alan wiped his mouth on his wrist and looked at her. "What's your name?"

She didn't answer. He started to rinse his glass at the woman's sink.

"My name's Natasha," she said finally, "you don't have to do that."

Alan had started on another dish. Soap stung the tiny cuts on his arms. The water revived his body but not his purpose; he worried Natasha would ask him to leave, or worse, that he would excuse himself.

"You're not the first person to get lost around here," Natasha said. "Were you camping?"

"I was wandering and I lost my pillowcase and...it had my things in it." Alan shut off the water and wrung his hands.

"I'd let you stay for awhile," Natasha leaned her head on her hand, "but my husband doesn't like to extend himself."

"I'm sorry," Alan said without thinking.

Natasha shrugged. "He's not home. Rusha is always keeping him late, since they're testing the girls."

Alan looked at her. "Girls from Earth?"

"Yes, I mean...oh, nevermind." Natasha shook her head. "I don't think I should have said that. You really look so much like our old Larque boy, how old are you?"

Alan remembered the pain of stretching in the morning on morning after morning, enough for a year or two, or to realize he was hesitating. "Seventy," he said, "I've been on Kisslic since I was a teenager."

Natasha smiled. "I started in my early thirties. It really is better the longer you're on it." The smile disappeared. "I haven't offered you any!"

"That's okay."

"But you must be hurting for it!" Natasha rushed to a cabinet to retrieve a glass and beckoned to Alan, who followed her out of the kitchen and down a hallway. "I'm very sorry," she said, opening a door, and Alan covered his mouth.

It was the girl with the red hair. Not on a horse, on a table, in a white room. Natasha held the cup under a domed apparatus connected to the girl. Kisslic flowed, black and frothing.

Natasha handed him the glass. Through Alan's head was Micah's voice warning him against it, it's not good for you, it tastes like sweat. And it did. He couldn't take his eyes off the girl. "I thought, uh…I thought girls can't make Kisslic?"

Natasha made an equivocating gesture. "They've found a way to make it happen. This is sort of a beta test."

Alan gave the woman an uneasy smile and she took the glass back from him. "Feel better?"

A deep breath, let it out, imagine water; so Alan began his internal regimen against uncontrolled nausea. He nodded and followed her into another room and leaned on an armchair, then sat. He felt hot and cold at the same time. Natasha was speaking but Alan heard tinny and shivering. All sound blurred.

He was staring at a corner of something and it appeared to be an accumulation of dots or motes. And the wall behind it was not wall but more motes, and the air between them motes, and to a body called Alan Cope made of motes.

Natasha thought that the boy might be ignoring her, and then she heard him say, "all...this," and then the throttle of collapse when he fell, tense and twitching, on the floor.

Alan Cope was tired of not knowing where he was. He heard the articulation of speech and his comprehension straggled behind its reality:

"How long was the fit?"

"Maybe a minute, I don't know."

"Damn it, Natasha, you gave him a whole glass? We don't know how much that girl is going to make, or for how much longer."

"He needed it. He was lost, I told you."

"I know, I know." The speaker's breath came close to Alan and he realized it was a man. "He looks like the Larque boy we had that got out."

"I know."

Alan tried to look. Someone was picking up his feet.

"You see these shoes?"

"Yes, I did notice them."

"They look real."

"They might be." It took the quick of Alan's might to pull his feet back; he felt so weak.

"I think those are real. Where did he get real shoes from Earth, if not from Earth?"

"Terra Library?"

"No, you don't wear something from the Terra Library. Not if you get something from there, you don't wear it. It's not what you do."

"He said he had seventy years."

Alan heard someone say "Earth" twice, the carpet smelled like his mother, as if she were standing over him with pliers, he hated it, he lifted himself to crawling. "Thank you I have to go now."

"Well, sit down a minute."

"Nono." Alan stood. "Thank you for The Water." He ducked away from the man's gaze and went out the way he came. He walked into breeze until he heard the sound of waves. It's the shoes, he thought, bending to take them off, they are real and from Earth. He tied the laces together and hung the shoes around his neck with the socks in them, walking into sand. His heart beat in time with the shoes thumping his ribs, thumping his chest. Alan followed the rushing sound and watched his feet, which were larger than he remembered; the veins stood out in soft relief. Foam rushed around the ankles. He looked out at ocean. Everything was gray.

Alan tried to find something on the shoes, some word or something not black or white, but he couldn't. And they were too clean. Of course he was from Earth, anyone could tell. He took the shoes off his neck and swung them forth into ocean.

It took Alan a long walk to realize that the ocean had not been there for long. There was not enough sand. Wood floated in the water, he found several dead birds. It was not ocean, it was a flood breaking into Luna. The shoes washed up and around Alan's legs and he stared at the water until he could not discern waves from atmosphere. He wondered, if he walked into it, would it breathe him back out like it did the shoes?

He sat for awhile and considered the red headed girl. He wanted. He wanted to go back. He wanted to go back for her. He wanted to go back for her so much. He wanted to go back for her so much that he felt. He wanted to go back for her so much that he felt afraid. He wanted to go back for her so much that he felt afraid to do so.

The water was rising. Alan picked up the shoes and went back for her.

The way back was shorter. The night hid him. He got closer and closer and skirted the windows of the house. Alan did not have a plan, he didn't know what room the girl was in but only that it was windowless.

"You're back."

Alan jumped. It was Natasha. She wore a nightgown and it gleamed under the moons. "Did you come to rob us?"

"I, I'm. There's water," Alan stammered, walking backwards as she approached. "It will come and swallow your house if you don't move inland so I came back to warn you and then it got dark--,"

"We know.

"You...what?"

"We know it's coming. We don't want to move. You're from Earth, aren't you? You really are."

"I'm not wearing Larque."

"But you're from Earth. I can tell."

Alan flinched. "Please don't tell. Don't tell your husband."

"He's not home."

"Are you lying to me?"

"No. Do you want to come in? Come inside, come on."

Alan followed her into the house. She stepped in a hallway and looked at him. "You have the saddest eyes I've ever seen."

"I'm sorry."

"Sorry for what?"

"I have come to rob you. I know the girl that you have on Mycholia. I want to take her home."

Natasha frowned. "What's her name?"

"She's important to me."

"What's her name?"

"I don't know, I want to know. Can you tell me?"

"Where do you think you can take her?"

"I don't know. You can trade me. You can let her go and put me on Mycholia. I have a good yield, a great yield."

"How do you know your own yield?"

"Well, I don't have antlers, do I?" Alan said, getting frustrated. "I'm still young. I'm good at it. She's important to me. She touched me." After a pause, he continued: "do you have oral anesthetic? I can work the machine myself. I don't eat much, you don't have to feed me. I can cook for you. Trade me." His eyes burned and he couldn't account for it.

Natasha sighed through her nose. "Don't look at me that way. You can leave, and take her with you. Just...be sure to break a window from the outside."

"A window from the outside?" Alan was beside the girl, turning off the machine, unbuckling her.

"Yes, any window. So my husband knows that you broke in, it couldn't be helped."

"Tell him I had a knife."

"Ok, you had a knife."

Alan slowly lifted the mask off of the girl's face, he pulled the tube out of her mouth. She didn't cough and she didn't open her eyes. She was lighter than him and shorter than him and several minutes later he was stumbling away from the house with the girl in his arms. And when he walked the moonlight stroked him in pale strokes. The weight of this girl was pressing his shoulders and arms and he wished his shoulders were bigger, wider, like platforms for growth or spectacle or speech or safety, and he smelled Mycholia on her, and it gave him vertigo.

Alan thought he could feel Natasha watching him struggle, and wondered if she expected him to fall like a fool, split his lip on a rock and look up to find her husband staring down at him, like he found Roger staring down at him, or the man at the park or the boy at the f-house or don't think about that, and by then he was no longer visible from Natasha's house. The clouds had acquired a pink tint as though they were lit from within, their creases and edges dipping into purple.

As he stared at them, the girl started to slip off his shoulder. She was mumbling something. Alan set her down on a bed of leaves.

Nala lurched forward into a coughing fit. And it was while sitting there, watching the girl cough and not knowing what to do or what it could be like to be a girl coughing that Alan realized he was hungry. He looked into her face. "I saw you on a horse."

She nodded. "I feel sick."

"It's Mycholia withdrawal," Alan said, his voice dropping a register. "You'll feel pretty rotten, but it will pass."

Nala rubbed her head. "You look like someone."

"I'm Alan Cope. What's your name?"

"My name? My name..." She rolled over and vomited. Alan took hold of her hair, it was so red, and it felt like red, and he held it away from her face. "It's alright," he was saying, unsure if she could understand him under her headphones, "you'll remember your name sometime. We'll get water." He helped her stand. "We'll get some water."

They stumbled for awhile. A calm descended over Alan that he had never before experienced in the company of others. He did not know where to go at first, and had taken to following the mid-sized moon. They saw what looked like a group of chirping beavers with a purple hue, and these animals crowded them quickly, making Nala laugh and Alan tense. He perceived for a moment that she might be laughing at him, and he backed out of the scene to busy himself with climbing a tree in search of water. Alan found a firm branch and sat on it. His vision met an ocean and he remembered the flood. There was no freshwater he could see. He blinked. They could follow the beavers, he thought, they looked like they came from freshwater.

Alan looked down at the little red among purple. He was still for a long time, unblinking, until she looked up and met his gaze. I'll take her inland, he thought, to the safe center. They followed the beavers to a lake that Alan thought he recognized. He wanted to bathe but everything was too cold. The girl did not want water. Alan urged her to drink and would not leave until she sipped a little from his hands. Afterwards, they marched inland. Alan had tried to preserve a logical sense of their position in relation to the coast, but after some time both he and Nala felt as if they were responding to some rumble beneath their feet. It had become more instinctual than logical.

The way was steep. Alan took her hand. He learned her name. The further they moved, the heavier their breath became and their steps. And then Nala coughed. The sound was like a rack hitting Alan's shoulders, he looked at her, had felt the rising of a cough in himself and suppressed it, then said, "we're almost there." They stopped to rest and watch waves of black birds in the sky.

"They look like the ones at home," Nala said.

"Pennsylvania?"

She nodded. Alan picked a leaf out of her hair and held his senses open. The birds were going inland, too. The way Kris had spoken, it seemed Rusha always had people on the lookout. Alan coughed. He could pretend to be Nala's keeper, but not for long; Natasha's husband had surely reported the girl stolen.

Later, while walking, Nala tensed beside Alan and said, "don't look now, someone following." They coughed. Alan felt embarrassment before alarm; he was disappointed that he had not noticed the stalker first. They kept walking, his hand a little tighter on hers, his mind running through dialogue: we're walking, we can walk, she needs fresh air, Dad found her at auction. Go away. We're getting fresh air.

But it wasn't fresh air. Alan's abdomen ached from coughing. It all sounded as if they were in a vacuum. Nala noted the silence, saying maybe the animals had left because they couldn't breathe, and Alan said we should save our breath. He looked behind them. In their wake was a man, possibly older than Alan, with a flatness of affect enhanced by a vapor mask, its lobes glistening.

"Hey!" The voice behind them was filtered fuzzy from the mask, "hey pretty girl, you know where you're going?"

"Don't look at him," Alan uttered. Something hit the small of his back.

"Who's she, is she yours?"

Alan turned around. "She's mine. Got her at auction." The man's eyes made Alan shudder, so wide they were with wanting.

"You got any Kisslic on you?"

Alan shook his head. He turned away and kept walking. The man followed, ranting as he did so:

"You don't have Kisslic? You've got the girl, don't you? How old are you? Hey! Hey. Can't you share?"

Alan whispered to Nala. "I'm gonna get his mask. When I let your hand go, run."

The man kept talking: "I have an injection. Bring her over my house. What's her yield?"

Nala tore out of Alan's hand and ran. Alan threw himself at the man before he could go after her and bit into his neck. Blood filled Alan's mouth. The man was beating every inch of him he could reach, but Alan had his arms and legs around him, biting harder than he thought he could, consuming like a bear consumes, inverting his instinct of repulsion.

Alan heard something that he did not want to hear. He pulled elastic straps off the man's head and left him bleeding in the dirt to follow the sound of Nala's coughing. When Alan found her he put the mask over her mouth and nose and she held it fast. "Are you okay?"

"Yes." She passed him the mask. "Take a breath."

Alan sucked air with his eyes shut. It smelled like silicone. He passed it back to her. They were both shaking. "I'm sorry about him." He coughed. "I got him bad."

"You got the mask, it was worth it."

Alan nodded. "Almost there." He kept moving, marveling at the energy that Nala's trust provoked in him. They took turns with the mask, passing it off when the other person met a respiratory fit. And then, when it was night, Nala lifted her arms to take the mask off her face and Alan stopped her. "You keep it."

"You're coughing," she said.

Alan shook his head, holding the mask on her face.

"You'll suffocate."

"So would you," Alan said, wheezing. "Please keep it."

"I won't."

"Then I'll force you."

Nala's eyes glittered under moons' light. "Don't say that."

Alan coughed and got down on all fours. He swept leaves aside and swiped his finger
across dirt to form words:

I'M SORRY.

Alan sat back on his heels, his head bent over the apology, coughing with his mouth shut, coughs shaking his body like the leaves shivering in wind. Nala put the mask over Alan's head. He felt her fingers at the nape of his neck; she was taking off his jacket. He could not look at her.

Nala held the jacket over her face and breathed through it. She rubbed out Alan's words and wrote:

IT'S OK. TELL ME WHAT'S WRONG.

Alan squinted at the dirt. "I don't want to talk about it. I want to be alone."

WE ARE ALONE.

and then:

I LIKE THE WAY YOUR JACKET SMELLS.

Alan was glad that she couldn't see his face. "I killed him, though. I killed him."

Nala coughed. NO.

"I did. He begged me to stop. He used my name. I don't know how he knew it, but he did."

WHAT DID YOU DO?

"I bit him. He's bleeding in…in the trees." Alan took off the mask. His breath vaporized. He lay in the dirt, smudging WHAT DID YOU DO? Nala tried to put the jacket over his shivering arms and he gently returned it to her. She put it back on him, saying "you'll freeze, I'm wearing fur."

Alan put his arms through the jacket and then around her while they tried to sleep. One of the mask's filters fell off during its exchange. They could not re-affix it in the dark, so they were left to breathe through one side with Alan's palm sealing the other. They went through the night like this, take a breath now take a breath here take a breath, the skin on the back of Alan's hand cracking and bleeding and Nala uttering jokes and words of comfort. They missed the sun. I will stumble into the center, Alan thought, I will have to carry her, she will black out, I will walk without breathing until I collapse.

Roger did not recognize his brother. He saw someone stumbling up the hill with a quality of constant affliction that reminded him of Alan, but still he did not recognize him. Bambi sat at his canvas, behind Roger, not paying attention.

Roger looked at Bambi's face: bright-eyed, tense under his shock of blue hair. It was a visage that, for him, stirred reservoirs of childhood memories. "Someone's coming up the hill, bimbo."

Bambi didn't look away from his painting. "Are they wearing Larque?"

"Nope." Roger looked back out the window. "Oh, there, he's just passed out. I think it's a guy. Pretty sure it's a guy. Came a long way, I guess."

Bambi had joined him beside the window. "He must have heard about the flood. I'll go and get him."

Roger watched Bambi and his father, Quinn, crowd the prone figure outside. Roger sat back in his chair. He'd never felt so old in his life. Of course, he thought, chuckling, I'm older than I've ever been before. Being old is always new. But often troubling. And there was nothing he could do about it. Oh, what a warm heavy feeling called Nothing I Can Do, respite with my splintered arm, ah, me and the war about lobotomy. It was good, he thought, to be safe. Rusha's men had tried to kill him, yet here he was by love and mercy and circumstance. How fickle this or any world.

Quinn had seen the letters in the coffee grounds. He told Micah about the plans to lobotomize children, which pissed him right the fuck off, and now all the knowledge of Larque would die with him. Rusha was still convinced that Quinn was his protege, but he couldn't prove it. The Larque boys were dying without Micah's adjustments.

Any more children from Earth, as far as Roger knew, would die on Luna's shores.

Alan saw a blue-haired man with a dimpled face standing over him, holding up his own hands, speaking.

"How many?" Bambi said for the fifth time, "how many fingers am I holding up, man?"

Alan thought hard. He held up two fingers.

"Alright, cool." Bambi nodded. "Try to stay awake, alright? Alright? Keep that thing on your face. I'll be right back." He headed out of the room, saying "mother!"

Alan slumped back into cushions. He was awkwardly repose in a loveseat and could feel blood beating in his feet. The walls around him were cerulean blue and senselessly curved. A piano blocked a doorway, and on top of it was a glass cylinder filled with clear liquid, like a vase but too enormous to function as such. Alan felt as though he were in a dream or a movie: he perceived time but no sequence of path. He wanted to see the girl, and knew he had probably dropped her when he himself fell.

Bambi returned with a tiny glass jar. "Mom. Mom, he's got a vapor mask on, still."

Out of sight, a melodic voice answered, "make him take it off."

Bambi nodded at Alan. "Take that off."

Alan was puzzled. Hadn't he left the mask on Nala? He reached up; there it was. He removed it. "Is the girl okay?"

"What girl?" They stared at each other.

"The girl." Alan stood up and the mask fell off his lap. "Is she okay?"

"I think you'd better lay back down."

Alan grabbed Bambi's shoulders. "I was with a girl."

"I was with a girl, too, once. Things change."

"Are you listening? I gave her the mask, now I have it," Alan took a breath. "I carried her inland."

"Yeah, I know," Bambi said, and Alan knew a breath of relief. "You definitely came up the hill." He shrugged Alan's hands off and opened the jar. "Didn't see a girl, though."

"But..."

"Now look, you're in shock, so hold off until we've tested you. We have to take a sample. I'm gunna hold this jar on your mouth and I want you to say your name in it and try not to breathe so much."

Alan said Alan Cope and Bambi sealed the jar. He paced over to the giant cylinder and placed the jar on the surface of the liquid within. It floated there for a moment, then sank to the bottom. Bambi leaned over, watching the jar. His clothes were black, yellow and pocketless. He looked fit—Alan felt like he'd been in his presence before, even though he'd never seen him. "What's your name?"

"Me? I'm Bambi."

Then the jar floated slowly up, coming to rest in the middle of the cylinder. Bambi made a soft sound. "That's very rare." He looked at Alan. "You're very rare."

"What happened to my girl?"

"I didn't see any girl. You're probably imagining it."

"Imagining it!?" Alan racked his brains, wishing that he had not lost consciousness on the hill. "How long was I out?"

"Maybe ten minutes. You're not the first to come through here, you know. Lots of boys trying to get to the middle since the big breakout at Rusha's facility."

Alan shook his head. "What are you talking about?"

Bambi blinked at him. "Wow, I thought I was out of touch. But you knew to come here, didn't you?"

Alan kept shaking his head. "I was supposed to bring her here for safety. Otherwise I came all the way for nothing."

Bambi frowned. "What's her name?"

Alan rubbed his head. "Nala."

"And your name is?"

"I told you—," Alan froze mid-sentence.

Bambi nodded grimly and clapped Alan's shoulder. "Right...I'll make some tea." He left promptly through an arch in the wall. Alan heard him climb stairs.

The jar floated. Alan folded himself back into the loveseat; he felt as though an internal organ had vacated his body. His heart suffered whiplash. He had not been alone with the girl. He had been alone, period.

The floating jar was the closest thing to company, he sensed, and he did not even know what it was for. His plan of action was useless, foiled. His intentions felt as scattered and senseless as the room around him. He felt it was not even possible to have intentions, he was being pulled in an endless undertow of events outside his control. Alan pressed the right side of his face into a cushion, and then there was yet another whistling sound, the sound like a dog whining, only this time with an acoustical resonance that did not at all compliment the space of the room. He rubbed his eyes and looked around for a moment, hands cupped beneath his face. The sound steadily grew in volume. Just as Alan noticed the cylinder vibrating, it shattered and its contents sprayed everywhere.

Alan jumped up onto the loveseat. A woman appeared in the archway through which Bambi just left, and Alan recognized her as Bambi's mother by her melodic voice:

"Was that your jar?" Alan looked into her gently wrinkled face and nodded.

"You broke the water."

"I'm sorry."

"Don't be sorry, it's fine." The woman tread barefoot across the room, glass shards snapping underneath her. She offered Alan her hand. "Please come down." Alan put his hands against the wall behind him. The room had begun to smell wet and too familiar: pine trees, sweating shirt, summer popsicle, blood and sun.

"It's alright, my friend." The woman stopped in front of the love seat. "I'll get you another jar. Where are you from?"

"Outside," Alan said simply.

"The real world?"

"Sure." He scanned her: dark clothes, red trim, palms open, younger up close.

"Did you meet my son?" When Alan said nothing, she stooped and dipped a hand into the liquid. "It doesn't hurt, see?" She held out her hand at the level of Alan's stomach. He touched it and it was, indeed, just a wet hand.

The woman nodded, raising her eyebrows a little. "You're tense as glass. No give at all. Full of tiny fractures."

Alan pulled his hand back. "What's the jar for?"

"Holding vibrations. Holding human patterns." The woman cocked her head. "I can show you my jar."

"What about your name?"

"My name is Lady." Her voice was very soft, now. "And you're right."

"Right about what?"

"You are alone."

Alan swallowed. He followed her into a room of shelved jars. The room was fitted with black-lights. He could see a network of glowing paint lines on the ground and his shoelaces standing out in sharp relief, as if they were moving of their own accord.

"This is my library," Lady said, "I've filled most of these. Those are thoughts," she pointed to a row of square jars, then triangular ones. "These are all dreams...memories," she added, pointing to a third collection, "hopes, names, emotions...."

"Whose emotions?"

"Mostly yours. Let's see...you need a nice round one...."

Alan edged closer to a series of humming vials. "These look like they're about to crack."

"Away from those!" Lady grabbed his neckline and tugged him sideways. "It's dangerous, darling, follow the boundaries."

Alan looked back at the lines on the floor, but they made about as much sense to him as a topographic map for a foreign planet. "I didn't touch them."

"Would you want a stranger so close to you?"

Alan rubbed his neck and didn't answer. Lady sighed with her stomach, her whole being seemed to tremble with it. "Forgive me, I know better." She moved to stand beside him. "Now, why do you suppose those jars are about to crack?"

"They're humming," Alan said.

Lady smiled. "That's good, you're listening."

"I think I understand."

Lady squinted. "Can you share?"

"Um…" Alan adjusted his sleeve. He couldn't recall the last time he had explained something to another person. "So you say something into a jar, and you can play it back later? Like, um. Like a stereo recorder?"

"I forgot how those work," Lady said, "but yes."

"Could I ask you something, then?" Lady nodded and Alan twisted his mouth in the silence, trying not to think of Nala. "Why did your son just ask for my name? What's the use in that?"

Lady started nodding again. "The jars are self-reflective, they know what they contain. So when you give me your name, you are giving me everything you understand about yourself."

"What's self-reflexive?"

Lady led him to a stool. "Sit down, little rock."

Alan obeyed, watching her carefully. She leaned over a barrel of jars and searched through it. "Now, you're very sensitive, tight like a drum surface. So I will word this carefully—it would be best if I didn't at all, but it seems I have to, with the approaching flood. We'll go in small steps. One question at a time. What do you know about stories?"

Alan clutched his stomach. He had a feeling like she was about to violate a contract for which he had no proof or understanding.

"When you hear a story, do you feel like you're in it?" she continued.

"I have to go." Alan stood. He felt disarmed and frustrated, as though he had been spied in the shower after forgetting to lock the door.

Lady frowned. "Go where?"

"I'mnotwellrightnow," Alan walked backwards, then turned on his heel. "I'll see myself out, thank you."

"Hold it." Lady followed him out of the library, heard him step in water and saw him panting near the piano. He was looking around the room like a bird on alert.

Alan rounded on her. "There was a doorway here!"

"It'll be back."

"Be back?" Alan threw up his arms. "Where did it go? And how did this pole get here?"

Lady tapped her lips. "That *is* puzzling. It's usually in Bambi's room. You can try climbing it, if you like. You might get out that way. But it's generally used for going *down*, if you know what I mean."

The pole did indeed extend into a large hole in the ceiling, which presumably opened to the floor above. Alan looked back at the woman. He huffed. "I was upset."

"Clearly."

"I can't remember what about."

She came up beside him, one hand on his arm and the other on his back; his throat burned. "Why do you look so sad?"

"Nothing makes sense. None of this makes sense. Nothing will ever make sense again." He paused, felt like the floor was falling out from under him. "I don't want to go back to Earth, but if I have to...is there any way for me to get home without...without losing my memory of everything here?"

She made an equivocating gesture. "I'll go and get one of my jars, and let you listen to it. That might help."

Lady retreated into the recesses of her library while Alan waited on a stool, his head bowed. She came back slowly, cradling a jar in both hands like it was a fragile nest. "This is me telling about the day after my son was born. Please be careful."

Alan considered asking what exactly he should do with it, but he could already feel long slow waves as he reached for the jar. It felt embarrassing; as if he had touched the woman herself in some intimate way. The jar shuddered, sending a vibration through him. He passed it from one hand to another and the shame transformed into an overwhelming affection for the jar, for the woman, for everything, affection so hard it sent pangs through his midsection, and a fear that he could taste.

He leaned over the jar, wanting to lift the thing to his face but knowing it was too heavy and fragile for that, he thought he heard a baby crying, he wanted to stop the vibrating, it was too much and too precarious for this bundle so precious.

"Take it," Alan breathed through gritted teeth, "take it back."

Lady relieved him of the jar. Alan rubbed his back. "That was heavy."

"A surprisingly apt description. I barely remember it at all."

Lady disappeared for a moment behind shelves. Alan swallowed, staring at his glowing laces and the guidelines on the floor. He could only imagine that his own mother hated him with as much fervor as Lady loved Bambi, who was now coming up behind him.

"Funny thought," Bambi said with his lilt of a voice. "I don't mean to interrupt, but I have some questions, Alan. And you need some tea. Mom?"

Lady reemerged. "Darling, don't come without knocking."

"I have tea. Can't you both come out and sit for a minute? It's so dark in here."

"Bambi..."

"He just got here, mom. Come on," He beckoned to Alan.

"Wait!" Lady leaned forward with an open jar. "Your name, little rock."

"Alan Cope."

Lady grinned and slammed the jar closed. "Thank you."

They followed Bambi to a rose-smelling room with a narrow white table. Alan sat in front of a brass teapot. While Bambi poured in cups Alan stared at a bowl of glistening rocks that he wanted to touch. "What are those?"

"Oysters. My dad brought them in from Micah's estate."

"Micah's estate?"

"Yeah, that's what I wanted to ask you about." Bambi pushed a cup towards Alan, who could feel the woman watching them. Bambi looked at his mother. "I was going to ask someone else, but you-know-who is so sensitive these days."

Alan swallowed. "What's your question?"

"My dad knew an Alan Cope." Bambi sat. "But he was younger than you, and he was from Earth—,"

"I'm from Earth," Alan interrupted.

Bambi dipped his head. "Do you know Roger?"

"He's my brother."

Bambi laughed. "Stay right there." He left the room. Alan heard Lady's voice behind him.

"Have an oyster, Alan."

"That's alright."

"Please." She pushed the bowl across the table.

Alan picked one up, stared at it for a moment, then cracked the thing against his palm. Water ran down his wrists. He rubbed his thumb over the shell's pearly underside.

"Are you angry at your brother?"

Alan shrugged. "I don't know."

"Do you want to see him again?"

Alan put his mouth over the shattered shell and sucked its fruit out. He chewed pensively. "Miss Lady, how did you know I am alone?"

"Because you have no one to rely on." She scratched her head. "I suspect that Bambi is upstairs planning to surprise you. Are you alright with that?"

"What kind of surprise?"

"Your brother is here."

"What do you mean?"

"He's in this house." Alan could feel a tension creeping over him. Lady stood. "I want to go and examine your jar. Help yourself to more oysters." She left the room.

Alan was turning a shell around in his hands when he felt a gentle breeze on his right. Two off-white curtains glowed from behind, swelling and contracting before an open door. Alan stepped between them and found himself standing on an outdoor balcony. Wind philandered his hair. He could only see mist and a handful of treetops peeking out of it. He examined his wet palms. They had hardened somewhat from his time in the forest, from grabbing rocks and trees for support.

Roger was here somehow, somehow, and he would appear at any moment, any moment. Tall and loud and unpredictable, but familiarly so. And with the memory of his older brother came the threat of crippling dependency, dependence tender, like an internal pressure shift, Alan could feel it in his neck and joints. He heard his name behind him and turned to face his brother.

Roger's shoulders visibly softened. "I didn't recognize you."

Alan walked past him into the room. "You broke your arm."

"It was broken, yeah. Rusha's men got me. They got me pretty good. They had real-world questions." Roger watched his brother, taller than before, long-legged, pouring a hot drink. "Yup. I was *interrogated.*"

"You want some tea?"

Roger reapplied his weight against the table. "They wanted to know more about lobotomies. Probably to stop us from aging or something....You're not wearing any magnets."

Alan cradled his cup of tea. "I trained my way out of it." He leaned against the table and propped one foot on a nearby chair.

"Trained out of it, huh?" Roger's smile was fading. "Can you show me how that's done?"

Alan sipped his tea. Roger came up beside him to pour his own cup. He nudged Alan with a splinted arm. "Would you look at me?"

Alan put his cup down and faced the man. He felt uncomfortably devoid of emotion.

Roger shook his head. "Well?"

"Well, what?"

"Well, I missed you."

Alan merely blinked, wishing he could say the same. He could feel a frown deepening in his face.

Roger mirrored the expression. "Aren't you curious to know how I got here?"

"Not especially. I suspect it has something to do with vodka."

Roger laughed. "What?"

"Yup." Alan nodded, squinting. "Definitely lemon vodka, I remember that much." He uncovered a plate beside the tea to reveal little cakes. He stuffed one whole into his mouth.

Roger stared at him. "Are you being serious right now?"

"You swore you wouldn't drink and then you did." Alan licked frosting off his thumb. "You broke an oath."

"I'm sorry, kid, but you don't know what you're saying. You can't make judgements about things that you don't understand."

"You're right, I don't understand it." Alan took another sip of his tea. "Putting us in danger and breaking a promise for temporary gratification? Can't say I understand that."

"Where do you get off using a word like that, *gratification,*" Roger scoffed. "That's being a grown-up, kid, you just haven't learned it yet. You want everything to be fair, but it isn't. People break promises, they hurt others to get what they want, and you will, too."

"I won't."

"There's no way around it, Alan. Nothing in life is a fair exchange, you're just spoiled."

Alan forced another cake into his mouth; his anger made it taste like ash. Roger was still trying to make eye contact with him. "I was under a lot of pressure. I was scared someone would find us, Alan, they would have taken you away and committed you."

"Committed me. Put me away. Lock out the world. Keep me inside."

"Yes! I was all nerves, Alan. It was uncomfortable —,"

"Yes! Life is uncomfortable!" Alan stood out of his chair and faced Roger again. "Be scared, be under pressure! Be uncomfortable! That's *being a grown-up*!" He quit the room, rubbing his hand over his ear and neck. He found a door to the outside and took it. The breeze cooled his eyelids. There was work to be done, he knew, questions to be asked and answered, about Nala, about lobotomies, about why he was anticipating a flood and whether it would ever come. But now, he didn't want to be bothered.

Alan settled himself against a smooth rock and internally begged his heart to steady itself against the oncoming storm. He had a hunch that he would be returning to Earth soon, that it was out of his control, but he did not want to return to Earth. On Earth he felt like a used bottle on concrete. Alan watched a squirrel search the ground. There was a time, he realized, for activity, and a time for rest. The plants beneath him were soft and it wasn't long before he fell asleep.

Bambi removed a needle from between his teeth. "Don't touch it, Roger."

"But it itches."

"And you'll pop another stitch if you don't listen to me."

Roger lowered a hand from his neck. "Can I sleep on it?"

"I wouldn't." Bambi packed bandages into a shiny red box.

"Alan is napping on the carrots," Roger said. "I'll go and wake him."

"Don't."

"He'll ruin the carrots."

"No, he won't. He needs time to rest and think."

Roger snorted. "He's always wanting to rest and think. He thinks too much."

"Still," Bambi stowed the first aid kit on a shelf near his unfinished painting. "It's his first time in the center of Luna. You remember how bizarre it was for you when we met. And anyway, Alan is different from you."

Roger watched his friend walk away from him. "Bambi, everything's fine, isn't it? With Alan. You think...you don't think there's anything really wicked going on?"

Bambi paused in the doorway. "I can't say. Mother is trying to sort it out."

"But when you find out, if you find out, you'll tell me, won't you?"

Bambi looked back over his shoulder. "It's hard for me to understand the future like that."

"Okay. Okay. But you've got to tell me, Bambi, if something is happening. Or help Alan tell me. I'm all he's got."

"I'll do my best, Roger."

"Really, though." Roger stood. "We're alone in the city right now. No one knows where we are—,"

"Stop it." Bambi rounded on him. "That's for Alan to figure out, that's what the jars are for."

"But—,"

"It's got to come from him."

"But what if he doesn't know?"

"Your brother is different from you." Bambi's posture softened. "I know you're worried about him, or you wouldn't be here. But you are here, both of you, for rest."

Roger sat. "He keeps talking about a flood."

Bambi laughed. "Don't worry about the flood."

Alan gasped awake; it was raining. He rubbed his eyes, sitting up on what was quickly turning to mud beneath him. He stumbled to his feet, shielding his eyes with an arm.

Quinn was running towards him and shouting something. He pointed at the ground. Bambi appeared at Alan's side and a little while later the three of them walked inside with armfuls of glistening carrots, turnips and potatoes. It was good, Bambi had explained, to harvest in the rain.

Cold water trickled down the backs of Alan's arms; he had taken off his jacket in the storm and it rested, dripping, on his shoulder. He soon found himself alone in the kitchen with Lady, skinning the freshly plucked veggies. She said she wanted him to come back to the library.

"The library with the jars?"

"Yes. Yours is especially heavy, I can't make it out. It broke my scale."

"I'm sorry. I feel really awful about it."

"About what?"

"I don't know, everything. Like premonition. Roger would get real upset, you know, to hear me talking about Luna. Like I was sick or something."

"Perhaps you'll know what you feel awful about after the flood comes."

"Maybe I will." Alan washed beets in a strainer. It seemed a given, for Lady to know what he was thinking, though he could not account for why. The whys seemed to matter less and less as time went on. He tasted the sour of worry. "I'm going to find out something awful, aren't I?"

Lady didn't answer him right away. "We can talk after dinner."

Roger and Bambi exchanged stories about their childhood exploits, which somehow Alan could hear but not quite make out, and while his older brother was absorbed in this dialogue, Alan noticed that Bambi was giving him nervous glances.

Midway through his meal, Alan felt a hand landing on his knee. He looked down and saw nothing. Roger was looking at him; they all were. Then a cramp suddenly seized Alan's midriff and he doubled over.

Thunder and lightening came at once. Alan felt another wave of tension ripple over his stomach and he backed out of his chair. Roger gave him an empathic look.

"It's alright, kid, it's no big deal. Do you want to lay down?"

"No." It was Bambi. "This is my job, let me handle this."

Lady stood up. "Bambi, no."

"What?" Alan snapped, frantic.

But Lady was looking at Bambi. "You're not ready."

"I am so."

Alan gripped the back of the chair and gasped. He was in so much pain he could barely speak; it seemed like a rod was crushing his spine; like tiny, unbreakable threads were winding tightly around his ribs.

Bambi was suddenly in front of him, with the lip of an empty jar under the rim of Alan's mouth.

"Help me," Alan said, and as he did, blood spilled from his lips into the jar—then, in a fluid movement, before his mother could stop him, Bambi drank it.

Quinn, who was still at the table, made a horrible, broken sound and covered his mouth. Lady held her son while he slowly sank to the floor. Alan's pain ebbed away and he closed his eyes, relieved. He heard Bambi:

"Oh—*Ow.* Mama..."

Roger's voice: "No big deal, Bambi, just wait. It's okay. Doesn't last long, usually." His voice was getting quieter. Alan opened his eyes and would remember forever what he saw:

Bambi took short, shallow breaths while his mother held him, his neck corded and tight, his face red with agony. Roger kneeled beside him and held his hand, whispering assurances; as he did, there was light—it was *light*—issuing from Roger's mouth.

Then came the sound of flickering, and from the same source. It sounded to Alan like a film reel. He crouched next to his brother, turned his face towards himself, and peered between his open lips...

...to see Alan lying on his side, face swollen. Awake but not moving. He dabs an ice-filled grocery bag on Alan's cheek. Why won't you tell me what happened? Say something. Say anything. He'll kill us. I feel like he's going to kill us. Speak. Speak—

"Did you give him drugs at the party?" Roger's voice.

"What?" A stranger's voice.

"I said—I'm—what did you make him do at the party?"

Suddenly, Alan was yanked backwards by Quinn and landed flat on his back.

"Don't look out there."

Alan sat up. "That's my real life!"

Quinn shook his head. "That is no life. You don't want to be there."

"But that's my life."

Quinn lifted him roughly and held him close. "It's no kind of life."

"It's *mine.*" Alan wrenched himself free.

"There are villains and victims, Alan. You are a victim. Accept your lot and let us swallow the worst of it."

Bambi suddenly gasped and took an enormous breath. Quinn took off his shirt and tucked it around his son.

"It's my life," Alan said softly to himself. No one seemed to hear him. Quinn took the bloody jar from Bambi, corked it, and walked briskly away. Alan followed.

"Gimme that jar, Quinn. It's mine."

"It's done."

Alan sped up—so did Quinn—the hall twisted and dipped. They broke into a run and heard Roger behind them:

"Give it to him! Let him have it, Quinn!"

Realizing then that he was near the library of jars, and therefore near every memory of his existence, Alan pivoted sharply with both men still following.

He burst through a door to the library, its floors aglow. Quinn landed on Alan, and Roger on Quinn. Alan clawed at the arm around his neck.

"I can't breathe!"

"It's his life, Quinn!"

The arm loosened—Alan stood—and Quinn punched Roger in the face.

They all went quiet, panting with exertion. Quinn flattened Roger against the floor. "Did you like your life?"

Roger said nothing. Alan watched; he felt like he was standing at the edge of a pooler deeper than he could survive.

"Did you like your life, Thumper?"

"I wanna live—"

WHAM—Quinn hit him again. "Did you like your life, huh? Did you like having sex with truckers in Washington?" WHAM. "Denver!" WHAM. "Missouri!"

"NO! No."

"Did you like your life?"

"No, sir."

"Tell him!"

Quinn turned Roger's face with his boot. Alan stared at him. "Tell him." When Roger said nothing, Quinn held his hand towards Alan.

"Come on, now, son. We'll spare you the worst of life. This whole world is yours. Get away from those jars. Trust me. Trust your brother—look at him. This is not someone who liked his life." Alan stood still. "Roger. Tell him."

But Roger's eyes were fixed somewhere on the floor. Alan looked: and there, just a step away, was the jar with Alan's name in it.

"Anything you want, Alan. Stay here. And have anything you want."

Alan took a deep breath and stepped closer to Quinn. "I want your boots."

Quinn bent to take them off. Alan put them on slowly. They were warm. He savored the wax laces in his fingers, the handsome shades of black and brown, the skin-like feeling of wear in every place broken by Quinn's many years of work. He savored his last pain-free moment.

Then he stomped on the jar—it cracked—and the walls, the ceiling, the floor, caved in—crushed by the weight of water.

"The Most Merciful taught the Qur'an, created man,
and taught him speech."
—*Qur'an, 55:1-55:4*

V

Alan's Flood

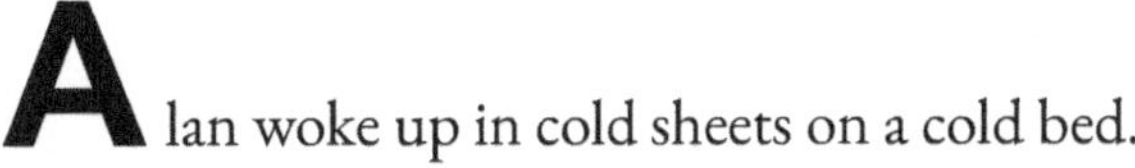lan woke up in cold sheets on a cold bed.

He was back on Earth. Where on Earth, he did not know. And he felt as though he were being watched, although he heard no one else in the room. He slowly sat up and then froze.

He was staring into a glistening lens.

The camera in front of Alan looked hideously familiar. He shut his eyes, feeling a tugging within himself, urging him to action.

Get up.

Alan resisted the temptation to fold himself back into sleep. The flood had happened. He couldn't go back. He stood and walked past the camera to a shielded window. Alan quietly peeked between the blinds.

Fourth floor apartment, he thought. He turned around to take better stock of the room, and although it was spatially familiar (he knew, for instance, that the door on his right led into a cramped bathroom, and that the one in front of him led out of the apartment), he still didn't recognize it.

There was a large bed, and a nightstand littered with tissues and syringes.

And a doorway blocked by a wardrobe.

Alan peered past it into the space beyond. He saw a kitchenette, a tv, a stained couch and a desk with a laptop on it.

He fought the urge to cough. The whole place smelled terrible and difficult to catalogue. Under the stench of cigarettes and sweat there was something of his brother. And something else; someone else. Certainly a man.

Just as surely as Alan knew where the bathroom was, he knew that he had to be very quiet. He sat on the bed, still as a rabbit on alert, waiting. He wanted to encounter Roger before anyone else, but the first man to enter the apartment was not Roger.

His hair was long, tied back and streaked with grease or dirt or dye. His eyes were worse than unkind; they seemed too shallow for even the capacity for kindness. His clothes were old and unfitting. The man walked past Alan as though there was no one in the room and stood for a moment behind the camera. He took the camera off its three legged stand and tossed it on the bed, where it landed by Alan's knee. Then he crossed over to the bathroom, unbuckling his pants as he went.

Alan glanced at the camera. And then, as if by muscle memory, he reached for it and opened a tiny panel in the side. Alan picked out a slip of plastic and hid it in the pillowcase behind him. The man came out of the bathroom sniffing and took up the camera with an unwashed hand. "Your brother's a sucker," he said. Alan watched him edge past the wardrobe into the other half of the apartment.

Alan opened his mouth to call the man back; he wanted to know where Roger was. But whether from fear or caution, he found it impossible to speak. Then something caught the corner of his vision: It was the back cover of a notebook with several words printed in what was clearly Roger's handwriting. Alan picked it up off the floor.

YES

NO

MAYBE

OKAY

TIRED

AFRAID

JUICE

Alan flipped the notebook over.

COLD

HOT

MEDICINE

SOUP

MORE

It was filled with such lists. Alan perused them, looking for some kind of order that would break the words into categories by time or intent, but he could find none. Intermittently he encountered folded pages that, when opened, revealed his own handwriting; and accounts of interactions he had in Luna.

Alan softly closed the notebook. The pages had been sticky and he was in the bathroom to wash his hands when he heard strange sounds coming from the other side of the apartment. It was something thudding, and someone choking. Then the bathroom door opened and the man seized Alan's forearm. Alan instantly dropped, making himself heavy as he was dragged back into the bedroom.

"Stop it," the man said when Alan started pulling away from him. "What do you think will happen to your brother," he continued, grabbing Alan's other arm, "if you don't give me what I want?"

I don't even know who you are, Alan wanted to shout, and he didn't; but he knew the danger he was in, and the familiarity of the sounds behind the wardrobe did more to serve his fear than his fortitude. He faltered at the mention of his brother and the man heaved Alan onto the bed.

Alan tried to kick him and then realized that his hand was on a snow drift.

He was lost among snow like strokes of white gesso, he could identify only space, and fur around his shoulders....

Stop it, Alan thought, *it's not snow, it's sheets, damn it, wake up and fight him off!*

Something hit the floor. Alan's muscles burned from exhaustion. His blood sounded like a train hurtling between his ears. He thought of nothing but getting as far away from this man as he could. Alan reached for a syringe and lost his wrist to the man's grip.

"*No!*" Alan writhed like a fish and the man suddenly leapt off him as if he were something poisonous. Alan rolled off the bed and hurled himself at the door just as keys were turning in its lock. The man slipped behind the wardrobe. The choking sound stopped.

Roger was on the other side of the door, which opened to an outdoor balcony made of iron. Alan sobbed with relief.

"You're back."

Roger looked incredulous. "What?"

"You're back, you're here."

"No, *you're* here," Roger said, pulling his brother into a crushing embrace. "Say something else."

"Say what?"

"Oh my God!" Alan felt Roger's voice vibrating though them: "He's talking, Jay, he's talking!"

"Not for long," The man said from behind the wardrobe. Roger didn't reply. His tears soaked Alan's shoulder. Jay went on: "You're home early."

"Yeah." Roger drew back, giving Alan's arms a final squeeze before opening a drawer in the syringe covered nightstand. "I finished putting in the fountain."

"Did she tip you good?"

Roger let out a half-hearted laugh. "Sure, I gave her the royal treatment." Alan heard him utter "poor woman." He hadn't the slightest clue what they were talking about, and he didn't care. He grabbed the back of Roger's coat.

"Be right there," Roger kneeled in front of the table, unravelling a wrinkled ziplock bag. Alan watched his brother's fingers, long and sensitive and in love with Leena. He heard the threat against them echo in his head. *What do you think will happen to your brother if you don't give me what I want?*

Alan glanced uncertainly at the door and tugged Roger's coat again. "I know," Roger kept saying, "I know, Alan, sit down, just for one second, okay? Please." He raised his voice. "Jay, I need more."

"You owe me for rent."

Roger didn't answer. Some ritual was occurring with the artifacts on the table that Alan neither understood or liked. Roger sat on the bed and wrapped a belt around his arm.

Alan's mouth was so dry it hushed his voice frantic. "Roger. Roger, come on. Come on, we gotta go. What're you—nono, don't do that!"

Roger moaned and a syringe slipped out of his hand. His pupils glided open.

"No no no, don't fall asleep." Alan stood up and tried to pull Roger off the bed, but he was as good as gone.

Alan stared, shivering and wishing with all his might that he could turn back time by a few moments and knock the syringe from Roger's hand. He wished he could go back to Luna, too, but now he hardly knew whether he had even been there in the first place....

He retreated to the bathroom and threw off his shirt. Alan had a merciless uncertainty about what Jay wanted from him, and he prayed that the altercation that had just transpired was an isolated incident. And then, of course, he had to ponder how long this man had known him to begin with; both he and Roger had acted as if there had been no rupture in their status quo, except for the suggestion that he, Alan, had just spoken for the first time in a while.

The shower was warm but not hot. Alan was uncomfortably close to the conclusion that Luna was not real, or at least not real enough to take him physically from

Earth. Yet his excursions there had been entirely involuntary.

He had been gone in mind but present in body.

Alan picked up a bar of soap and dropped it when he felt the hair clinging to its slimy underside. He looked past the shower curtain, half expecting Jay to kick the door open. Alan squeezed water out of his eyes, yearning to feel but needing to think. They were no longer on the farm, nor did it seem like they were anywhere near the suburbs in Cortland. Roger had gotten a job; he was, Alan recalled, wearing some kind of work uniform when he came in. This meant he was likely still disconnected from Arden, who, Alan thought bitterly, would never have let this happen.

His hair was longer than he remembered. He shut off the spout, and, glancing uncertainly at a stringy towel draped over the sink, started to swipe water out of his hair. And then, for the second time since waking, he heard someone choking. Alan struggled back into his clothes, cursing as they stuck to his skin. He searched around the sink for something he could use as a weapon, he found nothing, he stood behind the door with his fists raised.

And nothing happened. The choking, Alan realized, sounded more present than before, and somehow wet. He peered out of the bathroom. Bile sprayed out of Roger's mouth: he was suffocating. Alan rushed forward and shook him. "Wake up! Get up!"

"Surprised he hasn't died already," Jay said.

Alan turned to the wardrobe. The voice went on: "Turn him on his side."

Alan obeyed, thumping Roger hard on the back. Vomit sprayed over the sheets. Jay started to speak again.

"Leave me alone!" Alan spat. There was a nick in the floor beneath his foot and he felt suddenly that it was yawning larger and larger, it was a canyon that he could fall into or was perhaps flying above.

"Come here," Jay said.

Numbness took Alan's extremities. He approached the wardrobe and edged past it with glassy eyes, as if he were watching a film without a plot. Someone snapped at his face. Jay sat at the desk with his legs up on it. He looked at Alan the way he might have looked at a bean bag. "I don't like you to talk."

"I don't like *you*," Alan retorted. They stared at each other until a bird hit the window, THONK. "What happened to Roger?"

Jay shook his head. "You really have a shitty memory."

Alan's eyes watered. He refused to blink. "I've gathered that much," he said, "and I know when my brother's being someone's bitch."

The man had a dry chuckle. "You're everyone's bitch, Alan, he could take lessons from you."

Alan flinched. Jay took his legs off the desk and opened a drawer with a box in it. He lifted the lid and held up a tiny sachet. "Do you even know what this is?"

Alan felt his tongue twitch, but he did not answer.

"This is what your brother shoots up, Alan. Do you know what's in it?"

"Stop using my name," Alan muttered.

"What?"

Alan shook his head. "Nothing. I don't know."

Jay closed the box. "Well, Roger doesn't either. But I know. I know what's in it, and I can change it if I want." Jay's legs were back up on the desk. "Don't give me any trouble, and don't give my friends any trouble and keep your mouth shut unless I say otherwise."

As Jay spoke, Alan could feel an echo of the threats somewhere in his memory, stirring at the presence of this confrontation. He knew the man was at least as serious this time as he had ever been, if not more so. "I won't give you trouble."

Alan had not known such fear since the day he was kidnapped. The sight of Roger on the bed reminded him wretchedly of the plush tiger in Pennsylvania. Alan wanted to be there the moment his brother woke up, but Jay kept him in his side of the apartment to prepare dinner. In his numbness Alan witnessed a peculiar personhood in the food; he couldn't help wondering how it was that a zucchini could yield so under his knife. Roger shuffled in just as Alan was quietly spitting on a plate, which he then set in front of Jay.

"Smells amazing." Roger rubbed his face. "Innit he the best, Jay? You're the best, kid."

Alan wordlessly handed him a plate of steaming casserole. Roger looked over Jay's shoulder. "You still have my camera?"

"Yeah. I'll take my footage off tonight."

Roger tidied Alan's hair. "You feel like talking anymore?"

Alan glanced at Jay, who said, "he's been pretty quiet."

"S'alright," Roger said, but Alan could sense his disappointment. He poured a glass of juice for Alan, who nearly wept at the gesture and wanted nothing more than to grab his older brother and run to the nearest safe house. But Roger seemed perfectly happy; Jay asked him about work and Alan gathered that Roger had gone into landscaping, that he had a long commute, and that he had made some woman very happy that day.

Alan's tongue twitched, and he swallowed his words like so many hot orbs. After dinner he sat on the bed and Roger put a tiny screen in front of him.

"You just keep watching these videos," Roger said, "and you'll get it, Alan, it'll click." He snapped with this last comment and Alan watched the little screen. Someone was explaining how you could say a word with your hands, like *woman* or *house* or *shoe.* He took some pills that Roger offered to him and soon fell asleep.

Later, in the dark, Jay landed on him and smacked him awake. "Where's the card?"

"What?" Alan gasped.

"The memory card!" Jay shook him. "You took it, didn't you?"

Alan shook his head. "No, no I didn't." Jay hurled him from the bed. Alan landed hard and slowly sat up, rubbing his shoulder. Jay threw on the lights. "Help me look! Useless bitch."

Roger snored away, sleeping more soundly than Alan had ever seen. Alan went around to the side table and vaguely searched a drawer. He opened his mouth to ask what the card looked like and then froze.

Was it possible that Jay was referring to the chip that Alan had pulled out of the camera? Almost as soon as this thought entered Alan's head, another, much stronger voice took its place:

Don't give him the card. Keep it hidden.

Alan nodded to himself. He had trusted the impulse to take the card, and now he would obey the instinct to hide it. Suddenly Roger sat up with his eyes still closed, pointing out at the room.

"Shut up," he said. Jay and Alan stared at him. "Shut up. Work tomorrow." He promptly fell back into the pillows. Jay grabbed the back of Alan's neck and pushed him into the bathroom.

"You take the card?"

"No."

Jay's hand started up Alan's shirt and Alan shoved it aside. Jay sucked at his teeth for a moment. "Baxter's coming in the morning," he said, eyebrows flicking as though he expected some sort of reaction.

"I don't know what that means," Alan said, "and I didn't take your damn card."

"Fine, don't tell me," Jay said. "You can forget about Vicodin tomorrow, just suffer through it." He left the bathroom and Alan followed suit, shutting the lights off and lying awake in bed. When all was quiet, he plunged an arm into his pillowcase, felt around, and came up empty. He must have put the card in Roger's pillow. Alan watched his brother sleep and tried to remember what Vicodin was.

After Roger left in the morning, Jay showed Alan another screen, this one with an aerial view of a house on it. "You recognize that?" Jay asked.

Alan squinted at it, sitting on his hands on the bed. He was looking at a picture of Arden's house. He shook his head.

"Like hell you don't." Jay put the screen in his back pocket. "I'll bet your cousin wouldn't give me more trouble than she's worth."

Alan swallowed hot orbs. How much did this man know about him?

"Where's the card?"

"I dunno."

"Let me tell you something, you little shit. I get hunches. I know when someone's being a liar." They stared at each other. "What'd you do with it, huh? Give it to your brother? Toss it out the window? You think someone's gunna catch me, is that it?"

"You're a villain."

Jay slapped him across the face. "Tell me where it is."

"I don't have it."

"You're a liar, Alan."

Alan sat very still. The pillow next to him seemed to throb. Jay jerked his head at a corner. "Go stand over there."

Alan obeyed, looking for a nick, a scratch, any abnormality in the wall that he could dive into. He was very scared. He did not want to be there and his imagination was failing him. Perhaps imagination really was just a faculty, an ability rather than a place or a state of being. His mouth went dry.

Baxter, whoever he was, did not show up. Jay cursed over the phone about it. He put the camera on three legs and pulled Alan out of the corner.

"Don't make a sound and don't touch me," Jay said, and then he hit him repeatedly.

It was very painful and pain is very easy, Alan thought, you just have to breathe into it. So he focused very hard on breathing. He tried not to look at the man's face even though Jay was wearing a mask, and it's all okay, Alan thought, as long as he doesn't know where the little card is and anyway it'll be over soon.

Jay was saying harsh things to him all this time, he kept asking if Alan was going to cry but Alan wouldn't. Then Jay grabbed his neck and Alan's hand was halfway up before he remembered he wasn't supposed to touch Jay, and his hand stayed there, suspended between instinct and instinct. Two things flashed through Alan's mind at once: the sound of the word "trachea" and the crumbling of an eggshell. He fainted. Jay let the boy drop. He kicked him in the ribs.

Perhaps pain was not so very easy. It was dull in some obvious places and sharper in those more hidden. Alan rubbed cigarette ashes off his face and sneezed. He was on the couch and wearing an unfamiliar sweater. Jay sat in front of him.

"Guess what I found?" He held a little square card with two fingers. Alan swallowed and tried to sit up. Jay slipped the thing into his pocket. "Why'd you take it, Alan?"

Alan shook his head. "I didn't take it."

"Bullshit."

"I dunno, I'm sorry, Jay, I don't know why I took it." It felt like tiny bones were in Alan's tongue, so hard was it to speak and to be clear. "I don't know what it's for, I'm very sorry."

"Where is it?"

"You just said—,"

"That was a different one!" Jay stood over the boy. "I knew you took it. Get up and show me where it is."

Alan nodded as he struggled out of the couch. Shocks of pain flew up his back like darting fish. He frowned. His pants were missing, but he knew better than to ask about it. Alan stood up straight to get past the dresser, then hobbled to the bed with his hands pressed into his side. He reached into one pillowcase, then the other. His breath shallowed. "It's gone." Alan pulled the pillows out of their slips. "I put it in one of these."

"Which one?"

"They look the...same to me."

Jay ripped the sheets off the bed. Alan darted backwards.

"Munna kill you, Alan," Jay seethed, "you and your fucking—fuck!" His words collapsed into growling incoherence. He paced in a circle and then pointed at Alan. "I'm killing your brother."

Alan held the man's gaze and nodded, trying to absorb the man's anger with compliance.

"He's dead, Alan."

"Okay."

"You pull another stunt like that…"

"Yes."

"…I will bring your cousin here myself to replace you."

Alan nodded again, desperate to appease him.

"You're dead. You are dead. Don't move."

Alan shook his head with his eyes shut. "I won't move, Jay."

The man had already crossed over to his side of the apartment. Alan saw his pants in a far corner of the room, and his shoes in another corner, closer to him. He heard Jay on the phone:

"I think you should get here quick, Roger, that's all I'm saying. He's really doing it again."

He drifted back into the room and handed Alan two pills. Alan swallowed them numbly, straining to understand Roger's words on the other end of the phone.

"I tried," Jay was saying as he watched Alan swallow the medicine. "He's locked himself in the bathroom. He's really thinking of doing it."

After a moment of staring, Alan opened his mouth to prove he'd swallowed the pills, and Jay retreated again, still on the phone.

Then Alan was assaulted by a life-saving vision of himself on the floor. Dead. Bleeding from the mouth.

Alan picked up his shoes. He opened the apartment door. He stepped out of it.

The iron steps were cold. Alan took them at a steady pace. He walked barefoot on concrete, on a shard of something, on a bottle cap that stuck to his sole and he kept walking....Away and away until he was out of sight of the apartment.

Then he ducked down to put on his shoes and started running.

Alan ran for longer than he thought he could. He stopped in an alleyway to pull off the sweater and tie it around his waist. Cars and buildings had shimmering edges, presumably from the heat, but Alan found it hard to get a good look at them. Everything blurred. Someone slammed the lid of a trashcan and Alan laughed. His sides no longer hurt. It could be the medicine Jay gave me, he thought, yes, medicine is a prime suspect!

Alan took a step forward and yawned, thinking absurdly of a balloon emerging from his mouth. Pop! What delirium! Not very safe. I ought to find a safe spot. But everything is so much like syrup. Perhaps if I move forward.

"Perhaps, perhaps, perhaps," Alan said, leaning on a brick wall for support. When did walking become so complicated? Yes, medicine *is* the culprit! "I won't get anywhere," Alan went on in a loud voice, "without any pants!" He marched forward. "I'll perish. Without pants! Perish, perish, parsnip."

Alan settled into a patch of grass before he could fall; his sense of balance was waning. The ground was incredibly soft. He tried to feel the earth turn beneath him, and then realized that it was not spinning, but rocking. How had no one come to notice this before? All the science behind cameras and tiny screens and everyone still thought that the earth was spinning! I can't perish now, Alan thought. I've got to tell the people.

A coy-wolf bobbed across the street. Alan barked at it. A couple of young people crouched over him.

"Are you okay?"

"I saw a dog. Wait!" Alan pointed at them. "I'm perishing. I need some pants."

They laughed and Alan joined them, then suddenly stopped. "I think I'm dying. I had too many pills. I'm perish."

The couple standing over him looked so absurdly concerned; their faces were twisted with it. "What did you take?"

"I dunno, my roommate gave it to me." Sleep beckoned Alan like a red headed woman. "Vicodin," he said, and then shut his eyes. The couple walked away.

Roger had a flat tire. There was no use trying to fix it, he'd always been hopeless at that sort of thing. He growled at his phone; Jay was not answering. Roger had thrown a white towel over the front of the truck. He didn't own it. He suspected that there was an insurance number for him to call but he couldn't find it anywhere.

Roger's hands flew into prayer position as a crowd crossed the intersection. A man who was taller and heavier than Roger leaped out of its mass, all but quivering with self-importance. "You got a flat?"

"Yes, yes I could really use some help—,"

"No problem."

"Really?"

The man shut his eyes and nodded. "Open the hatch."

"Thank you!" Roger rushed around the truck. "My brother's got a death wish, he's seriously depressed. I've got to get home."

"Is it far?"

Roger swiped his hands through his hair. "Of course it's far, man, it's far enough. My roommate says he's locked himself in the bathroom, I don't know if he's taking pills or what."

"Well, call the cops, have you called the cops?"

"You think?"

"Yes," the man said, nodding. "You should definitely call someone. Maybe paramedics."

Roger climbed into the car. He had thought of this, of course, of what would happen in the case of a true emergency. He'd be arrested and charged, eventually. It had always been inevitable and it wouldn't be pretty....

"Nine one one, what's your emergency?"

"I need paramedics for my brother."

Roger stared through the window at a flashing marquee. Someone asked him his name. His address. Location. Brother's location. Would you like us to give you a call back?

Roger hung up and kept staring at the marquee, feeling sick. Then Jay called him back and he sat forward. "Is he okay?"

"Listen, Roger...."

"Oh-my-God-Jay you break into that bathroom or I will break you—,"

"Relax, Roger, listen to me. He left the apartment."

"What?"

"He's not here. He got out."

Roger stared at the dashboard. Alan had always flinched at the suggestion of doing so much as stepping out on the balcony. "He got out?"

"Yeah, I can't find him."

Roger shuddered and bit his finger. "Okay, um. Did he take any pills?"

"Yeah."

"Alright. Jay, I've, I dunno if you done it already, but I called the paramedics, so..."

"YOU WHAT?"

Jay dropped the phone. He poured his coffee over the open laptop on his desk. He put a pot of water on the stove and threw syringes into it. He piled all the sheets and towels together and ran down to the laundry room. He was leaning against the rhythm of a washer when he remembered the card. He picked up his phone. "Roger."

"What?"

"Where's the memory card I was using?"

"I don't know," Roger said, watching the stranger work on a bolt in the tire. "That's not my...not my problem." He realized somewhere along his response that he had found a memory card while he was running late for work that morning. It had given him a bad feeling, finding it in his pillow like that. Like someone was trying to hide it. He'd slipped it into his tool belt next to a pair of shears.

Jay had ended the call. Roger stared at his phone for a moment and then crouched to watch the stranger work. How could finding that memory card be more important than Alan's safety, even to Jay?

Alan was in a hospital and wanted so badly to speak, but the stuttering exhausted him. He penciled his name onto a prescription pad with an unsteady hand.

"Okay." A pretty nurse sat next to Alan's bed. She had been the one to tell him when his vitals were normal. "Is that your name?"

Alan nodded, pointing at the sheet and then at himself. *Arden Cope is my guardian,* he wrote, *my brother Roger Cope is in trouble. Roommate wants to kill him. Please help.*

He handed her the pad and held a steady, earnest expression while watching her read. The nurse did not seem alarmed. "Where did you get the pills?"

Alan groaned with frustration. What relevance could that bear? He pointed at the word *roommate.*

The nurse handed back the pad and continued in a deadpan voice. "Did you think that the dose of pills you had could be fatal?"

Alan thumbed to a fresh sheet. *I figured it out when I was having trouble walking.*

The nurse nodded. "Have you been harboring any suicidal thoughts?"

What's suicidal?

She seized the pad and squinted at it. Alan suddenly remembered what the word meant and tried to take the pad back, but she wouldn't let him. Tears were forming in her eyes. She stood up and left the room.

He lay back and sighed. Someone would come to take his fingerprints, he decided, just like they had the last time. Then, hopefully, he'd be on his way home.

(The nurse, by the way, took the pad to her father's house. She ripped off the sheet that said *what's suicidal?* and slipped it into a plastic frame next to a photo of her late mother).

Alan was told that until Arden was back in town, he would be staying with strangers. He tried not to think about it, even when a mousey social worker came along with new pants and a pack of crackers shaped like fish. He said his name was Steve. Alan mimed writing.

Later, Steve gave Alan a notebook from the trunk of his car, which held dozens of them. Steve looked tired, but he waited patiently as Alan wrote.

Are you a real social worker?

"Licensed social worker and clinical psychologist."

I want a co-ed house please.

Steve shook his head. "Not likely. But I'll try."

Alan resolved to prepare dinner wherever he ended up, so as best to avoid animosity and unwanted conversation. He sat in the passenger's side of Steve's car and started drafting a letter for Arden. Steve spent a lot of time on the phone. They eventually stopped outside a condominium with a tall dark man out front who smiled and waved at them. Alan tried to return the notebook but Steve told him to keep it. He gave Alan a notecard with several numbers on it, including Arden's. Alan held it so tight he could feel blood beating in his fingertips. What good was a phone number when you couldn't speak?

The place was not co-ed. It was full of discarded jackets and snack wrappers and sleeping bags. The floor was cold linoleum. It was colder than Alan's hands. From the window he saw a stocky, curly haired boy stride up to the back door, which he slammed shut behind him. "Bird!" He said, "Marco took my eye pod."

The keeper of the house, who was still outside, called back in a booming voice. "Alec I am talking to the social worker sit your butt down somewhere!"

Alec glanced at Alan and leaned out the front door. "Who's this in the kitchen?" Bird pushed Alec back into the house and shut the door. Alec sat on the table. "Marco took my eye pod and I'm gunna get him back," the boy said in what he probably thought was an aggressive voice. When Alan didn't answer, he said: "Are you retarded or something?"

Alan shook his head. Alec grabbed a handful of nuts from a container on the table. "You look like a girl," he said, and then stomped back outside.

The men out there were still talking. Alan approached a messy desk and searched for a marker. Then, with the notebook still clutched under one arm, he wrote the word NO across his left palm, and YES across his right.

Bird ordered pizza, foiling Alan's plan to cook for everyone. As if anticipating that Alan would be less likely to fall upon the food as the others did, yelling and reaching over each other, he handed Alan a small flat box and said, "that's yours." Alan took it and retreated to a corner.

In the morning, there were vans outside the condominium. They had satellite dishes on them. Several boys went outside to boast at the reporters and photographers who awaited them, yes, they said, we've seen Alan Cope. He's pretty weird. He's pretty normal. Looks kind of like a girl.

Arden watched from the end of the block. She turned up her collar, took a deep breath and got out of her car. Questions pelted her as she made her way around to the back door of the house. Someone cracked it open and, seeing Alan, she grabbed the front of his shirt and pulled him over the threshold. Cameras flashed. "Keep your head down," she said to Alan, then put her arms around him and marched them both back to the car.

Roger took his time coming home. He did not want to face Jay. He never did. Alan had been an endearing item, a buffer more effective than the dresser that split the apartment in two.

Jay said he would call if Alan came back. Roger watched his phone. It was Jay's fault, he realized. Jay is a tool. Jay is a snake. He can keep his fucking heroin. He let my sick brother out.

While on the subway, Roger was prepared to confront his roommate. He was prepared to cross between the dresser and the wall to yell at Jay. He was not prepared to find the man on the floor, holding a flashlight and poring over a drawer that he'd ripped out of the nightstand. Roger tossed his tool belt on the bed and went into the kitchen. Jay was probably still looking for that memory card, Roger thought as he watched coffee drip. Perhaps he would keep it a little longer, then, just to piss him off.

Roger had heard other men talk about the height of anger. About red-zoning. He could feel a buildup now, tension mounted on his spine like the units of an office building, and as oppressive. He tented his hands on the counter.

Roger crossed back over to where Jay was still searching for the memory card and sipped his coffee. "You wanna tell me why you're looking for a piece of plastic instead of my sick brother?"

Jay didn't answer. Roger smacked his lips and walked over to the window. He would wait until Jay was asleep, and then he would do something. He would find out what the hell was on that card, to start. He put a hand in his pocket. Another unit mounted his back.

Arden's hair had a pale streak in it; the kind that came from exhaustion. Her eyes were surrounded by lines and hollowness. Alan was afraid for her. When they were well away from the crowd she pulled over to the side of the road and acknowledged him at last.

"Are you my cousin?" She asked.

Alan glanced at her face and saw some of her old discernment there. He nodded.

"Look at me." She stared longer. More discernment. "What did I get you for your last birthday?"

Alan wrote the word "stereo" and showed it to her.

Her frown deepened, it was almost comical. "Why can't." She took a deep breath. "Why can't you talk?"

Alan flipped to the letter he wrote her.

Dear Arden: I don't know how long it's been, and I really need your help. I can't speak anymore, please read on. We may all be in lots of trouble. When Roger and I left we went to the old house in Tioga and I started getting sick. We were fighting. I know we were there for awhile but I don't remember much after that. I think I drifted in and out for a long time, I'll tell you about it later in case it's important.

At some point I woke up in Roger's apartment. It makes me sick to write this, it makes my stomach hurt, I am scared it will get found, maybe burn this after you read it. I don't know the address but it's not far from here, it has metal stairs on the front and the doors face the outside. It's very small. I guess we lived there with Roger's roommate, God I feel sick, Roger's roommate is named Jay and he says he'll kill Roger and kill me and I think he knows where you and Jenna live. This guy is serious, he's empty, Arden. He'd kill with his eyes open. He socked the light out of me for fun. I tried to tell Roger but I couldn't, it's been getting harder and harder for me to talk. We have to get Roger away from there. I know he ruined your life but we have to help him.

Arden stopped reading. She tried to hand the notebook back and Alan wouldn't let her. He pointed at the page, he crossed his arms. She wiped her eyes. "I'd rather wait until we get home."

Alan shook his head and tried to say the word "sorry" but stopped after several halting hisses. Arden swallowed and kept reading:

Jay said if I talked or ran off he would get Jenna to replace me because she won't give him any trouble.

"Alan I swear to God if you're making this up to get attention—"

Alan punch the dashboard and shook his head. He was seething, he wanted to talk so bad. Words piled over his tongue like so many broken birds. Arden turned the page.

Tell me is Jenna okay?

"She's okay," Arden said, and Alan breathed. Arden took out her phone. "Leena, please call me when you get this. I need someone to pick up Jenna from the library and stay with her until I'm back, it's an emergency." She handed Alan the notebook. "Do you trust me?"

Alan nodded. Arden went on: "I *will* read the rest of this when we get home. I want you to keep writing. Write anything and everything you can remember."

I wrote all I can remember.

"Write more. Every detail counts. What brand of cigarettes was Roger using? How did the shower work? How did the fridge open? Everything, everything."

Can't remember. I was blacking out.

Arden shook her head. "You have to try, Alan. Give me something I can use." She put the car into drive.

Alan was afraid when he saw Jenna, but he didn't know why. He barely heard a word she was saying. He interrupted her with awkward, frantic hugs. When the night came, he would not leave her room. He lay on the floor, watching the fish she had kept for him while he was gone. It had a tank with lights and bubbles. Alan continued his letter to Arden. He tried to remember every detail. It quickly became a list.

- ° Kitchen has gas stove
- ° Orange juice in fridge
- ° Shower doesn't get hot
- ° Roger had a tiny screen

Etc., etc....

Arden was smoking for the third time in her life when Roger called her. She had been advised: in the event that Roger calls you, answer him. Do not get angry. Let him talk. Try to get him to stay on the line as long as possible. Try to get a location, but don't push it. Get out your second cell phone and call the police.

This was all assuming, of course, that Alan was still missing. But Alan was upstairs, safe, pretending to sleep when Arden checked on him. Something wicked was happening to her blood pressure. She didn't want to talk to Roger; she wanted to smack him and sue him.

Arden picked up the phone. "If you're calling about Alan, I can't help you." She heard nothing for a long time. And then, from some immutable instinct, she added, "he says your roommate wants to kill you, or something."

"Arden."

"What."

"Arden, I...." There was a deep breath, or wind noise, but knowing Roger it was probably a deep breath. "Are you still a lawyer?"

Arden thought of saying that it was none of his business. She thought of dropping the phone on the couch. But curiosity was uncoiling inside her. "Why?"

"I think I killed someone by accident...I mean I didn't mean to...."

Arden sat forward. "Where are you?"

"Seneca."

"Okay. Get a pen and paper. I'm going to give you the number of an officer there. I want you to call him and say you have information about a murder, then go where he tells you to go and—,"

"Arden, I can't, this is my one call."

"You've been arrested already?"

"Yeah."

Arden stared at the blades of the ceiling fan; they were furred with dust.

"Roger, don't say anything. Don't answer any questions. Tell them you're waiting for your lawyer."

In Seneca, Roger swallowed. "Who's my lawyer?"

"I am." And then: "Sorry I called you Thumper."

Jenna woke up at 7 AM and stared at Alan on the floor. "Wake up." She threw a pillow at him. Startled, Alan woke and launched himself across the room. "Sorry!" she said as Alan wrote furiously, "got it, okay, no throwing. Sorry."

Alan wrapped a blanket around his shoulders and trotted out into the hall. He found Arden in the kitchen and put the notebook beside her. She held a tiny screen over it. "I'm taking pictures of each page, so we don't lose it," Arden said, and Alan had to fight the urge to swipe the notebook away from her.

Arden skimmed the writing as she went. "Your brother is safe from the roommate, he's in prison. I can't tell you any more than that."

Alan pulled up a chair and sat. He tried to gather a few words together; they were everywhere. "Keh...ken you...." He stopped, frowning at the table. Arden patiently watched him. He pointed at the little screen.

"What, this?" Arden gave him a pitying expression. "This is an eye phone."

Alan shook his head; why *eye?*

"I'll get you one like it," Arden said, and she kept snapping pictures. "Jenna's going to school on the internet, on the computer. She'll show you how to get enrolled, okay?"

"Oh....kay."

Arden left the kitchen and came back with a fresh notebook. It was spotted. "You can use this, now. I need your sizes for clothes and shoes, okay? What do you want for breakfast?"

Alan went to the fridge. He reached in with both hands and pulled out a carton of eggs. While cracking them, a sharp pain alighted in his jaw. He rubbed it and got out a fork. Arden scratched his shoulder affectionately.

"You wouldn't believe how many false alarms we had. People came right up to my door and claimed they were Alan Cope. I don't even know how they found out where we live." Alan gave her a quizzical look and she nodded. "You'd be surprised," she said, and he would have been. He would have been surprised to know the number of people who wanted to be him, or whatever they thought was him, online and in reality, the blogs, the the speculating, the choose your own ending. She kissed the side of his head and then sat down. Her phone vibrated and she closed a hand over it.

They would be poor, probably forever. That much Arden knew, and that much they would have to know.

Alan did not want to leave Jenna's side in the days that followed. He was scared to be alone and could see that Arden was too insensitive to this to tolerate his hovering for long. Arden had taken him aside and told him that they wouldn't have to worry about Jay, but he still felt that he and Jenna should supervise each other in some capacity. She explained to him about the internet, about how it *really* worked, and he took classes online. Jenna had one friend, who was equally busy, and so she studied most of the day and Alan followed her lead. He learned about social media but Jenna said not to do it, so he didn't. Catching up with school was surprisingly easy.

Nothing else was easy. Arden told them very little about how she spent her days. Only that Roger would be on trial soon about a Very Serious Issue, and that they weren't allowed to buy anything they didn't need. Jenna started clipping coupons. She and Alan looked for work, but they didn't tell Arden about it.

The emotive shorthand of using his hands to communicate exhausted Alan. The control he had to exert over his facial expressions seemed robbed him of headspace; it was harder than ever to think around other people. Particularly when that new pain in his tooth could strike at any moment....

"Are you okay?" Jenna asked, and Alan held up a finger. He was sitting through a shudder of pain, pressing a hand against the side of his face. When it passed, he took a deep breath and then nodded. Jenna's hands started moving. He recognized the signs for *where* and *live.*

Alan tented his fingers, separated his hands and then brought them down flat. *House.*

Jenna grinned. "This is so cool."

Alan gave her a weak smile. He couldn't help but think that there was something Jenna would rather do than practice sign language with him. They heard Arden come in through the kitchen.

"Did we sell the house yet?" Jenna asked.

"Nope." Arden was looking fuller these days; still worked to her limit, but in a more hydrated sort of way. "I fired the real estate agent, though. I think we can do it ourselves."

Alan said nothing. He knew Arden was trying to get almost half a million dollars for the place. Even with repairs, it was worth less than a tenth of that. The point, she had explained, was to rent it out, but to list it to buy. He couldn't understand what she meant, and he was sure that there were crucial pieces to her plan that he was not privy to.

"Alan," Arden said his name in a painfully gentle voice. "We have to talk for a bit."

Alan closed Spot (the spotted notebook) over a pencil and followed Arden into her office. He was learning to type, but was still better at writing by hand.

Arden looked at Alan's hair. "You cut it yourself, huh?"

Alan nodded.

Arden sat beside her desk. "Listen, Alan, when you...hmm." She rubbed her neck; she was nervous. "After all...after whatever it is that you've been through...."

Alan failed to suppress a mirthless chuckle, and along with it arrived a tiny flicker of resentment.

Arden went on: "I realized that when you returned home, the best thing I could do for you was to protect your right to privacy." She looked at him. "And I'm trying to do that. I'm trying much, much harder than you know." She took a breath. "Still, I think in some ways I violated that when I demanded that you write everything down, even if I have good reason. I'm very sorry."

Alan flipped idly through Spot. He had never asked what her reasoning was, and he really didn't care. He wanted to say, *who are you and what did you do to my cousin?* The flicker in him was getting hotter. He remembered trying to absorb Jay's fury with appeasement, *yes, Jay, I know you will kill me, I know, okay.* Where had that anger gone? Arden watched him. Alan realized that she was waiting for him to write something. He closed Spot with a snap.

Arden blinked. "Are you mad at me?"

Not at you, Alan thought, and he shook his head.

Arden leaned forward. "Alan, you know what could happen to your brother."

Alan nodded. He opened Spot. *You should tell me more.*

Arden nodded. "You're right, I should. I didn't want you to be involved at all, but I have to ask, are you willing to get involved? Because if you are, I still can't tell you everything. And I might have to confront you with some uncomfortable facts. And the thing is—and I know you're trying hard, and I read what you wrote—but Alan. I can't tell what's going on. There's a lot that is missing."

Alan was looking at the salt lamp on her desk. He'd never touched it, but he wanted to. He looked down and wrote: *Will it help Roger if I get involved?*

"Yes, it will. Almost certainly."

A shock pulsed through Alan's mouth again. He dropped the pencil and rubbed his jaw, feeling a little panic as the pain took a longer to subside than usual. Arden picked up the pencil and Alan slowly took it from her.

I want to help. But I can't. Every time I think about it —you are asking too much. I'm trying but I can' do it I'm sorry. Also I think there's something—

Pencil lead broke. Alan threw the thing in the trash and grabbed one off the desk. *wrong with my tooth.*

Arden swallowed. "Does it hurt?"

Alan wrote the number 10. Circled it.

On the way to the dentist it occurred to Alan that going for an X-ray would be as useless as an intake for speech therapy. He was too tired to write all of that down, though, and he soon found himself sitting on a strange chair. He was alone with a nurse who had just learned his name. She unfolded a piece of plastic with gloved hands and told him where it would go. Alan took the plastic from her and put it in his cheek. She peered in and shook her head. "It has to go even farther back than that," she said, "almost like—,"

"—you don't even care what I do to you," Jay was saying.

Alan's veins burned from the kind of anger that only appears in the face of injustice. "Roger will kill you if he knows—,"

"No," Jay's voice lowered. "He'll kill himself if he knows. He's already shooting up because of you. Put the razor in your mouth and if that doesn't shut you up I'll get more creative."

Alan heard someone in the dentist's office say something and remembered where he was. His blood pressure returned to normal. He blinked and took the sharp plastic out of his mouth. *So that's what they call a flashback,* he thought.

Alan was anxious to get home and write it down, just in case. Upon seeing his X-ray, however, all thoughts of the flashback fled his mind.

"What is *that?*" Arden pointed at the light box. Alan nodded beside her.

Dr. Kelly, as specified by her name tag, sighed and put on her glasses. "Well, there's a couple of different things going on. For one thing, your wisdom teeth are coming in, so that's likely what's causing the pain to escalate. Let's hope they don't." She took out a pen light and asked Alan to open his mouth.

"Had to see it for myself," she said, drawing back. She pointed at the troubling area of the X-Ray. "This here is a baby tooth."

"Baby tooth?"

"Yep. Never came out."

Alan and Arden glanced at each other. "Is that common?"

"I've never seen it before. You're seventeen, right?" she asked, looking at Alan, and he nodded. "Yeah," Dr. Kelly went on, "that's not very common." She pointed again. "So this here, it looks like it tried to come in, but it impacted. See how it's kind of at an angle?"

Looking at his own teeth was starting to make Alan feel rather sick. The doctor asked him to chew gum while she pressed in front of his ears. "Let me ask you something," she said, and Alan tried very hard to pay attention because something about this exam was making a pleasant tingle pour all over him, "do you get dizzy spells or lose your balance a lot?"

Alan said, "Uh-huh."

"He's kind of slow," Arden supplemented.

"Do you get headaches here?" The doctor drew a line up Alan's temple and he nearly fainted dead away.

"He gets a lot of headaches."

The doctor backed away from Alan and circled around him to her desk. "Okay," she said, "you're showing some signs of chronic TMJ, which means your jaw has been misaligned for awhile and its giving you problems. I would recommend surgery in two parts—,"

"Two parts?"

The doctor shrugged. "We have to get that baby tooth out."

"But what about his wisdom teeth? You said they were fine."

"They're fine for now. Usually they get impacted, and it's better to prevent that while we still can, or at least keep an eye on it." She looked at Alan. "Once you've healed, we can get you fitted for a mouth guard to wear when you sleep."

Just in case you forgot, Alan's eyes were enormous. He followed Arden into the lobby and waited next to a water cooler while she talked to the receptionist, who was young and nervous-looking.

"Can you please give me the amount for the deductible?" Arden said.

"That is the deductible."

"No, hun." Arden showed him the bill. "The deductible is what I pay after insurance."

The boy took the bill with one hand and rubbed his mouth with the other. "This is after insurance," he said in a hesitant voice.

Arden handed him her insurance card. "Can you just run this again, please?"

The boy took it and pecked at his keyboard. "You're covered."

"Okay, so what's my deductible?"

The boy pointed at the bill. "This is the deductible."

"That's the deductible?"

"Yes, ma'am."

"But this is more than half!"

The receptionist nodded and returned her card. "I guess it is, ma'am. You can call your insurance company. Would you like to schedule the next appointment today?"

That evening, Alan helped Jenna move the fish tank to his room on the condition that she wouldn't have to clean it. He plugged everything in and stared at it for awhile, trying not to think of his teeth or surgery in general, or that he couldn't get away with sleeping on the floor of her room any longer and would have to spent a long, terrifying night by himself. Nearby, Spot glowed in the watery light. Alan picked it up.

It was like I was there but I wasn't, that's why I think it was a flashback. I knew I was at the dentist, but my blood did not. Also my ears did not. Anyway, Jay and I used to argue when Roger wasn't home, he would bother me.

Bothered...how long could he use that word, *"bothered?"*

Alan looked up, squinting and trying to remember. His stomach churned and it was hard to focus. For some reason, all he could think of was when the wolf had sniffed his mouth in the cabin while he was still in Luna. He clicked his pen.

I know he bothered me while the TV was on. I was angry at him, and really freaked out. He didn't want me to talk to Roger about something with his business...
Jay had a business.

The fish moved. Alan couldn't remember what Jay did for money, only that it was on the internet.

It was a business he did on the internet, and he didn't want me to talk to Roger about it. He always wanted to shatter any interaction we had, he eventually didn't want me to talk to Roger at all. I think we were arguing because I said something by accident and he told me to put a razor

Alan crossed his legs.

in my mouth all day

Rubbed his jaw.

so that I could practice quiet. Quieting down. It must have done good on me because it's so, so hard to talk now.

That razor blade had had a circular hole in the middle that felt so perfect to Alan's tongue, and that memory had to be at least as sharp as the blade itself because in that moment, while Alan leaned over his paper, it struck a fault line between his eyes that would never go away.

He marked the page for Arden to read and curled into bed with the lights on, with his clothes on, with his shoes on.

At 2:30 AM Jenna burst into Alan's room and he sat up in bed, heart racing.

"Arden's crying."

Alan's jaw dropped. He shook his head.

"I know," Jenna went on, "I don't know what to do!"

They made their way down stairs and peered into the living room. Arden was sobbing over the coffee table. Dumbfounded, Jenna and Alan stared at her and then at each other. Alan piled his fists, twisted them, then cupped one hand and circled the other: *make tea.*

Jenna nodded. "You do that, I'll get a blanket or something."

Alan set the water to boil and then walked around Arden, trying to read the shape of the space around her.

She was crying out of anger, he realized. She took a blanket from Jenna and wiped her face on it. "Roger sucks at being in prison," she cried, and Alan nodded.

Arden sniffed, collected herself and reached into her bag. She pulled out a letter-size envelope and handed it to Alan. "You're gonna have to look at the photos in there and tell me if you recognize any of those kids."

Alan busied himself with the fastener and Arden put her hand over it. "No—not now, honey."

Jenna tugged on Alan's shirt and he followed her into the kitchen. "Arden hasn't called anyone 'honey' since the dog died," she whispered.

Right, Alan thought, *I'm the new dog.* He shrugged at her; he was very tired of shrugging.

Alan didn't recognize the children in the folder. He looked at the eyes in the photos and tried to remember, but he couldn't and somehow the effort made his stomach sick. Arden kept asking him about children, and it gave him a bad feeling.

"Are you sure Jay didn't bring anyone else into the apartment?"

I'm sure I don't remember. Alan was typing, now. He carried a laptop everywhere. **He just**

mentioned Baxter once, like I told you. But Baxter never showed. He was pissed.

"And then Jay hit you and the camera was there that time."

Yes. I really don't remember anyone else, and he didn't mention anyone we know except Jenna and Roger.

"You didn't see him watching any videos of children?"

I just heard the choking a lot, but I never saw it. No one else was in the apartment. I'm not saying that he wouldn't hurt anyone else, I just didn't see him do it.

"Did he say anything as if someone was watching from the camera?"

I already told you he was just telling me to cry and calling me names and that. I really don't remember much, I was trying to catch my breath, Arden.

Arden tented her fingers and rested her chin on them. Alan inserted a page break and then circled his wrists: Jenna had sent him an article about carpal tunnel. Arden put her hands down. "I can take you to see Roger tomorrow."

Alan lurched towards the keyboard. **Really?**

"Only if you want." Arden sat back. "You won't be able to talk for long, but it would do him some good to see you, and, I mean...it might help jog your memory, as awful as that sounds." She watched him for awhile. "You miss him, huh?"

Yup.

"He misses you. He always asks if you're talking yet."

I don't want him to be disappointed.

"You'll talk again," Arden said firmly, "when it's time. But tomorrow we're going to see him. You have to touch base about what's going on."

Okay. Did you get to find out what was on that memory card?

"Right, the card." Arden pulled a legal pad out of a drawer. "The files are unreadable; it means they won't open. Prosecution's going to do everything they can to fix that, my hope is that it won't work. I want this memory card thing to disappear."

But why? Isn't it supposed to make Jay look bad? I'm sure it's important, Arden, he was so crazy about the thing. You should have seen him. I know it's important.

"I thought so, too, but they're trying to prove that it's Roger's memory card and I don't know where that leaves us."

Alan leaned his head on one hand and pecked with the other. Is he pleading guilty for murder or innocent?

"Well, to begin with, I'm trying to get a manslaughter charge, not a murder charge." Arden blinked. "Do you think he did it, Alan?"

Alan chewed his lip. He used to say he'd kill anyone who hurt me. We were little. But he meant it………………… Alan made a train of dots whenever he wanted Arden to wait for him to finish a thought. It was the only thing that really made typing better than talking. He didn't know Jay was that bad, though. He couldn't have known. We hid it.

Arden's pen slid across her legal pad and Alan's leg bobbed. He pushed the laptop a few inches and she looked up to read his comment. Her face looked pinched.

"I heard some things yesterday that are a little inconsistent with what you've shared with me, Alan." She rotated her pen in front of her and Alan waited for her to continue. "I know that...I know that Roger didn't know that Jay was so violent. But are you sure he wasn't angry with him about something else? Or jealous?"

Why would he be jealous?

Arden spun a little in her chair. "Well, Roger had to be at work while Jay was in the apartment with you all day. And then you stopped talking to him."

I didn't stop talking to him, Arden, I just stopped talking. You have to read Spot later.

"The notebook?"

Yes, with the spots on it. I remembered why I can't speak.

Before bed, Alan brought Spot downstairs and left it in Arden's office. She read about the razor blade while he dreamt of it and woke up spitting.

Driving to the prison took a long time, and Alan had a little panic at the sight of it. Roger Cope, in prison. Jail. Lockup. His brother. It had felt as if Alan were missing a limb that he seldom used but always needed. He didn't want Arden to see them reunite, to watch the crushing embrace that Alan was sure would ensure, but it didn't happen that way. He and Roger were separated by plexiglass.

Alan's hand was up on it, pressing hard, wanting Roger to press back but he didn't. The relief in his face was exhausting to watch. They had to use cord phones to talk, Roger was twisting both hands around his.

"Hey, kiddo. You still holding your vow of silence?"

Alan's mouth quivered. He had never seen Roger tremble in that way, as if he was terrified of himself.

"Don't worry, Alan. Everything's fine, it's better now, isn't it? Arden says you've been really here. Not checking out like you were before."

"It's...aw...awful," Alan managed, and Roger gulped.

"Did you go to Luna?"

Alan's fingers twitched on the glass. He had just realized how thin Roger was, how dull his skin looked. Like a listless tank pet.

"I thought it was the right thing to do, telling you all those stories. I wanted you to grow up different than me, to have something to believe."

Alan huffed. How could Roger bring this up now, with only a handful of minutes to talk? They stared for a moment, at a mutual loss for words. Then Alan seized the pad and pen in his back pocket. *Tell me another one.*

Roger scratched the side of his arm, thinking. His bruised eyes blinked a few times. "Once there was a…I forgot what they're called. A sheep-keeper. The sheep-keeper wanted attention so he cried *wolf wolf* and the villagers came and when the villagers came there was no wolf and they left the boy alone. All the sheep were shocked but one.

"The sheep-keeper wanted love, so he cried *wolf wolf* and the villagers came and when the villagers came there was no wolf and they left the boy alone. All the sheep were shocked but one.

"The sheep-keeper wanted protection so he cried *wolf wolf* and the villagers came and when the villagers came there was no wolf so they left the boy alone. All the sheep were shocked but one.

"The sheep-keeper wanted to show everyone the one sheep who was never shocked, who was always there, his best sheep. so he called *wolf wolf* to summon the villagers but the villagers did not come. The wolf finally did, and all the sheep left but one. The wolf bit the boy around the ankles and around the veins in his neck, and the sheep stayed by his keeper's side while he lay dying.

"The villagers found the sheep-keeper dead and questioned the loyal animal by his side. They asked, 'What happened to your keeper?' and the sheep gave no answer... because it could not speak."

I don't understand it, Alan thought suddenly, and he started to cry a little.

Roger shrugged. "It's just a story, Alan."

Alan ducked his head and busied himself with the pen. Roger was being lifted from his chair. He brushed his hand on the plexiglass and by the time Alan glanced up it was too late to touch back.

When they were outside, Arden threw her keys at Alan and he barely caught them.

"It's a big lot here," she said, "you wanna go around a few times?"

Knowing that this attempt to cheer him up would probably have worked on anyone else, Alan kept his face neutral when he shook his head and tried to return the keys. Arden closed Alan's hand over them.

"Come on," she smiled. "It's about time you learned to drive."

Alan shook his head and got in the passenger's side of the car.

"You're more hormonal than Jenna," Arden said. She turned the radio to a news station that had an atrocious hissing behind the dialogue. Alan tried to tune it all out but he couldn't escape some notion of what was said.

"That's some of the weather, then," a man's voice said, "and after that, it looks like we can expect more weather. Up next, we have a watered down version of Vivaldi's four seasons, and then more news."

Someone jabbed at a piano for awhile, and then a woman's voice took the lead: "Lots of things happening in the news today. There's still some war, people are talking about that. Also, a teenager in a place made another cure for cancer, but it appears that he's waiting on a go ahead from a Very Big Company. For more information you can follow us on social media at social media dot com. You can also subscribe to our new media channel and digitize us at alternative media slash internet.

Alan groaned. He pushed his head against the window and watched a car that looked like Roger's. The news went on; he thought he heard something about Larque boys and then Arden finally turned it off. Alan sighed, trying to remember what had really been said before realizing that he didn't want to know, anyway.

When they got home, Jenna was in the living room, and Arden took the opportunity to sit them down and explain that they needed make make money for their own expenses. Alan and Jenna looked at each other.

"I've got a job already," Jenna said, "and Alan's looking."

Arden looked bemused as she lowered herself into a chair. "...you didn't ask me for money for your car payment."

"I know."

"Are you behind in school?"

"No. I did extra in the summer, remember?"

"Shh!" Arden threw one hand up between them and put the other on her own forehead. Alan looked away. Seeing Arden confused was almost as unbearable as the tooth pain.

"It's not a big deal," Jenna uttered, and Arden stood up so fast that her chair slid back a foot.

"It is a big deal, Jenna! I have to know exactly how much money is coming into this house! And you!"

Alan, who had been trying to slink out of the room, jumped a foot in the air when Arden pointed at him.

"Stop acting like everything's dandy! I'm tired of waiting on you to open your damn mouth and tell me what the hell you need already!"

Alan shrugged. Arden picked up a decorative bowl and threw it across the room; Jenna hurled insults at her sister and Alan slid down the wall, wanted to disappear into the fissure of the baseboard behind him. He saw the clouds that preceded loss of consciousness and knew that he must be hallucinating, because Arden and Jenna were suddenly having a frantic argument not about money, but about Luna.

"There's *more* of them!" Arden was saying, "there's like a dozen new boys coming out with the same story about the island and antlers and its public and what the hell, Jenna!"

"I know, okay, calm down!"

"Did you do it? Are you behind this?"

"No, Arden, oh my God! I'm not doing it and he's not doing it, okay? We can't control the fucking public!"

"Is he on Facebook?"

"...no, Arden, he's not on Facebook. Look, Alan are you on Facebook?"

Alan frantically shook his head.

"No, he's not, okay? See? We can't control every person on Earth that wants attention, alright? They probably just dug up some old interviews with Roger..."

"But his contracts Jenna they were all five year I made sure—,"

"Arden!" Jenna shouted, "it's the *internet!* There are. No. Contracts!"

Arden sat down. "This is bad, Jenna, it's bad."

"I know." Jenna went to the pantry and retrieved a paper bag. She shook it out and gave it to Alan, who started puffing away.

"We have no money."

"I know."

"It's very bad."

"I know."

Alan went upstairs. He took off his shoes and turned off the light. He settled into his bed. I am finished, Alan thought, like a plastic spoon in the trash. He started to sleep.

Arden was going to explain things to Alan, but she couldn't wake him. Jenna said they should wait until morning, but they couldn't wake him then, either. Alan stayed asleep.

The trial started without him. Arden knew she couldn't understand Alan's willful slumber and there was no time to try.

Alan dreamt of the trial. Water steadily filled the witness stand; he was trapped in there. Attorneys asked him questions without context. What time was it, Alan? Did it hurt? What did it smell like?

"Please excuse me," Alan answered, "I am resting."

The rest of his dream-state was mostly on a beach, he languished in a lagoon while pretty women came upon him with delight and took pictures. Sometimes he heard things from Outside, like about Arden needing to send him away. That was alright, Alan thought, rubbing sand between his fingertips, they'll move my body somehow. We ruined Arden's life. She tried her best. I just hope that they don't sentence Roger for a very long prison term. Because the world is a better world without Jay.

Some...some sound eventually joined Alan in the dream-state. It wasn't the first sound, but it was the only one he couldn't quite characterize. Alan turned over in the sand, waiting idly for it to quiet down. It didn't.

Usually sounds from the outside compelled him to get up and walk around, but this did not. It was decidedly not music, but also not talking. Talking went up and down. Music went back and forth. But this? This seemed to vibrate right through him. It was uncomfortable in a strange, undemanding way. Like trying to sleep when your body was sore from a restless day.

But I'm already asleep, aren't I? Alan thought, and he rolled over again in the sand. But this sound—this language he didn't know—it persisted.

It was not uncommon for Alan to cough a little in this sleep, but Jenna was shocked when she saw blood spraying all over his face. She shoved him onto his side.

In his dream-state, Alan knew that there was a pearl in his mouth. He was terrified to let it out.

No one else was in the room when Alan finally did wake up. It was dark; there was an IV in his arm. He thought for an instant that a razor blade had finally got his tongue because he tasted blood, but then he remembered that that was over, that Jay was gone and Roger was on trial for killing him. The only relief in regaining consciousness was that the pearl in Alan's mouth felt smaller than in the dream. He spat it into his palm—and there was the tooth..

Alan shed a handful of silent tears and hid them in a pillowcase. It took the sum of all his energy to sit up. The sound that had woken him—whatever it was—had stopped.

The people who came for Alan came with a baby sheep. A white lamb with a black head. "We are here," they said, "from the Healing Center for Introverts, Empaths and Other Highly Sensitive People."

Alan nodded and they helped him out of bed. He knew he was being Sent Away. Arden was there but he would not look at her and she would not look at him. He looked at the lamb.

It was a three hour drive to the Healing Center for Introverts, Empaths and Other Highly Sensitive People. Alan sat in the truck bed so he could be with the lamb. It stumbled a lot; it would not sit down. They had a long three hours. Arden followed them in her car.

They arrived at a quiet farm. Alan tried to convince himself that he was still dreaming but the fuzz of waking reality filled his ears like white noise. He tried to lift the lamb out of the truck but it flailed its tiny limbs and fell on the ground. The driver held Alan's gaze for a moment. "Can you Fetch That Lamb," she said, "and Put it with The Rest of The Flock?" Arden looked at her.

"What About his Intake?"

"Intake," Alan murmured, testing the word in his mouth.

"The Lamb is Part of his Intake."

Alan wandered after the animal. There was something Decidedly Different about the Words He was Hearing, As if they Were All being Spoken for the first time. Weak though he was, he managed to secure the lamb several yards from the truck and carry it beyond the fence of its pasture. He walked up to where Arden and the driver were waiting and followed them down a gravel path.

"It's only Three Months," Arden said while they took their tour. "See those Rows, Alan?" They plant their own food."

Alan nodded with vigor. He wanted her to keep talking.

"It's okay, I promise. I did my Research. I know it seems like a Long Time, But it's Not. The Trial will Be over by then. Look, Alan! The Horses Are there."

Alan smiled at her excitement. He wanted to suggest that she spend some time here as well, but he didn't know how, so he said, "I Know They Are Horses."

"See?" Arden's eyes glinted. "You're feeling Better already."

Alan Nodded, although he almost couldn't stand the thought of Not Going Home. He indicated the Need for Pen and Paper after the tour and asked Arden about it. *Just For A Little Bit,* he wrote, and he capitalized the words because he was suddenly so excited to have each one of them.

"Of course you're coming back home," Arden said, frowning. "What are you talking about?"

Alan rubbed his face, eyes widening. It Felt a little like sandpaper. He searched among his palate of words. It was like searching a hillside for interesting rocks. "Hard Times," he said after a moment.

Arden tugged her ear and turned in a circle. "I need to tell you: I don't talk to my mom anymore because she had bad boyfriends." She was speaking very fast and Alan strained to listen. He had never heard Arden speak about her mother before then. "Dangerous men, you know, and they Got Abusive sometimes when she wasn't around, and I told her and she didn't believe me. She kicked me out. That's why I stepped in to get Roger and took Jenna in and that's why you don't live with your aunt, alright? I want you to live in a home where you'll be believed." She put her hands on her hips. "You don't have to feel bad, because you're like me that way, Alan. When life shits on you, you stay focused." Arden lost her breath to a sudden hug.

Alan was introduced to a tiny room with a clean bed. He spent his first evening alone, scrolling through tutorials on equine care, as it was incumbent upon him to help with the horses during his stay. They would let him ride one if he did a good job. Alan pulled the blanket up to his chin. It smelled like sugary dough. Next to the bed was a salt lamp a little smaller than Arden's, and very warm.

Roosters crowed when the sun came up. An envelope slipped through the little brass mail slot in Alan's door. He stretched and crossed the room. In the envelope was a map, a schedule and a handwritten letter.

Hello, Alan!

Welcome to The Healing Center for Introverts, Empaths and other Highly Sensitive People. In the spirit of independence and respecting personal space, I would encourage you to explore the grounds and discover the many quiet spots to think and reflect. Your mandatory work schedule is in bold. All other events are optional. Breakfast starts at 7:30 AM. Remember to meet with your counselor, Dr. Jones, at 2 PM today...

The letter was signed by Doris, with a number and email underneath.

Alan did find a lot of quiet nooks. The center had three separate libraries. And the people he encountered were, for the most part, different. They listened. They made space for you when you walked in the room. Alan had always practiced these behaviors, but it had never before occurred to him how rare it was to find those habits in others. He was more comfortable than he had ever been. Despite this, anxieties that had been easy to ignore because they were so wholly unique to him suddenly had a desperate relevance. Alan did his best to ignore them.

Meanwhile, at Roger's trial, the nurse who saw Alan through his Vicodin scare was called to the witness stand. She had already exchanged several glances with the hopelessly adorable defendant, and it didn't do much to soothe her nerves. At Arden's bequest she had turned over the sheets from the prescription pad that Alan had used to communicate in the hospital. She was there to corroborate that he had indeed claimed that Jay posed a threat to Roger Cope.

Arden had a notebook with many things crossed out in it. They had established Roger's dependence on narcotics—there was no hiding that—and that Jay was supplying them. They established that Jay sold child pornography on at least two occasions. She leaned over the her checklist.

Roger waited with his head down, always almost crying, trying to look innocent and trying even harder not to remember what he did.

This is what Roger did:

He put the memory card in Jay's laptop while the man slept on the couch. He opened the drive. He clicked a file. He watched *longer* than the eleven seconds necessary to know what was happening to his brother.

Roger did this because he wanted to know the extent to which he himself had been wronged. Fury mounted him up to the eyes. He yanked the card out and got a glistening knife out of the kitchen.

Roger stabbed Jay twice before shouting at him. The stabbing was easy. The shouting was easy, too: "Why is it so important for you to get off, Jay? Will the world stop turning if you don't?"

While he was shouting, Jay struggled off the couch and grabbed the side of Roger's neck and Roger slashed the man's stomach. That's what killed him. He didn't regret killing Jay, but he didn't have to fake any emotions on the stand because guilt lived in him like a sharp toothed animal. It fed on Roger's conviction that he had killed Jay for vengeful satisfaction, and not in defense of his slip of a brother. The guilt was rough, sharp, would sneak up on him always, like blackmail with anthrax.

The cafeteria at The Healing Center for Introverts, Empaths and Other Highly Sensitive People had a conveyer belt for used dishes. It drifted into the kitchen, where Alan was standing with his back to the sink. He had left the library early after trying to ignore a nearby conversation about the narrative arts. It incited an intense mixture of frustration and pity for the teenaged Roger who had first introduced Luna to him. Alan wanted very much to ignore those emotions for the time being, at least until they could be easily and safely assessed (which, realistically, they could not).

To his left, He heard the clink of dishes pushing into each other. Scarlett (known as "Scar"), had kitchen duty with Alan that evening, but she hadn't shown up yet. He stared blankly at the conveyer belt. A glass of water was incrementally pushed towards the edge. It shattered beside Alan's foot and he looked at it, unmoving. Then came a bowl. Then came spoons. Then came a plate with a loud sound. They were disgusting. Full of spit and oils and the slop of others. He did not feel like himself.

Scar finally shuffled in wearing an oversized sweater and rubbing a tissue across her nose. She looked at the floor. "What happened?"

"You're late."

"I'm taking a sick day." She looked at him. "Doris said that if you cover for me you can take tomorrow off. I wanted to tell you myself." Scarlett rushed forward to stop another glass from falling. "Alan, come on. Pay attention." She put it in the sink. "Are you going to cover for me or what?"

"I'm not your bitch."

Scar gave him an intense look. Alan stared right back. She was infuriatingly calm. "I am not cleaning these dishes," Alan said, "They are not mine." He took off rubber gloves and threw them at her feet. He walked right into the main office, rang the bell, and waited. An attendant he barely knew approached the desk.

"I will not do kitchen duty anymore," Alan said to the puzzled face across the desk. "I do not like to be around dishes and sinks. I am a Highly Sensitive Person. If I am told to clean dishes again I will break one and use it to cut this artery." He pointed at the side of his own neck. "Is that clear enough?"

The attendant gave him a condescending look. "I think you need to see Dr. Jones."

"I am going to put this in writing," Alan said, lifting a pen from the desk. "I want it noted that I have threatened no one but myself." He had never felt so simultaneously angry and apathetic, but he was convinced that he was giving the desired impression. To what end, he did not know. Something simply had to change.

The man walked away from the desk while Alan kept writing. It wasn't long before he was escorted to Dr. Jones's office.

"What's Going On, Alan? Do you Need to Talk? Is there something you're Not Telling Us?"

Alan sat down with a straight back and huffed. "Lots of things," he said, "I have a Bad Brother. I was Fucked Without Permission. I think Luna is real."

The attendant beside Alan looked suddenly interested but Dr. Jones just gave them both a harsh stare. "I think it hardly matters, Alan, whether Luna is real."

There was a tense pause. Alan rounded on the attendant. "Do not be a man touching me," he said in the lowest register he could manage. The attendant released Alan's arm, then said, "were you really kidnapped?" Alan's mouth dropped open.

Dr. Jones threw down his glasses. "Oh my God, David, you can't just ask people if they were really kidnapped."

"But he just said—,"

"Get out, alright?" Dr. Jones's raised his voice as much as anyone dared at the Center. "Wait outside." David slipped out of the office and left the door open in his wake.

"Why does he think I wasn't kidnapped?"

"You shouldn't encourage them, Alan."

"What are you talking about?"

Dr. Jones stood up and closed the office door. "There are some who believe that your disappearance was part of a guerrilla marketing campaign."

"Marketing campaign...you mean to *sell something?*"

"Yes."

"Sell what?"

Dr. Jones returned to his desk. He put his glasses back on. "To sell a novel. Don't panic, Alan, I know what you're thinking."

Alan had such large eyes! He looked at Dr. Jones. He looked at his own knees. He looked directly at you. Then he shut his eyes and ran a hand through his hair. "Micah was right. I. Am not. Real."

"Alan. Does it really matter if—"

"It matters, doc!" Alan was shaking. Since arriving at the Center and regaining his ability to speak, the two of them had had several conversations about Alan's mounting suspicion that he was Being A Created Thing.

"Lie down, Alan."

"Don't tell me what to do. I know I'm created. I'm made-up. I *know* it."

"How do you know it?"

"Because," Alan said, flexing his hands, "I feel so... finite. Finished. You see my hand?" He held it out. "I'm just....here." He looked up.

"You're anxious, that's what it is. You're perseverating."

Alan had nothing to say to that. His thoughts were like quicksand.

"You said that you're not religious, Alan."

"I'm not. I don't even think about religion. What's that got to do with it?"

Dr. Jones sat back in his chair. "It's a fine distraction, isn't it, Alan? All these deep, existential questions: Am I real? Am I fictional? Very distracting."

"Distracting from what?"

"From your healing."

Alan snorted. He could feel a lecture approaching.

The man went on: "Did it ever occur to you that you may come closer to the answers you seek if you took a moment to address your feelings about real things?"

"Like what?"

"Like the fact that your brother might spend the rest of his life in prison for killing a rapist."

"You really have a way with words, doc."

They sat in silence for a moment. Alan waited for the man to continue.

"Whether or not you consider yourself to be real, Alan, has no bearing at all on your problems. And it doesn't address the anger that keeps bringing you back to my office."

"But you know I'm on to something, don't you?" Alan said. He had never felt so heavy in his life. There was another awkward pause. Dr. Jones picked up a slip of paper off his desk; it was the note Alan had written detailing his threat. He asked Alan who he should call.

"Call about what?"

"You are thinking about hurting yourself."

"No, I'm not. What are you talking about?"

Dr. Jones flicked the note. "Says here you're threatening to cut yourself."

Alan fisted his hands so hard that his knuckles cracked. "I said that because I don't want kitchen duty."

The man crumbled the note in his fist. "Unlike life with your brother, Alan, life here does not necessitate you making a scene in order to be heard. Alright?"

Alan did not say anything.

"You want a different job?"

Alan nodded.

"Why?"

Alan wondered, then realized: "...Roger drowned me in the sink. While I was cleaning dishes." Alan's eyes were on fire. David passed him a box of Kleenex.

"He didn't drown you. You're alive. You're here. To drown is to be dead." After a medically sufficient pause, he went on: "Can you help in the library, instead of kitchen duty?"

Alan nodded.

"Alright. I'll talk to Doris. You can go now."

Alan slipped out of the office. He was walking with his head down when Scar violently shoved past him in the hallway.

The following afternoon, after unsuccessfully trying to distract himself all morning, Alan worked up enough gumption to form an apology. He was expecting to see Scarlett at dinner.

Are these turnips or radishes? Alan wondered, looking over his share of pot roast. He surveyed the dining room but didn't see any sign of her. He nestled into a bean bag and picked up his fork. The doc talked a lot about how the body of a highly sensitive person could internalize criticism and conflict, how it could cause nausea. Vomiting, even. Anorexia.

Alan lifted a dripping lock of meat. He believed it was true. Food was so much more appealing when Roger wasn't around to suck up emotional validation like a parasite. Alan picked up a turnip that could have been a radish. It wasn't useful to have such thoughts, he recalled, especially during mealtime. He felt strange after yesterday's outburst. After a short, quiet conversation, he'd been able to switch out kitchen duty for clerical work.

He almost didn't believe it, and expected someone to play some sort of joke on him when he showed up for the shift, but it passed without incident. The matter had been so simple that Alan flinched at the thought of his threat. The doc was right. Making a scene was the kind of thing you had to do if you lived with someone like Roger, because Roger liked scenes. He was good at them and he always wanted to play the game his way. Before yesterday, it had never occurred to Alan that simply asking for a change could result in his being heard.

Alan swirled one of the radish-maybe-turnips across the gravy on his plate. You had to hand it to them, they had disarmed him completely, and it was a relief. When he finished his plate Alan stood up and squinted. He couldn't find Scarlett and people were filing out of the dining hall already. She was probably still sick, he realized.

As Alan made his way across the short gravel path to the girl's dorm, he watched his reflection in the front doors. The regular meals and manual labor made him look sort of pleasantly aggressed. He knew he looked good when he was out working the horses; he saw the girls talk in the library, the dining room, after group therapy—he could feel when they were looking at him. Alan reached for the door handle and froze, reading the sign he missed:

Co-ed visiting hours are from 9:30 AM to 4:30 PM

Alan felt his stomach churn. Of course he couldn't visit a girl so late...he had forgotten....

Alan darted away from the dorm before he could be seen. Such rules, impersonal though they were, had become a source of profound discomfort for him. His frown deepened as he stepped away from the gravel path and towards the paddock. That's how Roger seduced all those women, Alan realized, by making himself seem safe. But how could anyone? The world is scary. Alan did not think anyone could put him at ease. He suddenly wanted to vomit for the first time in weeks.

The horses at the center were free-roaming animals. Alan stood at the fence and made kissing noises. There were no horses in sight. He kissed again and heard a sound like distant thunder as the herd approached. Alan held his hand over their noses, which huffed so warmly. He loved Honey, the horse he imagined was the same color as butter.

"How come you're not scared of me, Honey?" Alan flashed his teeth. "You ought to be scared. Men are very scary. We can't visit in the night." Alan pulled a burr our of her forelock. "I can hardly look myself in the mirror."

Speaking of being looked at, was he? Honey seemed, like his hand that stroked her, to be an expression of creation. Alan looked at you. "Are we the same?" he uttered and then looked at the sky. The night arrived, and it seemed more light than dark when he looked at the stars. As if the sky were a cheesecloth that covered them all against the light of some cosmic refrigerator. Honey nickered and the horses left Alan's affection to continue foraging. He could hear their teeth cropping grass in the dark.

Less clear, but still audible, was the sound of talking, or something like it. It was more persistent than talking but somehow Alan couldn't make it out. It was a sound that went right through you, a language he didn't know. The same sound that penetrated his long sleep at home.

He followed it until he realized it was floating out of an open window in the girl's dorm. Alan stared up at the window for a long time and was suddenly reminded of breaking Natasha's window when he rescued Nala.

This window was only inches above his head. Someone was in there now, someone closer to the sound than he. Maybe she was awake, listening in bed with her legs up the wall. Maybe she knew what it meant.

Alan thought of punching the screen in. He could launch himself through the window and shush her and do nothing, just be there, closer to the sound and safe. She would remember it: A man broke into my room and shushed me and did nothing, he just wanted to be closer to the sound and safe, and it was.

But that would not do. Alan started to walk away. It wasn't as though he was a man in a story…was he? He glanced back at the window. He listened for a long time. If he found Scarlett tomorrow, he would ask her about it. She might know whose room it was.

While brushing his teeth, Alan's phone lit up with a message from Jenna.

Trial did not go well today. Prosecution is a bitch.

Alan parked the toothbrush in his cheek and picked up the phone.

Alan: **What's going on?**

Jenna: They make it look like roger was in debt or something. Can arden call you tomorrow afternoon?

Alan: Sure no problem. What do you mean in debt

He stared at the phone. Jenna was taking awhile to answer.

Jenna: Nothing alan they're just trying to make him look bad, anyway arden can explain better she will call you tomorrow okay

Alan: Ok

Alan turned on the faucet. The sight of the toothbrush projecting out of his mouth reminded him so acutely of the razor that he—nay, this boy in the mirror, this Mirror-Boy—he flinched.

Mirror-Boy was kind of tall. Mirror Boy was one to watch. Alan leaned closer, peering at him. "Don't leave me," he mouthed.

Mirror-Boy smiled, and Alan saw his reflection pick up his phone:

Alan: hey Jenna listen tell Arden I will testify ok

Jenna: Alan are you sure? It's a pain in the ass it takes a long time

Alan stood still for a minute, until his hands were the same as Mirror-Boy's hands, until he could say: yes, I got it. I can do it. Tell Roger it'll be ok.

Scar's bedroom door had her name on it. She sat up in bed to read Alan's apology letter. "Who told you to write this?"

"No one," Alan said a little too loudly, "I know I acted like a jerk, that's all."

She sneezed. "This is sweet. Thank you. I'll keep it."

Alan scanned the tissues littering her bedside table. "Still sick, huh?"

"Yes." She buried herself back under her blanket. "Flu."

Alan pursed his lips, nodding. "Well," he said after a moment, "I catch easy." And he exited the room.

It was such painfully awkward departure that he felt compelled to return that afternoon. He had forgotten to wish her a Get Well Soon, let alone ask about what he'd heard the night before; and he heard it again when he came back.

In her fever, Scar thought for a moment that a horse was standing over her. She saw Alan in a vapor mask. Scar cleared her throat and reached over to the phone. The sound stopped. Alan blinked as if he were leaving a dream.

"You sound like a horse breathing in that," She said.

"I didn't want to catch the flu, so I borrowed a mask from the art room."

Scarlett took the covered bowl he offered and lifted the lid. "This is soup."

"You're sick...It's a, it's a Get Well Soon Soup."

"You brought me sooooouup." She looked both tired and delighted, and then, so quickly that he might have imagined it, Alan detected a flicker of worry.

He pointed at her phone. "What were you listening to?"

She blew her nose. "Kind of hard to explain it."

"What language is it?"

"I'm not sure, to be honest."

"Do you understand it?"

"Not really. Not at all." She lowered a spoon into the soup. "Thanks, Alan. You're a very good person."

"You're welcome," Alan said, and then his phone rang.

Scar watched him retreat to a corner of the room. He pulled down the vapor mask; it hung around his neck.

Alan tapped the phone with an impatient finger. "I thought I could stay here a bit longer."

Scar took an enormous slurp to cover the crack she perceived in Alan's voice. She couldn't hear whoever was on the line (nor was she interested in eavesdropping to begin with), but she couldn't help but notice the subtle transformation in his face.

Alan ended the call. "I'm leaving tomorrow," he told her.

Scarlett stirred the soup. "So soon?"

Alan nodded. "I might be able to come back, but... probably not." he said, but he sounded more resigned than hopeful.

She looked sideways at him: his downcast eyes and his hair in the way of them. She looked at an embodiment of the word *crestfallen.* "Don't leave without giving me your number."

Alan looked at her. "You want my number?"

Scarlett handed him her phone. "Text yourself."

Alan held her phone for a moment. "I don't know my own number," he realized aloud, and she laughed. It sounded like a smattering of raindrops. Alan felt as though a net were tightening around his heart. "Can I have your number instead?"

"Sure, Alan. Just promise me you'll try to smile," she said, and he did.

Alan spent the evening on a horse. He thought of the girl in Pennsylvania, and his ability to eat and hear after his encounter with her...she had looked exactly like Nala, now that he thought about it...she, too, may not have been real....

Scarlett, on the other hand, seemed quite real, and made him feel the same. Pleasantly helpless. Surprisingly capable.

Alan spent a while lunging Honey after his ride. He needed to see Dr. Jones but the man was also down with the flu. Without the doc to make a phone call about being Too Traumatized To Testify, Alan would have less trouble making due on his promise to do it—of course, that also mean there was no way out of it, now. Arden said that he was being summoned by the prosecution. He could try getting a note out of one of the other therapists, but his stomach churned at the thought of trying to convince them overnight that he couldn't even—,

—*make popcorn without burning it. Look at this good-for-nothing fuck, he can't even puke straight, right Alan? Think you can aim for the trash next time?*

Honey nickered. Alan blinked. He'd been standing still as stock in the arena. The lunge line was looped twice around his torso. "Sorry Honey," he said as he disentangled himself. "I'm distracted. I'm afraid. I have to sit up in front of a jury and tell them what it's like to get pushed around." But Alan wanted everyone to loathe Jay. He wanted them to spit on the man's grave.

Leading up to the court date, Alan remembered more. He remembered terrifying nights in motel rooms, pills dissolving on his tongue, being ushered into fresh clothes before Roger came back from work. And then the day came when he would be asked, yet again, about things he could remember.

Enter Jack Minnow, litigator. Intelligent, disciplined and attractive by conventional standards. Standing at the front of the courtroom, he is holding an 18x24" whiteboard that he shows first to a jury, and then to the young man sitting in the witness box. "Is this the floor plan of the apartment you shared with the defendant?"

"Objection." Enter Arden Cope. Lawyer and relation of the defendant. Also attractive by conventional standards, and at least as intelligent as her opponent. Hopes to break into real estate.

The judge watches. "Sustained."

Jack takes a breath. "Do you recognize this floor plan?"

The young man squints at the whiteboard and says, "yes, sir."

Arden writes "Alan needs glasses" on her notepad.

Jack looks at the whiteboard. "Must have been pretty inconvenient to have a dresser blocking the doorway like that, Alan. Any reason for such an arrangement?"

"Not that I know of. But I had no problem with anything that got in between me and Jay."

"So you didn't put the dresser there?"

"Not that I can recall, sir."

Jack hands Alan a dry-erase marker. "Can you put an X on the place where you most often slept?"

Alan draws an X where he used to sleep. Then he's asked to put another one for Roger. Another one for Jay.

"So you shared the bed with your brother."

"Yeah, it was a large bed."

"How big was it?" Even though Jack asks the questions for Alan to answer, he is looking at other people in the room.

Alan shrugs. "Big enough."

"Was it a full?"

"Objection." Arden taps her pencil.

"Overruled."

"Was it a full bed?"

Alan frowns. "It was full when we were in it."

The judge looks at Alan. "Do you understand the question?"

"Not really."

Jack spreads his arms. "Was the bed any wider than this?"

"A little wider than that, yeah."

"So there was enough room for both of you."

"Yes, sir."

"It's a small apartment for three people, don't you think?"

"I guess so."

"Did you like it there?"

"Not particularly."

"Did you ever think about leaving?"

Alan shakes his head. "It wasn't safe to leave Roger."

"Did you think you were in his custody?"

"That's not why I couldn't leave."

"So you knew that you weren't in his custody?"

Alan doesn't answer right away. He looks at the judge and says, "I plead the fifth."

Arden tries to suppress a smile. Jack wanted very much to remind the jury of his insinuation that Roger may have already been guilty of kidnapping his brother. (Of course it was true in the eyes of the law, but Arden had never pressed charges). It would be a nice thing for the prosecution to couple with Roger's shop lifting incident in the 90s. But an honest answer from Alan would alternatively suggest that he could've left of his own accord, which would potentially incriminate him and give him the right to try and reject the whole line of questioning.

After a few moments of discussion with the judge, Jack turned back to Alan. "Why wasn't it safe to leave Roger?"

"Well for one thing, I wouldn't leave anyone alone with someone like Jay. And Roger was sick, he was shooting up."

"Shooting up what?"

"I don't know, but it made him sick."

"So you found it safer to stay in the apartment when your brother was home."

"Yes, sir."

"What about when he wasn't home?"

Alan hesitates. "I waited for him to come back."

"You waited in the apartment."

"Yeah."

"Do you know what Jay did for a living?"

"He had an online business. I didn't know what it was."

"Did he work from the apartment?"

Alan blinks. "Most of the time, as far as I know. I didn't have the details."

Jack gets closer to Alan. He leans against the witness box. "That's right, you have a selective memory, don't you?"

"Objection." Arden's throat is dry.

"Sustained."

Jack rubbed his forehead. "You said, in previous statements, that you don't remember everything. Can you tell us about that?"

"Yes, sir, I get blackouts. May I explain?"

Arden shuts her eyes. She begged Alan not to admit this, but she knew he would.

"Of course."

"Sometimes, if circumstances get especially unpleasant, and I mean really unpleasant, I check out completely. I'm not aware of what's happening and when I'm awake again, I don't know where the time went. Sometimes I remember what happened later, if I get some kind of a flashback. I'm just not aware at the time and it has to get triggered."

"When was your last blackout?"

Alan looks up and to the right. "It must have been the day before I had the Vicodin and was checked into the hospital."

Jack nodded. "So is it safe to assume that you remember more now about Jay than you did before you heard that your brother had killed him?"

"I don't have to remember much to know what kind of person Jay was."

Jack smiles. "I doubt that any of us would. Can you remember any conversations that you might have had with Jay about the defendant's drug use?"

"Yes, sir, we did have one conversation about it. Jay showed me a bag of powder—,"

"Powder? What kind of powder?"

"I haven't a clue, sir. Just like a sachet of powder. He told me that Roger was shooting it up, and he threatened to contaminate it if I didn't keep my mouth shut."

"How did he phrase that? Can you remember?"

"He said, 'this is what your brother shoots up, Alan.' And he said that he could put whatever he wanted in it."

"So he was threatening the defendant."

Alan takes a breath. "Yes."

"What did he want you to keep your mouth shut about?"

"Everything. And it worked." Alan glances at the jury. "It took months to be able to talk like this again."

Jack is scratching his chin. He paces the courtroom. Arden is gritting her teeth. Jack says, "Do you know how your brother was compensating Jay for drugs?"

"Objection."

"Sustained."

Jack rubs his forehead. "Alan, are you implying that Jay provided your brother with whatever he was shooting up?"

Alan is looking at his cousin, trying to understand why she objected to the last question. Then he says, "it did seem that way, yes. But I don't know for sure."

"Had your brother ever abused narcotics prior to living with Jay?"

"Not that I know of."

"Had he used any illegal substances at all prior to living with Jay?"

"Not that I know of."

"Do you know of any other source whatsoever that could have provided illegal substances to Roger, other than Jay?"

"No, sir, I don't know of any."

Jack was pacing again. "Did you ever see your brother pay his roommate in cash?"

"Yes, for rent."

"He said it was for rent?"

"Yeah, he always seemed to be owing Jay for rent."

"Do you know what kind of work your brother was doing?"

"I think it was landscaping. He's a fantastic gardener."

From his table, Jack picked up a large plastic bag with a camera in it. "I've got just a couple more questions for you, Alan. Do you recognize this camera?"

"It looks familiar."

"Do you know whose camera it is?"

Alan takes a moment to answer. "I'm not sure," he says in a soft way.

"Does your brother have a camera?"

"Yes."

"Does it look like this one?"

"Yes, sir..." Alan twists to and fro a bit in his seat.

"So there's a possibility that this is your brother's camera?"

"Yeah, possibly."

Jack returns the camera back to his table and picks up a photograph the size of printer paper, holding it below Alan's line of vision as he approaches the witness box. "I'm going to show you a screen cap, Alan," Jack says, "and I want you to tell us if you recognize the people in it." He lifts the photograph.

After Alan confirms the presence of himself and Jay in the photograph, Jack shows it to the jury. They look at it, and about half of them shift in their seat. Alan succeeds in catching a gaze among them and he returns it with a broken look. Jack seems to be considering another question, but for whatever reason, he refrains. Arden stands up to cross examine her young cousin. She has a speckled notebook in one hand.

"Can you tell me what this is?"

"That's my notebook."

"What do you call it?"

"Spot."

Arden looks at the jury. "Why do you call it Spot, Alan?"

Alan huffs. "It has spots on it."

Arden perches the thing on her arm and deftly flips through it. She plies the witness with questions to confirm the validity and use of its contents; the dates, the entries, the one line responses written when he could not speak. Spot, he asserts, is a trove of most accurate and honest memories. Arden thanks him, smiling like a cheshire cat, and he is dismissed.

Arden calls Jennifer Ward to the witness box. Jennifer is in her late thirties, divorced with no children, and appears to be simultaneously embarrassed and amused as she answers Arden's questions about Roger. She was a client of his.

"I hired him to do the lawn," Jennifer says.

Arden smiled. "I hire someone to do my lawn, too. I know what it's like not to have a man in the house." She is trying to put the witness at ease. "Occasionally someone comes along and does it for free, leaves a little flag out front and a brochure on the stoop. If you've lived in the suburbs you'll know what I mean."

Jennifer nods. "I get those."

"So is that how you came about hiring the defendant?"

"Objection."

"Sustained."

Arden glances at the judge and looks back at the witness. "Alright, Ms Ward, tell us how you met Roger."

Jennifer clears her throat. "The lawn got so bad after my husband left that I found a notice on my door, and to be honest, it upset me big time. I was on the phone with a friend when she told me about this landscaping company...."

"The one that Roger works for?"

"Yes, she recommended it and she said I should ask for him."

"Did she say why?"

"She said that she had a good experience with him and that he would chat me up a bit." Jennifer shrugged. "My confidence kind of sucked at the time."

"Did he flirt with you?"

"Yes."

Arden slowly nodded. "And did you find him to be in the least bit annoying or aggressive when he was chatting you up?"

"Objection."

"Overruled."

Jennifer shook her head. "No, he was really, um... charming. You know? Very polite."

"Did you tell your friend that you took her advice and hired him?"

"I texted her while he was working, told her I liked him. She said I should ask him about fixing my fountain, but my yard doesn't have one. She didn't really mean a fountain."

Jennifer still has the texts on her phone. She shares it verbatim. Jack Minnow is taking notes. Alan is sitting so far off the edge of his seat that he seems to be in danger of falling.

"How much did he charge you for extra services?"

"Objection."

"Overruled."

"Permission to approach the bench."

"Permission granted."

Arden curses Jack under her breath as she approaches the judge. She insists that she is not trying to give evidence of taxable income, but is only presenting suggestions for how Roger may have had the means to pay for illegal substances. They back away and Arden asks, again, "how much did the defendant charge you for extra services performed?"

Jennifer ducks her head. "A hundred dollars in cash."

Arden exhales. "So in addition to the bill for the work he did on your lawn, the defendant left your house with a hundred dollars in cash?"

"No. He left with a hundred and fifty in cash."

Alan's mouth drops open. He whips around to face Roger, whose face is in his hands.

Jennifer shrugs. "He did a great job."

Jack practically leaps out of his seat to cross examine her. "You expect us to believe that *this* defendant," (he points at the man in question), "came into your house covered in sweat and grass stains to give you a back rub, charged you a hundred dollars, and collected fifty in gratuity for extra services?"

"Yup."

"Were any of these extra services sexual in nature?"

"Not *really*."

"Hmm." Jack cocks his head. "So this wasn't a case of prostitution?"

"I plead the fifth!" Jennifer is practically trembling, she is so incensed. "Your honor, I reject this whole line of questioning!"

"Fine, fine!" Jack waves his hand. "Strike it, forget about it. No further questions."

Arden calls up an expert witness to share cost estimates for narcotics such as heroin. On the way out, she stops by a press conference to say few carefully rehearsed comments, and that marks the end of Alan's first day in the trial.

Alan huddled over his phone. Despite the fact that the interrogations so far had proved more benign than he expected, he felt thoroughly unsettled.

He sat on the floor of Jenna's room, staring blankly at the ground as she cleaned out her dresser. Around him were old socks, chipped plastic earrings, beaded bracelets worn to the point of disuse.

"Do you want to help?"

"No."

"Are you gonna move?"

Alan rolled an eyeliner crayon under his foot. "No."

"Well, I'm gonna dump out all my clothes. So move."

Alan spotted something glittery and circular in the mess. He picked it up.

"What's this?"

"It's a hand mirror."

Alan popped it open: there he was, Mirror Boy.

"You don't want this?"

"No, that's all trash."

Mirror Boy smiled. "Like me," he said, and Jenna laughed.

"I'm serious, you gotta move you're in my way."

"Can I have your mace?"

"Stop taking my stuff."

"I want to go to the library."

Jenna tossed the mace at him. "Go buy your own first."

Alan walked between shelves on foreign language, trying to ascertain how many books he could carry home. The silence of the library invited him to consider his next conversation with Roger; he had scheduled a visit three days before the next court date. When Alan walked home he practiced freshly learnt words, turning them around in his mouth like chewing gum and trying to remember if he had heard any of them coming from Scarlett's room. After several deep breaths, he even ventured a call to Scarlett, and she answered. He couldn't stop himself from speaking with a kind of virginal fervor over the phone, and he feared she might think he was stupid. Her responses were sober, but confirmed the contrary.

"Do you know that you're not normal?" She asked.

Alan thought for awhile. "I think that...I'm discovering my senses. For the first time. I don't know if that's being normal." He was outside the house now, but walking in circles on the driveway. "I can always feel when something is right, though. My cousins aren't like that, they're a lot more logical. I don't think I can do that, I can't seem to rule out things logically like they can."

"You have a different kind of intelligence," Scarlett said, "that's all."

Alan sat on the front stoop. "What kind of intelligence do you think you have?"

Scarlett started to answer, and a dark car pulled up outside of the house. Alan stood. "I have to go, I'm sorry," he said into the phone. "I'm being chased by the press. It's a long story, I'll tell you later. Bye." He hung up and darted into the house.

Alan was back at the prison; Roger's posture was wrecked. "So what's it like to talk again, kiddo?"

"Why do you sound like that?"

"I don't sound like anything."

"You're being a jerk," Alan said. Since his arrival, Roger had picked up the phone but not bothered to look through the plexiglass at all. Alan pounded it with his fist. "Look at me, asshole."

When his brother didn't answer, Alan leaned forward on his elbows. "How did you get so much cash out of that woman? She must have been lonely as hell."

"Not really."

"Then what did you *do?*"

Roger almost smiled. "I can't talk about it, I'm a gentlemen." Silence. "I'll tell you if I get out of here."

"*When* you get out of here," Alan corrected. "You saw what happened. Even with my amnesia, the prosecution has no case. There's no way they'll be able to prove you were in on it. I've never heard such a stupid bunch of questions in my life...."

Roger finally looked at him. "In on what?"

"Well..." Alan hesitated. "Forget it."

"No, no, what are you talking about?"

Alan rolled his eyes. "Roger, they think that if they prove that you were using me to pay for heroin, then they'll have another motive for the murder."

"How could I be using you to pay for something if you weren't even working?"

The brothers stared at each other. In between them, Alan knew, there was an invisible fulcrum; and something on it had just tilted. "Roger, they...they're trying to prove that you knew what Jay was doing. What he was selling."

"But I didn't!"

"I know." Alan ventured further: "Why are you playing dumb?"

"I didn't know, Alan, I met him at a party through a mutual friend I swear to God I didn't know!"

Alan tented his fingers on the plexiglass. "Alright, don't lose your cool. I believe you."

"You do? Are you sure you do?"

"...sure." Alan sat back. "And if I believe it, the jury will believe it. They're just people."

"He seemed so normal," Roger said, tugging on the phone cord. "Like a tool, but a normal tool."

"Normal's got nothing to do with it," Alan spat, suddenly furious. "He didn't hurt me because he was special, I was just there. It was convenient."

Roger dropped the phone and violently retched. He closed a hand over his own mouth and took a moment to recover before picking up the phone again. "There'd better be a hell."

"There is a hell." Alan said it with enough gravity to prompt an inquisitive look from his brother, but he didn't want to discuss his burgeoning religious feelings any more than was necessary at that moment. "I'm infecting this jury, Roger. I'm going to make them sick. They'll fill up with sin just to look at me."

Roger's eyes alighted with curiosity. "What do you mean?"

"Well," Alan spoke with care; he didn't want to further aggravate Roger's gag reflexes. "Maybe Jay was so much like a lot of people, with just a little less self control. Don't you think that's true?"

"Aauuugghhh."

"Good," Alan said, and the sound of his own conviction made a shudder travel the length of his body. "Most people don't decide with reason, Roger. They decide with feelings. Most people have a little guilt inside them. I'll make them feel guilty just for being human. You'll be the jury's hero."

Roger gave his brother a forlorn look. "There's someone in here who reminds me of you."

"Of course there is," Alan muttered. Eager to change the subject, he told Roger about Scarlett. "I don't know what to do next with her. Like, how do I...get her to feel safe. With me."

Roger rubbed his face. "Well you have to...you know...wear cute hats and stuff."

"What are you talking about?"

Roger pinched his eyes, then tented his fingers on the table before him. "You've got to appropriate the feminine item. Become like them. Women want themselves...they want themselves in a man's body, with a man's voice and stuff."

Alan frowns. "That sounds kind of advanced. I need, like...seduction 101."

Roger shrugs. "That's easy, just let her love you. Be nice. Tell her everything, let her love it. But you'll get your heart broken."

"No worries, my heart's already broken."

Alan would remember his second day of testimony as one of the longest and most intense of his life. He'd been ready to parrot the sentiment that had made Roger nearly heaving sick the other day, but was otherwise completely unprepared.

The opening statements are heated. Jack talks about money and drugs, facts and metaphor. Arden talks about a razor in Alan's mouth, and children who are missed by parents who live in agony.

Jack asks the defendant about the dresser. "I didn't put it there," Roger says, "I put it closer to the bathroom."

"How did it get in the doorway?"

"Alan put it there. But he won't remember that because he was asleep. He was sleepwalking."

"So he moved it during the night?"

"Yeah, he was throwing the clothes out and pushing it in front of the doorway. Woke me up."

"Did he say anything?"

"No," Roger pops two knuckles. "He was just making a big racket."

"Did you try to stop him?"

"Yes, but—,"

"How?"

Roger blinks. "I don't understand the question."

"How did you try to stop Alan?"

"I just tried to get him to come back to bed."

"How?"

The defendant narrows his eyes. "I threw the clothes back in the drawers and I yelled at him and then Jay got up."

"What did Jay do?"

"He asked me what was going on and I told him Alan was trying to block the doorway and he thought—," Roger's breath catches and he takes another. "He thought it was hysterical."

Jack seems happy enough with that. Arden is ready to cross examine; she paces the courtroom. She asks Roger about the one thing everyone secretly wants to know: the origin of Luna.

"Is Luna a figment of your imagination?"

"I don't like the word 'figment', but yes," Roger asserts. Everyone is tense as glass.

"When were you aware that you had made it all up?"

"I'm absolutely sure that I don't understand that question," Roger says without blinking.

"Well, when the press asked you about what transpired during your captivity, what did you tell them?"

"I told them that I was on an island called Luna and that I believed it was real."

"And did you believe it was real?"

"...Nope."

"Arden taps her lips and adopts a breathless sarcasm that triggers a smirk on her youngest cousin's face. "So you *lied* to the press?"

"Yup."

She rounds on the defendant. "You *lied* to ABC news?"

"Yes."

"You *lied* to Dateline?"

"I even lied to my therapist." Roger flashes a sarcastic peace sign.

"So you lied not only about Luna's existence, but you pretended to believe in it when in fact...you knew full well that it's not real."

"Yeah, I lied about the whole thing."

The jury shifts again. Public skeptics will come to love this day.

Arden picks up a folder. "I have here a transcript from a television interview that you did when you were sixteen. You were asked whether it was possible that Luna was a defense mechanism during your captivity—,"

"Objection.

"Overruled."

Arden glares at Jack and goes on: "Your response to this was, and I quote 'it definitely seems that way, but no. I was there, I heard it, I saw it, I smelled it, it was completely real."

Roger shrugs and tugs a lock of his own hair. "I wasn't under oath for *Dateline.*"

Arden lowers the transcript. "Did you expect anyone to believe you?"

"I expected to convince them that I believed it," Roger says, pointing at himself, "and it's like you just read, they did. They thought I used it to cope. I put enough links between my stories about Luna and what I actually went through; more than enough to support their theory."

"Seems like a tall order for a teenager with a lot of trauma, don't you think?"

Roger shrugs. "I spent a lot of time just sitting around in motel rooms. Plenty of time to think."

"Even so, you must have had *some* motivation to get that kind of attention. There is a syndrome named after you, Roger Cope."

"I didn't want Alan to know the truth."

Arden nods. "How old was he when you started sharing this narrative about Luna?"

"Nine or ten."

"Don't you think nine or ten is old enough to tell reality from fantasy?"

Roger sighs. "Not my reality and not if you're Alan."

Arden shrugged. "You didn't think he would believe a stranger on TV against the word of his big brother?"

Roger nodded. "Exactly. Why believe some other punk just because he has a microphone and he's talking about things you don't understand? Alan believed me because I told him the truth. Courtrooms care about accuracy, fine. Reality and fantasy, blah blah blah. But accuracy's got nothing to do with the truth for me."

He looks at his brother. Alan sits with one hand on his lap and the other on the seat beside him. He returns the gaze with one of deference, and holds this until Jack Minnow calls him up to the witness box.

Jack is holding Spot. "You testified that all the dated entries in this notebook are true *and accurate.*"

"Yes. "Alan sits strangely; he looks at Jack but his shoulders are facing the jury.

Jack rifles through Spot. "Do you know what a minnow is, Alan?"

"It's a type of fish."

"It says here there was a...minnow darting up your leg. While you were preparing lunch. Care to explain that?"

Alan blinks. "It's a metaphor."

"Metaphor for what?"

"Pain," Alan said baldly. "You'll see it elsewhere."

"Hm. So there wasn't a fish in the apartment with you?"

Arden crosses her arms and struggles to hide her eye-rolling behind closed lids. Alan adopts a look of healthy confusion. "No, Mr. Minnow, there was no fish in the apartment. No live fish, anyway."

"So you can attest to the fact that there are details in these entries that are not literally true."

Alan cocks an eyebrow. "I will attest to that, yeah, sure."

"Well then I'm wondering, Alan, when you make associations between things as far removed as pain and freshwater fish, how I'm supposed to discern how much of this is literal..." Jack leans against the witness box, "...and how much is metaphor."

Alan turns to face him squarely. "Are you quite serious?"

"Very serious," Jack says.

"Aw," Alan stares him down. "Must really bother you, having your name appropriated like that."

Jack snorts. "Appropriated." He's smiling.

"Yeah, appropriated. Pretty sure lawyers are supposed to know big words."

"Permission to treat the witness as hostile."

"Permission granted."

Jack scans the witness with his eyes and Alan clenches his fists. Jack's voice lowers. "You should be very careful, Alan, about using words you don't understand."

"You should be careful not to look at people that way, it makes them nervous."

"Drop the attitude, Mr. Cope," the judge says, and Jack steps away from the witness box. "It's alright, your honor. I'm trying to make a point, and anyway…" he stops at his table. "Alan's discomfort is more than justified." Jack turns to face the witness again. "When was the last time you had access to this notebook?"

"Her name is Spot."

"Oh, I'm sorry!" Jack says with derision, "I wasn't aware objects have gender. Are we in France?"

Alan leans forward. "It's a metaphor."

Jack rounds on him, brandishing Spot. "When did you last write in this?"

"The date's in there."

"You don't remember?"

Alan juts his chin. "I fucking don't know."

"Second warning, Mr. Cope. I can hold you in contempt of court and take you into custody."

Jack takes a deep breath. "You wrote that the defendant had no knowledge of what happened between you and his roommate, and I have to say, Alan, I don't believe you one bit!"

"I'm telling the truth."

"You can't tell the truth about something you don't know." Jack's voice gradually rises as he continues: "You're claiming, Alan, that your older brother didn't notice you being raped in his own bed, in the apartment that he came home to every single day to sleep and shoot up narcotics."

"He didn't know. I hid it from him." Alan glances at the defendant, then sits up a little in his chair. "We have a habit of hiding painful things from each other, as everyone in this room knows."

"You're telling me that Roger didn't notice you changing?"

"Objection."

"Sustained."

Jack bears down on the witness box. "He didn't need an explanation for why you stopped talking?"

"He had other explanations."

"Did he notice the bruises?"

"No."

"He didn't ask about the blood, Alan? Or the broken coffee pot? Or the vomit or the condoms on the floor, you hid all of that from him?"

Alan's chest is heaving. His heart is frayed to the stem and beyond. Jack's voice softened. "He was sick and poor and drug dependent, isn't that true?"

"I plead the fifth."

"You can't plead the fifth, Alan."

"Then yes," Alan says, "he was those things."

"Don't you think it's possible, then, that there's just the *slightest* chance," Jack pinches space between his thumb and forefinger, "that amidst all the things going wrong in the apartment, that the defendant may have noticed, on some...subconscious level...that something was off, but with all the stress, and the sickness, and trying to make enough money to feed two people, he had little chance of pinpointing what the problem was?"

Alan hesitates. His chest is still heaving, but he's breathless when he answers, "No. I've been throwing up since I was eight. I cut myself and told him I liked it. I'm a good liar. If something broke, Jay would tell him I threw a fit, and I did throw fits."

"What about Luna?"

Alan blinks, genuinely bemused. "What about it?"

Jack picks up a different notebook, a slimmer one with a spiral. "The defendant testified that he used this to communicate with you. You've written about Luna in here, haven't you?"

Alan swallows. "Maybe."

"This is your handwriting, isn't it?"

"Yes, but—,"

"So you told your brother that you were accosted by white coats who strapped you to a table, shoved a tube down your throat and forced you to take drugs you knew nothing about in a world that *he invented.*" Jack points at Roger. "And he never suspected that something was wrong?"

Click—Alan looks down at the mirror in his hand—then back up, more troubled than ever. He is unable to answer before Jack goes on: "You know what I think, Alan?" He steps away from the box again. "I think you're a resourceful kid who tried to fix the situation in the smartest, safest way possible so that you and your brother could escape Jay in peace."

Alan knots his hands together. He senses Arden's frustration, Roger's shame and pity, Jack's respectful anger all descending on him like sprays of acid.

Jack shrugs. "I guess your brother just doesn't understand metaphor."

"You villain!" Alan shouts and launches himself out of his chair.

Twenty minutes later, Alan was escorted to the cell where he would spend the night. There was another man there with his back turned, and when he shifted to face the newcomer, Alan elbowed him in the face.

They scuffled, but even after Alan's work at the farm he was no match for this fellow, who soon had him pinned to the ground.

"You'll get what's coming to ye, damn fool! Starting a fight at your size!"

"Get off me!

"Serves you right...." The man hesitated as he watched Alan's expression of fury mutate into one of abject terror. "Take it easy, now."

"No!"

The man release Alan and tried to help him up. He set a gentle hand on Alan's arm and Alan pushed it aside. "Don't be soft about it—,"

"Soft about what?" The man retreated and swiped blood out of his eye.

Alan's mouth was trembling. He tucked his face into his arms and cried. He cried about everything. He cried the way that your loved one cries.

The man's hands met his hips. He regarded Alan like a spill on the floor, and then dropped a blanket around the young man's shoulders. "Dinna stop yourself from cryin', boy."

Alan wept harder, and you wanted to hold him.

The next morning he awaited a ride home with his head bowed, his eyes swollen from crying the night before. He pinched his arm; there was a strange buzzing sensation all over his body. When he got his phone back it was laden with messages from Scarlett. She wanted to know how the trial was going, though she still had heard so little about its purpose.

Alan rubbed his mouth and pecked at the screen; he could not leave her waiting. He was interrupted when Arden lifted him by his shirt and marched him outside.

"You have a criminal record now, Alan! Why couldn't you look at me? Couldn't you hear all those pencils I was breaking!?" She slammed a car door. "I know you're angry but you can't do this!" She backed out so abruptly that Alan gripped his seat to steady himself. "The law is not kind to young men from broken homes, Alan. Consider yourself lucky that all you got was an overnight stay. I can *not* bail you out!"

"I wasn't saying—"

"Just because I practice law doesn't mean I have all the power in the world. And why, I just want to know, why can't you ever put your emotions aside? For anything?"

"You saw what Jack was like...."

"Jack is not your enemy, Alan, none of us are. You are the victim here, and it seems like everyone knows it but you."

"Roger's the victim," Alan's voice was hoarse from dehydration, "he could get a death penalty."

"I don't think anyone should be put to death for killing a practicing pedophile in a fit of revenge," Arden said firmly, "but that's just my opinion, it's not the law. And it doesn't make him innocent."

"He didn't know what Jay was really like!"

"Willful ignorance," Arden spat.

Alan watched her for a long time, lost in a mixture of empathy and hopelessness. "You've never been in denial about anything? You never ignored something right in front of you because it was too hard to bear?" He asked after awhile. "No one is perfect."

Arden reached over, hesitated, and then took Alan's hand. "Are you okay?"

"Of course not," Alan said, looking at her hand.

"I spoke to Jack yesterday, you're all done. You don't have to testify anymore. And I think..." she squeezed his hand and let it go. "I think you're brave as *fuck* for showing up, Alan."

Alan gave her a soft little nod. It was a matter of procedure for Arden to communicate with Jack, but it felt strange to think about it. He rested his throbbing head on his hand. He took a deep breath and asked the question he'd been pointedly avoiding since returning to Cortland. "Are you sending me back to the farm?"

"I'm sorry." Arden glanced at him. "You know I can't."

Alan glanced at his phone and then flipped it over on his leg. He didn't want to miss the sunset.

After Roger's death sentence was averted, after Alan found work at an animal shelter, after Jenna graduated, the three of them went for a day trip to the beach. They planned to meet Leena there; she had been gone for a long time for a fellowship. It was difficult to be with everyone but Roger.

Difficult, but not impossible.

The ocean was so dazzling that it almost blinded Alan. He meandered in the sand around Leena and his cousins, holding bags and towels, passing one side, then the other, glaring at any nearby men.

Scarlett accepted the idea of being with Alan with a kind of underwhelming calm, as if she had expected it long before Alan himself had considered the possibility. There were challenging things ahead, of course, discussions to be had about what they believed and what they expected—what they were going to do with life. But it all seemed so much easier than being trapped in an apartment with a monster behind the dresser.

I want you to know, Alan mentally reviewed her last letter to him, *that I am with you totally. You will never find anyone who loves you as completely and profoundly as I do...*

"Hey, Alan!" Jenna poked him. "What's that over there?"

Alan looked at the vine-like sculpture at which she was pointing, and shook his head. "I don't...Oh!" he saw a flash of Little Red next to it.

"Surprise!" Jenna said, and Arden and Leena grinned when he dropped everything and ran. Scarlett bounded towards Alan, crying just as much as he was, and they nearly fell over on impact. He rocked her.
When they were on the shore, when Alan felt her kissing the whispery part of his elbow, he asked: "Why do I have to call you Scar?"

"Because I hate 'Scarlett.' It doesn't mean anything."

Alan turned to face her. "It does mean something. It's a color."

"Don't be romantic."

"I'm not trying to be, it really is. It's like....it looks like the way something feels when it's on fire." He touched her bottom lip, knowing you would understand.

She looked thoughtfully at him, trying to imagine it. "I wish you could really show us what colors are like."

Alan looked out at us. "If you stare at the waves long enough, you'll start to see it." This is true.

Love—any kind of love—is fraught with complications, but it was not so with Alan and Scarlett. Theories suggested themselves, but in the depth of his heart Alan believed that he had simply been granted, finally, a reprieve.

Epilogue: Cope Syndrome
by Roger Cope!

Okay first of all this novel was not called *The Fox and the Stag* for all the time we were working on it. It was called *Cope Syndrome,* and I like that title best. But by the time we were putting it together for publication, that title was giving Ayah major headache because of all the pressure working on it so long, so she changed it at the final hour. As far as I'm concerned, this book is called *The Novel Formerly Known as Cope Syndrome.*

Now, on to the epilogue stuff: I eventually was released, and Alan and Scar got married. The first guy who kidnapped Alan also got out of jail. If you are one of the people who read *Say You're Sorry,* then you know what happened there.

The Healing Center for Introverts and blah blah blah is an *actual* fabrication—don't send your teenagers to centers like that, they're really bad and abusive in real life! Ayah invented this one for Alan because he needed a place to rest, it's a total fantasy don't take it serious.

Arden eventually sold the house but gave up on real estate after that. She fell in love with a woman who's nothing like her. Jenna never tells us what she's up to, and she doesn't want to be in any other stories so you probably won't see her again. She has a friend, Asiyah, who you'll meet down the line.

And then there's Jack Minnow, the lawyer who locked me up. He completely fell apart after the events in this book. Ayah made him his own screenplay, it's called *Missouri Angels* if any of you Big Hollywoods want to throw some money her way. She pities everyone, I guess.

As for my memoir: It's done. Ayah transcribed it for me when she was in high school.

I know she would help me edit it but honestly it's so bad, I don't know that I'll ever be able to put it out. Not unless Alan basically rewrites it for me *cough couch* HINT HINT.

I am so proud of Alan for all the work he did on this! For my part, I wish I could say it's been a pleasure—it hasn't.

I end up in jail in this one, which is only sexy for about three minutes. Also, I really don't remember putting Alan's head in the sink. I'm not saying it never happened, I believe him, I'm just telling you I don't remember it.

Good news is: I'm not real. I get to live many lives, over and over. I call them Timelines.

Overall, this novel is not my favorite Timeline. This one is a gift for Alan, through and through. I hardly feel like I'm in it, and not just because it makes me look bad. Ayah lied a lot on my behalf. I mean, I'm not this violent usually, but I'm a lot worse in other ways. I used to be really insecure that I'm not smart. I told her I want to use a lot of big vocabulary words and sound really sophisticated, so she indulged me a bit here but maybe it backfired.

I think I did that really because Micah gave me a total classical education: piano, Latin, drawing—I even worked on that painting of myself in his house, but I forgot most of it and I feel guilty about that. In truth, Alan is the most smart. There is another Timeline where he goes to Harvard—it's a screenplay called *American Boys* and it's my favorite because it's also the story where I meet my hotwife, Emma! So look out for that, it's a good one.

And that's really my luck: No matter what story I'm in, I'm always sexy and people feel bad for me—especially women. My bad luck is, my childhood is always trash. I have always been someone who looked into the eyes of evil too early and lived. That's not gonna change.

Alan has luck, too: every person he loves, loves him back. His bad luck is...well, he has to deal with me.

And that's our lives. We go from story to story, me broken and Alan getting smart, and sometimes if Ayah thinks she wants to write about someone else we just change our names and play pretend (but we can't fool her for long).

So in *my* opinion, that's why this book took so long. It was maybe a dozen different stories that she was trying to squeeze into one, because she didn't understand that we can have many Timelines. But by the time this was getting close to finished, Alan had finally figured out that he's fictional, too, and he explained to her about how I was messing around with the Timelines. Spoiled all my fun!

I was taking a walk recently with Ayah and I stepped on a snake and it bit me: two little holes showed up on my ankle. They looked hollow for a second and then filled up with blood. I happen to know it was not a poisonous snake but I didn't say anything and I let her suck the blood out just in case. Anyway, on the way back to her motel she was smiling hard and I was like, "What's wrong why are you smiling?"

And she says, "I love to pity you. I can't pity real men."

So then I was like *oh ow my leg still hurts* even though it was fine actually. I don't know if most real people are like Ayah. Alan says she is "cut from a different cloth" but just in case he's wrong, go ahead and feel bad for me if you want, idk.

Thanks for reading my chapter! Okay bye see you around!

Ayah Abdul-Rauf is an award-winning writer, filmmaker and professor. It is her solemn duty to share the many tales of the Cope brothers.

This novel was drafted by hand with legal pads, no. 2 pencils and B5 paper.

It was redrafted in WordPerfect, Microsoft Word and Scrivener without the use of computer-generated assistance wherever possible, including spell check.

It was typeset in Pages, with 12 pt EB Garamond.

The cover was designed in Adobe Illustrator.